NEVER TRUST A REBEL

Sarah Mallory

Published in Great Britain 2014
by Mills & Boon, an imprint of Harlequin (UK) Limited,
Eton House, 18-24 Paradise Road, Richmond, Surrey, TW9 1SR

ISBN: 978-0-263-90981-4

Harlequin (UK) Limited's policy is to use papers that are natural, renewable and recyclable products and made from wood grown in sustainable forests. The logging and manufacturing processes conform to the legal environmental regulations of the country of origin.

Printed and bound in Spain
by Blackprint CPI, Barcelona

'Would ... me goodnight?'

She knew she was taking a great risk but he did not look outraged, nor did he admonish her for her forwardness. When he maintained his silence she added softly, 'You are a rake, are you not? And rakes always want to kiss a pretty girl.'

He stopped, frowning down at her fingers resting on his sleeve.

'You would not be wise to pursue this, Miss Salforde.'

A tiny *frisson* of excitement ran along her spine as she heard the warning note in his voice. She moved a little nearer.

'Surely it would not be improper for my guardian to call me Elyse?'

Her excitement intensified as his gaze moved to her face, so piercing that for a moment it took her breath away. She read danger in his look but the wine she had imbibed had given her courage and she felt emboldened by the challenge. She schooled her face into a picture of innocence, at the same time leaning closer so that the lace at her breast was almost touching his waistcoat. She saw his eyes darken and felt a flicker of satisfaction.

'You are playing a dangerous game, *Miss Salforde*.'

AUTHOR NOTE

Ten years after Bonnie Prince Charlie tried and failed to reclaim the British throne for his father, Drew Castlemain returns to England to carry out his friend's final wishes. He meets Elyse, a spirited young lady and the belle of the northern spa town of Scarborough, but events conspire to prevent him from delivering her to her fiancé and instead they find themselves falling headlong into love…

This Georgian romance is set half a century before the Regency, when it was still usual for men to carry swords and for ladies to wear heavy gowns with hoops and layers of petticoats. Travel was slower, too, with poor roads and lumbering coaches—as my hero and heroine discover to their cost.

I really loved telling Elyse and Drew's story; they are a young couple who have to fight against the odds to win their happiness, but of course in the end they succeed, and I hope you will enjoy their journey as much as I enjoyed writing about it.

Oh, and on a final note, Drew and Elyse's whirlwind romance blossomed over a couple of weeks. Improbable, you might think, but it can happen—I met my own hero and knew after just two weeks that he was the one for me. We have just celebrated forty-one years together, so I think I might have been right!

Sarah Mallory was born in Bristol, and now lives in an old farmhouse on the edge of the Pennines with her husband and family. She left grammar school at sixteen to work in companies as varied as stockbrokers, marine engineers, insurance brokers, biscuit manufacturers and even a quarrying company. Her first book was published shortly after the birth of her daughter. She has published more than a dozen books under the pen-name of Melinda Hammond, winning the Reviewers' Choice Award from singletitles.com for *Dance for a Diamond* and the Historical Novel Society's Editors' Choice for *Gentlemen in Question*. Sarah Mallory has also twice won the Romantic Novelists' Association's RONA Rose® Award for *The Dangerous Lord Durrington* and *Beneath the Major's Scars*.

Previous novels by the same author:

THE WICKED BARON
MORE THAN A GOVERNESS
(part of *On Mothering Sunday*)
WICKED CAPTAIN, WAYWARD WIFE
THE EARL'S RUNAWAY BRIDE
DISGRACE AND DESIRE
TO CATCH A HUSBAND…
SNOWBOUND WITH THE NOTORIOUS RAKE
(part of *An Improper Regency Christmas*)
THE DANGEROUS LORD DARRINGTON
BENEATH THE MAJOR'S SCARS*
BEHIND THE RAKE'S WICKED WAGER*
BOUGHT FOR REVENGE
LADY BENEATH THE VEIL**
AT THE HIGHWAYMAN'S PLEASURE**
THE SCARLET GOWN

**The Notorious Coale Brothers*
**Linked by character

And in Mills & Boon® *Undone!* eBooks:

THE TANTALISING MISS COALE*

And in M&B:

THE ILLEGITIMATE MONTAGUE
(part of *Castonbury Park* Regency mini-series)

To the UK's brilliant NHS and all its dedicated staff,
especially in A&E.
In particular, Dr E B-G—thanks for the
(rather painful) memory!

Prologue

Paris—1756

The Porte St Honoré was crowded with the usual mix of smart carriages, heavy wagons and tumbrils, all anxious to reach their destination before dark. Suddenly shouts and an unseemly scuffle interrupted the steady flow of traffic. A group of liveried servants surged down the Rue St Honoré, dragging in their midst two figures whose bloodied faces, muddied frockcoats and torn lace ruffles suggested that they had been seriously manhandled. When the group reached the city gate they carried the two men outside and threw them down on to the cobbles.

'If you are wise you will not return to Paris, *messieurs*,' growled one of the servants, making a great show of dusting his hands.

'Aye, we do not take kindly to English dogs

cheating our master at his own card table,' declared a second, while several others aimed vicious kicks at the two men on the ground, before the whole group turned and made their way, laughing, back into the city. The excitement over, the traffic on the Rue St Honoré resumed its steady progress, passing on either side of the two bodies with barely a glance.

One of the men struggled to his hands and knees and stayed there for a moment, as if debating if he could get up. He made the attempt and stood, swaying. Then he pushed his long, unpowdered hair back from his face and turned to help his companion.

'Come along, Harry. I think it best if we heed their advice.'

'No choice, my friend. The *duc* will see to it that we are not made welcome in Paris for some time.' Harry gingerly touched his swollen lip. 'I can't abide a bad loser.'

'You were flirting with La Belle Marianne. That was damned reckless of you.'

'Faith, Drew, the lady gave me a blatant invitation to pursue her. And what of you? Madame le Clere has been warming your bed for the past se'ennight.'

'Someone had to amuse her, with her husband out of Paris. Not quite the same as dallying with the *duc*'s mistress under his very nose. You should have resisted.'

'Nay, my boy, where is the fun in that? Now, where the devil's my wig?'

Drew scooped up the sorry-looking jumble of hair and silk and held it out, saying, 'And you are sure you did not mark the cards?'

'Of course not.' Harry jammed the wig on his head. 'Stap me, boy, I should call you out for that.' He winced and put his hand on his back. 'Egad, but that hurts.' His grin faded and was replaced by a look of shock as he staggered. He collapsed against his companion, saying with a feeble laugh, 'By Gad, I fear they have finished me, old friend.'

'Come along, Harry,' Drew wrung out the cloth and wiped the ashen face. 'We've been through worse than this.'

He frowned as he regarded the restless figure on the bed. He himself was stiff and bruised from the beating he had received but he was recovering, whereas Harry appeared to be growing weaker, writhing in agony as the effects of the laudanum wore off. They had made their way to an inn on the Rue de Chemin Vert where the landlady quickly ushered them upstairs to a bedroom, declaring that the sight of them in their present bloodied state would frighten away her customers. Drew welcomed her ready assistance and suspected she was another of Harry's conquests. He felt a momentary irritation with his friend: they might not be in this situation now if Harry had been able to resist flirting with every pretty woman who came his way.

As the long night wore on he could do nothing but bathe his friend's face and administer more laudanum. In the long periods between he thought back over the years they had spent wandering Europe together. Three years ago Drew had been scraping a living as a mercenary, fighting for any foreign power that would pay him, but then he had met Harry Salforde. Drew was more than ten years his junior but the two men had struck up a close friendship. Harry had taken Drew under his wing, bought him a suit of fine clothes and introduced him to the gambling hells of Rome, Naples and finally Paris, where they had practised their skills at games of chance. So successful had they been that Drew had been able to put away a tidy sum. Thus he was not too concerned about their current lack of funds. It was one of the hazards of living by one's wits.

They had found themselves at the gaming tables with the richest and most powerful nobles in France, but those same nobles did not enjoy losing to their English opponents, and Drew supposed it was inevitable that one day their luck would turn. That the *duc* should have them beaten and thrown out of the city in such an ignominious manner rankled, but Drew bore the man no ill will. He had learned that much from Harry over the years. He merely shrugged off misfortune, learning from his mistakes and moving on to the next city.

Except this time it did not look as if Harry would be moving on for some time.

Drew spent a sleepless night, finally getting a little rest as dawn broke and Harry was sleeping more peacefully, but it did not last and as the morning wore on he grew restless again. Drew noted with some unease that Harry was sweating badly and he fetched a damp cloth to bathe his face. Harry looked at him with bloodshot eyes and for a while did not seem to recognise him. Then at last he gave a sigh.

'I think I'm done for this time, Drew.'

'Devil a bit. Rest is all you need, old friend.'

Harry shifted in the bed, wincing and Drew reached for the laudanum.

'Here, drink this, it will help you sleep.'

'No, not yet.' Harry grabbed his wrist. 'Before that, there's something I must tell you. Something you must promise me.'

'Of course. Anything.'

'I have a daughter.'

'I know. Elyse.' Drew forced a grin. 'You told me she is a rare beauty.'

'Aye, she is. She had just emerged from the schoolroom the last time I saw her but she was bidding fair to become a diamond, like her mother.' His face contorted in pain. 'Lisabet. Frenchwoman, y'know. Beautiful, spirited—only woman I truly loved. She died several years ago and since then Elyse has been in the care of her aunt, my sister, Matthews in Scarborough.'

'She is safe then.'

Harry's grip on his wrist tightened.

'No. There's more. That last time I visited her was just before I met you. Viscount Whittlewood was in Scarborough for his health and I chanced upon him at the gaming tables. Naturally we sat down together on several occasions.'

'Naturally,' Drew said drily.

'He—er—lost. We came to an arrangement. He would marry Elyse to his younger son, in payment of the debt.'

'*What*? But that's outrageous.'

Harry gave a laugh that was cut short by a gasp of pain.

'Whittlewood had lost an outrageous sum. There is nothing so bad about it. Elyse and William were dancing together at the assembly and getting on famously. Smelling of April and May, both of 'em. That is what gave me the idea. Contracts were drawn up, the boy proposed, everything was agreed, but the viscount asked that the marriage should be put off for a while until his son had reached his majority. I saw no harm in it. After all Elyse was only seventeen at the time and had much to learn about the world.' He coughed, wincing as the pain tore at his insides and it was some moments before he could continue.

'Whittlewood's son was one-and-twenty six months ago but he made no move to claim his bride. I wrote to the viscount, advising him that my patience was wearing thin. Play or pay up. Whittlewood agreed that I should deliver Elyse to him by Michaelmas, when she reaches her majority, and the marriage will take place within the month.'

'And what does your daughter say to all this?' asked Drew.

'What should she say, but yes? What girl in her right mind would turn down the chance to ally herself to the Reversons? They are one of the foremost families in England. Besides, he's a good-looking young man and they were fancying themselves very much in love even then. Don't look down your nose at me, Drew. I know that was a few years back but m'sister's last letter informed me that Elyse has been corresponding with Reverson and he is still eager for the match. So all that needs to be done now is to take the bride to her groom. Only I did not expect to cock up my toes before I could do it.'

'Do not talk such nonsense. You will be up and about again in a few days.'

Harry closed his eyes, one hand waving feebly.

'I don't think so, my friend, not this time. I won't be able to escort Elyse to her new family, so I must ask you to do it for me.'

'Me!' the shock of it surprised a laugh from Drew. 'Lord, Harry, you more than anyone should know that I can't go back to England. There's a price on my head.'

'You can change your name. It wouldn't be the first time. And what has it been, ten years since you went back? Who is likely to remember you?'

'That is not all, Harry. I have lived those past ten years by my wits and my sword, stealing kisses from other men's wives and daughters. A disreputable rogue! I am the last man you should entrust with such a task.'

'No, you are the perfect choice to look after my precious daughter.' Harry's voice was failing, but he managed a weak grin. 'Poacher turned gamekeeper. Help me sit up now, and I'll write a note for m'sister, then she will give Elyse into your care.'

Drew argued, but in vain. In the end he called for pen and ink and helped Harry to write his final letters. It took a long time, sitting up seemed to cause Harry even more pain and he fainted off more than once, but at last the business was finished and Harry leaned back, closing his eyes.

'There, it is done.' His voice was little more than a thread. 'Give this to my sister, she will find you all the documents relating to this business.'

'Hush, my friend, no need to talk more of this now. Wait until the morning—'

'I doubt I shall see the morning. The pain in my gut is damnable.' He waved his hand towards his frockcoat, thrown over a chair. 'You'll find some papers sewn into the lining, and a letter of introduction to a certain gentleman in Lyon. Go to him and he will give you access to my funds.'

'Harry—'

'No, let me finish.' He drew another laboured breath, the skin on his face as grey as old parchment. 'Take what you need for your journey, and give the rest to Elyse on her birthday. 'Tis her inheritance.'

'I will, Harry.'

'Do I have your word as a gentleman? And don't give me that rubbish again about your being a rebel. I knew you for a gentleman the first time I saw you!'

Drew grasped the hand, and not by the flicker of an eyelid did he show his dismay at the cold skin.

'You have my word, Harry. A rebel's honour, for what it's worth.'

'Good.' He closed his eyes and seemed to relax down into the pillows. 'Then I commend my daughter to your care.'

Within an hour Harry Salforde was dead.

Chapter One

'Miss Salforde, I prostrate myself at your feet. I am your slave!'

Elyse looked down at the portly gentleman kneeling before her, his badly powdered bagwig failing to cover completely his straggly blond hair.

'Well, you need not, Mr Scorton. I cannot give you any hope because I am promised to another, as you are very well aware.'

She tried and failed to stop the smile that was bubbling inside her. The gentleman, looking up at that moment, saw her lips twitch and struggled to his feet, saying in an injured tone, 'You are very cruel, fair beauty. If you will not countenance my suit, why did you agree to come outside with me?'

Yes, why had she?

Elyse pondered the matter. She could not

deny that the drawing room was very hot and crowded, but there had been no shortage of gentlemen offering to escort her out on to the terrace. So why had she favoured Mr Scorton?

Because he was the least likely of her many admirers and tonight she had decided to take pity on him. Elyse did not consider herself vain, but she was often called beautiful, so she supposed it must be true. Her figure was good, and there was something about her dark curls, brown eyes and heart-shaped face that seemed to draw gentlemen to her. All sorts of men, married or single, young or old, they crowded around her. They paid her compliments, teased her, flirted with her. She was happy enough to respond to them all, knowing herself safe from any serious courtship because she was in love with the Honourable Mr William Reverson, younger son of Viscount Whittlewood, and she was going to marry him. And her admirers, too, knew of her engagement and were content to enjoy a mild flirtation, a little amusing badinage with a pretty young lady. All quite harmless.

However, it seemed that Mr Scorton, with his pompous manners and badly fitting wig, was so smitten with her that he was not content to kiss her hand and whisper ridiculous compliments into her ear, he had actually had the temerity to propose!

It was a salutary lesson, and one that she knew regretfully she should have learned before this, but what was one to do when men were silly enough to shower her with praise and adulation? However, she had no wish to cause distress to anyone, and she realised she must be more circumspect in future. With a rueful smile she held out her hand to Mr Scorton.

'Why, sir, I came out with you for a little air, nothing more, but if I have raised false hopes in you then I am very sorry for it. Pray cry friends with me, sir.'

He clasped her fingers in his pudgy hands.

'Ah, so kind, so generous. I cannot let you go without trying to persuade you to think seriously of my offer.'

Before she knew what he was about he had pulled her into his arms.

'Really, Mr Scor—'

Her words were smothered as he covered her face with hot, ardent kisses.

He might only be the same height as Elyse, and as broad as he was wide, but Mr Scorton in the throes of passion proved himself immensely strong. She could not break out of his hold and was crushed against him, unable even to deliver a well-aimed kick to his shins because the thick folds of her black petticoats were in the way.

She twisted her head away, shuddering as his wet lips slithered over her cheek.

'How dare you, sir, I am in mourning!'

'And your sorrow makes you even more irresistible.'

'Enough sir, let me go!'

She did not expect him to obey, so she was more than a little surprised to find herself suddenly released.

Elyse staggered back and steadied herself against the balustrade that edged the terrace. As soon as she had regained her balance she raised her head, intending to deliver a blistering reproof, but the words died on her lips when she realised that they were no longer alone on the terrace.

A dark stranger was standing between her and Mr Scorton, who was clutching at his throat.

'For Gad, sir,' Scorton gasped, 'you have well-nigh strangled me.'

'I had to find some way of pulling you off the lady and my fingers in the back of your neck cloth proved most effective.'

This cool rejoinder brought a choleric flush to Mr Scorton's cheeks.

'Then by heavens you shall answer for it. Name your friends, sir.'

Mr Scorton placed his hand upon the hilt of his sword and drew himself up to his full if diminutive height, which Elyse could not fail to notice left him several inches shorter than the tall stranger.

'Don't be such a damned fool,' came the crushing retort. 'I am the girl's guardian.'

The effect of this statement silenced Mr Scorton, but it caused Elyse to give a little shriek. Both men looked towards her but it was the stranger who spoke, addressing Mr Scorton in a tone of weary boredom.

'I suggest you go away, sir, before I give you a bloody nose to go with your sore throat.'

With only the slightest hesitation Mr Scorton hurried away and the stranger turned towards Elyse. Her instinct was to step back, but her thick skirts were already pressing against the balustrade and she was trapped.

'Keep away from me,' she said, putting out her hand.

He had his back to the light that spilled out of the drawing room windows, so Elyse could not see his face and she was aware of an unaccountable stirring of alarm. His large frame stood menacingly between her and the safety of the house. She felt a stab of annoyance that her erstwhile suitor had gone off so readily and left her to face this man alone.

He made no move to approach, but his silence was equally unnerving and she said sharply, 'I have no idea who you are.'

'Drew Bastion.' He spoke curtly without even a bow or an 'at your service'. 'I wrote to you from France, to inform you of your father's death and the fact that he had appointed me your guardian.'

'I do not need a guardian.'

'From what I have just seen I think you do,' he retorted. 'I was surprised to arrive and find the house so full of company.'

'My aunt arranged this party weeks ago and decided we should not cancel. Once we heard the news about Papa we made it clear there could be no music or dancing.'

'You should also have made it clear there would be no flirting.'

'I was not—'

'From the moment I walked in I have observed you,' he interrupted. 'You have been constantly surrounded by gentlemen and your manner, the way you ply your fan, is most unseemly for one in deep mourning for her father.'

Drew paused, reining in his anger. Harry's loss was still raw and this lack of respect was an outrage. Yet it was hardly Miss Salforde's fault if men were falling over themselves to win her favour. Her dark beauty was everything that Harry had described to him. Luminescent was the word that came to his mind, despite her bereaved state. She was as covered up as a Jesuit in a bombazine manteau, but its dull black petticoats only enhanced the porcelain delicacy of her fine skin, which was innocent of paint or powder.

She had caught his eye as soon as he walked into the room. In any other circumstances he would have made his way to her and engaged her interest, for there was no denying the sharp tug of attraction he had felt as he took in her excellent figure and those luxuriant curls, the colour of polished ebony. But he had recognised her immediately as Harry's daughter, and honour would not allow him to trifle with a lady who had been placed under his protection. However, it was clear that the other gentlemen present were equally entranced and they had no such restraint upon them.

No, he could not blame her for attracting any man's attention, but he could blame her for responding in such a flirtatious manner. And what was Mrs Matthews thinking of, to allow the party to go ahead barely three months after her brother's death? Of course, this was the thriving spa town of Scarborough and not Paris, but surely the rules of polite society in England had not changed quite so radically while he had been away? As if reading his mind the girl put up her head, a challenge in her dark eyes.

'We are holding a quiet soirée, sir, as befits a house in mourning. The guests here came only to offer their condolences.'

His lip curled.

'That may well have been the intention, but the gentlemen crowding around you were certainly doing more than *offering their condolences* and you were doing nothing to discourage them.'

'That is outrageous. You have no right to say such things to me!'

He ignored her outburst.

'Then I come out here to find you flirting so

disgracefully in the darkness. By heaven you are as bad as your father.'

'How dare you malign my sainted papa!'

Her dark eyes sparkled with wrath but he found his own anger diffused by a sudden flash of humour.

He said drily, 'Your father was many things, including a good friend to me, Miss Salforde, but he was no saint.'

He thought she would fly at him for that, but although her eyes widened and the angry flush on her cheeks deepened, she bit her lip and regarded him in silence. He observed her resentful look, the shadow of doubt in her eyes. So she knew something of her father's life then. But he was not here to argue with her. He tried to modify his tone when he spoke again.

'Enough of this, Miss Salforde. Shall we go in and find your aunt?'

After the briefest hesitation Elyse laid her fingers on his proffered arm. Andrew Bastion. She recalled, now, that her aunt had mentioned his name when she had read out his letter, but Elyse had taken little note of it at the time, nor the fact that he had been appointed her guardian. She had been too shocked by the news of her father's sudden demise. Since her mother's death twelve years ago she had only seen Papa occasionally and for very brief periods. He would arrive, boisterous, laughing and bringing with him extravagant presents for them both, then he would disappear again for months, even years. He had become a distant figure, larger than life yet not quite real. That is why it felt so uncomfortable to be in deep mourning for a father she barely knew.

But that did not mean she would forgive this man for upbraiding her in such a brutish manner. A tiny prickle of conscience whispered that she might have deserved his reprimand but she was not accustomed to criticism. Mama had always spoiled her, and Aunt Matthews was of such a complaisant nature that she never made any effort to check her. It was the same with the gentlemen of her acquaintance. As soon as she had left the schoolroom she had been aware of their admiration. Why, even her aunt's elderly gentlemen friends gazed upon her with approval.

Elyse glanced up at her escort as they stepped back into the light of the drawing room. As a friend of Papa's she had assumed he would be of a similar age and she was surprised to discover that he was much younger—some years less than thirty, she guessed. As if aware of her scrutiny Bastion glanced down at her and she discovered he was also extremely handsome. Something, a flash, a bolt of attraction shot between them and she quickly averted her gaze, frightened by the sudden inexplicable feeling that came over her, as if she had always known this man. It could not be. She had never seen him before, although now his image was burned into her memory.

His face was lean, with straight dark brows above a pair of searching blue eyes. A coat of dark blue velvet embroidered with silver was moulded to his large frame and threw into sharp relief the snowy lace ruffles at his throat and wrists. His clothes were undoubtedly fashionable and had a distinctly French air. Despite the fact that he wore his own light brown hair unpowdered and caught back with a simple black ribbon she thought him very elegant, much more stylish than any other gentlemen present tonight.

Indignation welled up within Elyse. It would not do to let him know what she thought of him, especially when he so patently disapproved of her. But surely his disapproval would not last for long? He would come round when he knew her better. After all, she had not yet met a man who was impervious to her charms. She took another glance at the unyielding figure of her escort and a tiny doubt shook her. It was true she had never been short of admirers, but she had never before set out to attract a man. She shook her head at her foolishness. She was not trying to *attract* him, merely to make him like her. She buried her indignation and tried for a friendly tone.

'Are you truly my guardian, Mr Bastion?'

'I am. Your father left you to my charge. I have the papers with me, proving my identity, if you would like to see them.'

'I beg your pardon, I did not mean to question you, but when we read your letter—I expected someone older.' She flashed him a smile. 'Why, you cannot be much older than I am.'

'I am six-and-twenty, and old enough *not* to be bamboozled by your tricks and stratagems, madam.'

The glint in his blue eyes made the blush deepen in her cheeks. Had he guessed her thoughts? She was tempted to protest, but in truth she had been trying to charm him and decided it would be wiser to remain silent until she had the measure of Mr Andrew Bastion.

He took her back to her aunt, who greeted them with unruffled cheerfulness.

'So you found her, Mr Bastion. Was she on the terrace, as we thought?'

'I was, Aunt Matthews.' Elyse answered quickly, to prevent her companion from doing so. 'I had stepped out for a breath of air and Mr Scorton was so ungentlemanly as to forget himself.' She could not resist a flicker of a glance at the man beside her. He should not be allowed to think she had been indulging in a light flirtation. 'He made me an offer of marriage.'

'Did he my dear? How tiresome for you.'

Knowing her aunt's complaisant nature, Elyse was in no way disconcerted by her lack of concern, but Mr Bastion was much less sanguine.

'You appear singularly unsurprised, madam.'

Mrs Matthews opened her eyes at him.

'You are wrong, sir. I am very surprised, for everyone here knows Elyse is promised to Viscount Whittlewood's son. However, I must take you to task, Elyse. It is all very well for you to be friendly with the gentlemen here. After all, you have known them for years, but as for going out on to the terrace alone with one of them, that was not at all wise, my love.'

Elyse bit her lip. It did not need her aunt's

gentle reproof to tell her that. She could only be grateful that Mr Bastion did not disclose just how unwise she had been. Yet his silence on the subject only increased her irritation, since she was now doubly beholden to him. When another guest claimed her aunt's attention Elyse turned to Mr Bastion and began to offer him an apology. He cut her short.

'Save your words, Miss Salforde. You will not turn me up sweet.'

'I was not attempting to—'

'It is my opinion that you have been grievously indulged,' he continued as if she had not spoken. 'No wonder your father asked me to take you in hand.'

She drew herself up, an angry retort rising to her lips but before she could utter it he had pulled her hand on to his arm.

'Let us move away a little, Miss Salforde, where we may talk undisturbed.'

'I have no wish to talk to you.'

'I do not doubt that, but I am your guardian and I think I need to make a few things clear.' He led her to the far side of the refreshment table, which was currently deserted. 'You have been petted and spoiled and come to think of yourself as a diamond of the highest order.'

She gave a gasp of indignation.

'I think no such thing.'

'But you do think yourself up to every rig and row, and able to wrap any man round your little finger, is that not so?' She blushed a fiery red and he nodded with satisfaction. 'Let us get one thing straight at the outset, Miss Salforde. I am no callow youth to be dazzled by your smile, nor am I ancient enough to dote on you.'

She pulled her arm free and turned to glare up at him.

'You are insulting, sir.'

He leaned a little closer. She saw again that disturbing glint in his eye, but this time it held her attention. She could not look away.

'I am merely making sure we understand one another,' he told her. 'Your father appointed me to look after you, and not before time, from what I have witnessed tonight.'

He was towering over her and she had the strangest impression that she was enveloped in his shadow. His blue eyes bored into her as if he could see into her very soul. Her spine tingled, she felt threatened, imperilled, yet this man was her guardian, sent by Papa to protect her.

She blurted out, 'I think you are far more

dangerous than any of the gentlemen here tonight.'

The harsh look vanished and the corners of his mouth lifted.

'You may well be right, Miss Salforde, so you would be wise to tread carefully.' He gave a little bow, turned on his heel and left her to stare at his retreating form.

The remainder of the evening proved very long and frustrating for Elyse. She kept away from the infuriating Mr Bastion as much as possible, but she could not relax and enjoy herself. She was very conscious of every man who approached her, unable to respond to even the mildest compliment and instead she sought out her female acquaintances, determined that no further accusations of improper conduct should be levelled at her.

For once she was relieved when the guests began to take their leave, but even then her trials were not at an end, for she discovered that Aunt Matthews had invited Mr Bastion to remain behind.

'I have ordered wine and cakes to be brought to us in the morning room,' she told Elyse, directing a smile at the gentleman that showed how far she had fallen under his spell. 'There are papers I need to hand over and I made sure you would like to talk to him about your father.'

'I should, of course, Aunt, but perhaps it is a little late for Mr Bastion.'

'I have already assured you I am not in my dotage, Miss Salforde.' His eyes gleamed with a challenge as he anticipated her next argument. 'And everyone assures me that you have boundless energy.'

She shot him a smouldering glance but was not yet beaten.

'I have,' she responded sweetly, 'but perhaps my aunt may be fatigued.'

Aunt Matthews laughingly disclaimed.

'Not a bit of it. Why, it is not much past midnight. Now come along, both of you, let us repair to the morning room and make ourselves comfortable.'

She sailed out of the room and Elyse followed, head held high and ignoring the gentleman who fell into step beside her.

'I would not advise you to cross swords with me, Miss Salforde,' he murmured.

She gave a little huff of impatience.

'I have no wish to do so,' she hissed at him.

'But I will not allow you to browbeat me, you… you bully!'

He stopped caught her arm, turning her to face him.

'I shall do whatever is necessary to look after you as your father would have wanted. Is that clear?'

'Perfectly.' The harsh look in his face made her quail inwardly, but she kept her chin up and met his eyes with a defiant stare. 'But that does not mean I have to *like* you.'

To her consternation his frown disappeared at that and he grinned.

'I am desolated, of course, but doubtless I will survive.'

She gave a little gasp of indignation. How dare he laugh at her. Pulling her arm free she hurried on to the morning room, determined to be revenged upon the hateful man.

'So, Mr Bastion, you were with my brother at the end.'

Drew, Mrs Matthews and her niece were sitting around a small table in the morning room, wine and a selection of delectable little cakes provided by Mrs Matthews's indefatigable cook set out before them.

Drew sipped his wine, wondering how much to tell them. That he and Harry had been thrown out of Paris, ostensibly for cheating at cards? That might not shock the ladies as much as the real reason, that Harry had been having a liaison with the *duc*'s mistress. He glanced across the table at Elyse, looking very demure as she nibbled at one of the little cakes. She had probably inherited her beauty from her mother, but she certainly had Harry's charm of manner. She looked up at him at that moment, peeping at him from beneath her lashes in a way that immediately aroused his interest. He fought it down quickly and frowned. She also appeared to have inherited Harry's propensity for flirting.

'You said he died of an injury,' Mrs Matthews continued, when he tarried too long over his answer. 'Was he involved in a duel, perhaps?' She smiled when he looked up, his brows raised in surprise at her question. 'My brother was a scapegrace, Mr Bastion. An adventurer with an eye for the ladies. He never made any secret of it. Even when Elyse's mama was alive he could not change his ways and settle down, so you need not think to shock us.'

'There *was* a little trouble,' he confessed. 'In Paris.'

He paused, remembering how he had half-carried half-dragged Harry to the inn where Harry had told him he knew the landlord's wife. Drew's lips tightened. Harry's trouble was that he knew *every man's* wife.

Drew saw that Elyse was watching him, although he acquitted her now of trying to flirt with him. Her gaze was steady, direct. He knew she would not be satisfied unless he gave some explanation of what had happened. But her candid look made him uneasy. He wanted to protect her from the truth.

'Footpads. Harry was more seriously injured than we thought at first. I summoned a physician but it was no use, he died within hours, but before he did, he drew up certain papers. Including one making me your guardian, Miss Salforde.'

'Yes, I have been considering that,' Elyse said. 'Why should he do such a thing, sir, when my aunt has managed very well on her own for the past dozen years?'

He replied carefully. 'Your father was very conscious that Mrs Matthews is a widow.'

'And he thought you a more suitable guardian?' She raised her brows and he observed the faint look of disbelief before she shifted her gaze to the cakes. 'I believe you had known my father for some years, Mr Bastion.'

'That is correct. We had become close friends.'

Her hand hovered over the platter before she selected a tiny iced fancy, saying as she did so, 'If you were my father's friend, sir, and you were with him in Paris, it occurs to me that you, too, are an adventurer. And quite possibly a rake,' she added thoughtfully. 'I am well aware that my father had that reputation.'

Touché.

'What I was in the past is irrelevant,' he told her. 'As is the future. For now I have a task to perform. Before he died your father was in touch with Viscount Whittlewood concerning your marriage to his younger son, the Honourable William Reverson.'

'Ah, thank heaven for that,' exclaimed Mrs Matthews. 'Elyse and William Reverson have been betrothed now for three years and I was afraid they would never marry.'

'Quite,' said Drew. 'Harry considered the delay had gone on long enough and he was anxious to have the matter settled. He and the viscount came to an agreement, a date was set for the marriage and Miss Salforde will join the viscount's household a month beforehand, that she may grow accustomed to her new family.' He glanced at Mrs Matthews. 'It was also agreed that you, ma'am, should be invited to remain with your niece as chaperon—and honoured guest—until the wedding.'

'Well, of course,' said the widow. 'And that is even more important now, since I am the only relative the poor child has.'

Drew inclined his head at her before turning his attention to Elyse.

'On his deathbed, your father charged me with the task of delivering you safely into Lord Whittlewood's care by Michaelmas.'

The cake fell from Elyse's nerveless fingers.

'But that is my birthday, and less than a month away.'

'Yes.'

'But I shall still be in mourning.'

'Your father knew that, but it is his express wish that the arrangements stand. The wedding will take place a month later, at the end of October.'

'I cannot possibly be married so soon.'

From her startled gaze Drew knew that Elyse had not been informed of the forthcoming change in her circumstances. He felt a tiny spurt of irritation. It was just like Harry to want to keep such information to himself until he could return to Scarborough and whisk his daughter off to her new life. *He* would have considered the speed and surprise of the whole venture exciting. Elyse looked as if she needed more time to grow accustomed to the idea. In contrast to her niece's shocked countenance, Mrs Matthews was beaming at him.

'But of course you can, my love. Heavens, you have been waiting long enough. With Lord Whittlewood's money and influence behind the alliance everything can be arranged in a twinkling.' She turned her smile upon Drew. 'That is wonderful news, sir. I know Mr Reverson and my niece are eager for the match, but we did not know a date had been agreed. And, Elyse, just think of it. You will be with Mr Reverson for your birthday on the twenty-ninth of September.'

'Yes. I shall be one-and-twenty.'

'At which date my guardianship of you comes to an end,' stated Drew.

'And not a moment too soon.'

Mrs Matthews tutted.

'Now, now, Elyse, it was your father's wish that Mr Bastion should have a care for you and we must respect that.' She smiled at Drew. 'So you will be accompanying us to the viscount's principal seat, sir? I believe it is in Cambridgeshire.'

'No. Lord Whittlewood informs me he will be at his town house in London.'

Drew recalled the viscount's letter which Harry had passed over to him. It was unusually specific. Miss Salforde was to be delivered into his care by Michaelmas and not a day later, or he would consider the agreement null and void. Drew did not know how binding that last clause would be, but to drag the matter through the courts was unthinkable. It would not reflect well upon either party. The viscount's standing was sufficiently good for him to survive it, but Harry's name would fare less well, and the scandal attached to his daughter would ruin her for life. And as for his own part in the affair, Drew had no wish to attract the notice of the authorities.

He said now, 'I intend to deliver Miss Salforde to Lord Whittlewood in London by the end of the week. I will then remain in town for the two weeks until Michaelmas. That will give me time to ascertain that Miss Salforde is happy with all the arrangements before I relinquish my guardianship. After that she will be in the care of the viscount, who plans to remove the whole family to Cambridgeshire for the banns to be called.'

'Yes of course, but…' Mrs Matthews frowned. 'To be in town by the end of the week we will need to set out in a few days' time.'

Drew nodded. 'Wednesday at the latest, ma'am. If the weather turns we might easily take a se'ennight to reach London.'

Elyse had been listening in silence, but now she gave an outraged gasp. The news of her forthcoming marriage was shock enough, but to leave her home at such short notice was intolerable.

'That's the day after tomorrow,' she said. 'We cannot possibly be ready so soon.'

'I'm afraid you will have to be.'

'You are riding roughshod over us, Mr Bastion.'

His gaze flickered over her, the blue eyes cold and indifferent.

'I would have thought you would be impatient to join your fiancé. Perhaps you are not so eager for the match as you once were?'

'Of course I am, but—'

'But nothing, Miss Salforde. You have tomorrow to do your packing and make your arrangements.'

She sat upright in her chair, bristling with indignation.

'It is not long enough. Why, there are a dozen little things I shall need, including new gowns.' Elyse turned to look at Aunt Matthews, but she received no support there.

'We will manage with what we have, my dear. After all, we shall be able to go shopping in town, and think how much more exciting that will be. Do not worry, Mr Bastion. Elyse and I will be ready.'

'Good.' He rose. 'I will organise a post-chaise and send you word of what time it will call for you.'

Elyse felt her anger bubbling up inside. She had one hand resting on the table and it clenched tightly into a fist as she drew in a breath to retort, but Aunt Matthews covered her fingers with her own and squeezed them warningly as she repeated quietly, 'We will be ready, sir.'

'What an insufferable man!'

Elyse had struggled to contain herself until Mr Bastion had been shown out and the door had barely closed behind him before her exclamation was uttered, resonant with suppressed violence.

'Hush my dear, he may still hear you.'

'I am sure I do not care. I declare I quite abhor him.'

'Why should you do that, my love, when he is doing his best to carry out your father's wishes?'

'But in such a high-handed manner.'

Aunt Matthews chuckled.

'He does appear to be in a hurry to get you to the viscount, does he not? But there, your father's plans were never straightforward, so doubtless there is a good reason for it,' she added shrewdly.

Elyse tossed her head. 'He is the most arrogant, overbearing man I have ever met.'

'Is he? I think it more likely that he is the first man you have met who has not succumbed to your charms.'

Elyse flushed, not at all pleased at her aunt displaying such unwonted perspicacity. She said no more on the subject and presently took herself off to bed, where her rest was disturbed by dreams of an autocratic gentleman with searching blue eyes.

Despite a long journey and the bracing sea air, it was a long time before Drew slept. He had very reluctantly agreed to become guardian to Harry's daughter and now he realised that his qualms had been justified. Harry had described his daughter as intelligent, spirited and beautiful, but he had not told Drew just *how* spirited she was. Nor had Drew believed she would be so beautiful. A veritable diamond. Oh, Harry had described her as such but Drew had dismissed that as a father's natural partiality. And after all, Harry had not seen his daughter for three years, he could not have known with any certainty that the pretty seventeen-year-old would become a nonpareil.

As soon as Drew had arrived in Scarborough he had heard bucks in the taproom toasting the incomparable Miss Salforde and the way they had been clustering around her in her own drawing room convinced him that all the menfolk of the town were in thrall to her. It was not difficult to understand why. She was witty and beautiful and she had a smile that could light up a room. And those large pansy-brown eyes—he had no doubt that her local swains had written odes to them. He had seen for himself how they could be velvet soft or sparkling with anger. He imagined they would be heart-stoppingly glorious when they were shining with happiness. Or love.

The thought had him turning restlessly in his bed. He might not have his old friend's weakness for a pretty face, but he could not deny the attraction he felt towards Elyse Salforde. What was it that Harry had said?

'Who better than a rake to look after a beautiful woman? Poacher turned gamekeeper, my friend.'

Well, perhaps there is still a little too much of the poacher about me, thought Drew.

There was no doubt that he found Elyse Salforde too damned tempting for comfort. It wasn't just her beauty, but something within her, some force of nature that shone out. When their eyes met it seemed to call to him, like a kindred spirit.

By God he was turning into an old fool. He pushed himself up and thumped his pillow before settling down again and pulling the blankets more securely around him. He was honour-bound to carry out Harry's dying wishes and he would do so. He would deliver Harry's daughter safe and sound to her bridegroom if it was the last thing he did.

Chapter Two

The next morning dawned bright and clear and Drew lost no time in making his arrangements. These went well and with the late-summer sun beating down upon him he began to think the task ahead was not quite so onerous. A few days on the road and once they reached London he could hand Miss Elyse Salforde over to Lord Whittlewood. Mrs Matthews had sent him a polite note, inviting him to join them for dinner and he had grinned as he read it. He doubted her niece was in favour of the idea. She had spent most of the previous evening glaring at him, and in truth he knew he had deserved it. He had ridden her hard and given no sign that he found her attractive. She had more than enough admirers and he was not going to add to their number.

Amongst the fashionable beauties of London she might not stand out quite so much, but in a provincial spa town like Scarborough she was undoubtedly a diamond, and far too conscious of her own worth. It would do Miss Salforde no harm at all to be brought down to earth a little and if she tried her tricks upon him then he would do it.

Having finished his business he made his way to the beach to watch the horse racing. He spent a pleasant couple of hours discussing horseflesh with other observers, placing wagers, losing a little money, winning even more before quitting the sands. It was still early and there was time to spare before he needed to change for his dinner engagement, so he decided to stroll through the town. The streets were busy and it was not long before a familiar figure caught his eye.

Miss Salforde was coming towards him in the company of an elderly lady and gentleman. She wore a dark grey cloak over her black gown and it looked out of place against the more colourful attire of her companions. As they approached he recognised the couple as Mr and Mrs Oliver, guests at Mrs Matthews's party last night. He was relieved to see that Elyse was not escorted by any of her young swains. It seemed the chit had some proper feeling, after all.

It soon became apparent that the Olivers

had recognised him. When they came up they stopped to acknowledge his bow and exchange courtesies. Only Elyse looked less than pleased to see him, standing back from her friends and looking beyond him with every appearance of haughty indifference.

'We are making our daily visit to the spa,' offered the old gentleman, the improbably brown hair of his bagwig making a stark contrast to the white whiskers and eyebrows that adorned his aged face. 'But first we are escorting Miss Salforde to the circulating library and home again.'

Elyse looked a little self-conscious when she realised she was the centre of attention, lifting her hands to show him the books she was carrying.

'I must needs return them before I leave town.'

'We called upon Mrs Matthews to thank her for her hospitality last evening and she told us the exciting news,' explained Mrs Oliver. 'You are all off to London! I am sure the ladies must be very pleased they have you to escort them, Mr Bastion. One can hire a courier, I know, but there is nothing so comforting as having a gentleman in attendance.'

Drew bowed.

'Indeed, ma'am. But—is the library not out of your way?'

'Oh, nothing to speak of,' replied Mr Oliver gallantly. 'We will make a little detour, of course, but we are happy to do so, since Mrs Matthews would have had to send her maid, and she has told us how much there is do if everything is to be packed up in time. We do not begrudge a little extra walking, do we my dear?'

His wife concurred readily, but Drew's eyes dwelled thoughtfully upon the way the old gentleman leaned upon his stick.

'If you wish I would happily accompany Miss Salforde to the library, and save you the extra journey.' He saw Elyse's start of surprise, her look of alarm.

'Oh, but I could not possibly impose upon you,' she began, flustered.

He gave a wide smile that encompassed all three of them, saying easily, 'It is no imposition. I have nothing to do until dinnertime and would enjoy the diversion.'

'Well, that is exceeding kind of you, my boy,' declared Mr Oliver, beaming. 'And nothing could be better, Miss Salforde, for there can be no harm in leaving you in the company of your guardian, what?' He gave a wheezy chuckle.

'And I've no doubt you will much prefer to be accompanied by this handsome young fellow, eh?'

'No, indeed, Mr Oliver, I am more than happy to remain with you and Mrs Oliver.'

Elyse's response was heartfelt, Drew was sure, but her elderly friends thought she was merely sparing their feelings. They laughed aside her protests and said goodbye, strolling away and leaving Elyse standing beside Drew. She was regarding him solemnly, a discontented frown marring her perfect features. His lips twitched.

'I have no doubt they are very kind,' he said smiling, 'But to escort you to the circulating library and back again would have added a good mile or so to their perambulations.' He held out his arm. 'Shall we walk on?'

Elyse knew she had no choice. The streets were busy and to refuse his escort and walk unaccompanied through the town where she was so well known would expose her to censure, and there was even the risk of being accosted. Also, she thought indignantly, she doubted he would let her walk away from him. How she wished now that she had declined Mr and Mrs Oliver's kindly offer and waited for Hoyle to come with her—or she could even have sent a footman on the errand.

Curbing such futile regrets she assumed her chilliest demeanour and placed the very tips of her fingers on his sleeve as they set off through the busy streets. She was aware of the attention they were attracting. She acknowledged politely the sly smiles and nods of her many acquaintances but ignored their knowing looks. She noted too the admiring glances that were cast at her escort. His height immediately drew the eye, and there was no denying that his figure was good. It showed to advantage in his russet coat of superfine wool with its silver-gilt buttons. There was no creasing or straining of the material across his broad shoulders or where it tapered gently to his waist before flaring out, and even then a vent in the heavy folds allowed his sword to pass through without marring the elegant lines. In normal circumstances she would have been very pleased to be seen on the arm of such a handsome gentleman, but the circumstances were far from normal and she could not forget his odious behaviour towards her the previous evening. He interrupted her reverie by remarking with a laugh in his voice,

'It behoves us to have some conversation, Miss Salforde.'

'I did not realise I was obliged to entertain you.'

'To escort such a beautiful lady is entertainment enough.'

She could not resist a glance at him as she said drily, 'Trying to turn me up sweet, Mr Bastion?'

'Could I do so?'

The glint in his eyes challenged her and she fought down the impulse to smile back at him. Instead she looked away and said in an indifferent tone, 'You have certainly charmed my aunt.'

'I have no doubt she is relieved to have someone share the responsibility for your guardianship. You must be a sad trial to her.'

'That is not it at all,' she retorted, nettled. 'I am not the least trouble, I assure you. In fact I am of great use to her.'

'Oh?'

'I practically run the household.'

'You rule the roost.'

'No, not at all, I—' She bit her lip. 'You are making a May-game of me, sir.'

He merely laughed at that, and as they had arrived at the circulating library she said no more.

Mr Frear, the library's elderly owner was behind the counter and immediately came forward, his friendly greeting balm to Elyse's wounded pride. She handed back her books and explained that she would not be requiring more.

'Ah yes, I have heard that you are leaving us,' he declared. 'Your going will be a sad loss to the town, Miss Salforde.'

'By heaven, word travels quickly.'

'It does indeed, sir, when it concerns Scarborough's brightest star,' replied Mr Frear gallantly.

Elyse glanced up at the gentleman beside her. That should show him she was held in some esteem here. And he could not accuse her of flirting with old Mr Frear.

Her errand complete and spirits raised somewhat by her reception at the circulating library, Elyse and her companion set off back towards Aunt Matthews's house in Northfield Square. Her escort behaved with such civil courtesy that she was emboldened to try once more to delay their departure.

'Is it imperative that we quit Scarborough tomorrow, Mr Bastion? Surely an extra day would make no odds.'

'We may need that extra day if the weather

should turn. We are a long way from London, Miss Salforde. I would have thought you impatient to see Mr Reverson again.'

'I am, of course.'

She could not avoid the heartbeat's hesitation before making her reply. Marriage to William had been her future for so long that she had come to take it for granted, but the knowledge that she would soon be making her home with William's family was a little frightening. After all, they were almost strangers, even William. She had not forgotten the pleasure of dancing with him, the elation she had felt at his shy proposal, the thrill of the chaste kisses they had exchanged in secret, but they had been together for such a short time.

William had left Scarborough soon after they had become engaged. Elyse had been heartbroken for a week, but then she had settled down to life as one of the belles of the town, happy in the knowledge that she need not join the other young ladies in their scramble to make a suitable alliance. It amused her each Season to watch them pursuing their quarry at the routs and assemblies but she envied none of them their husbands. Apart from headstrong Jenny Malden who had eloped with an actor and been disowned by her family, they had all married sensibly and although they all appeared to be happy enough, not one of them had married for love, which is what she would be doing, as well as marrying into one of the highest families in the land. How could she not be proud of her achievement?

She said, more confidently, 'I cannot wait to be with William again. I received a letter from him only recently begging me to come with all speed.'

'Is he a regular correspondent?'

'He writes to me when he can. He is very busy.'

She would not tell him that it was the first letter she had received in months.

'But you have not seen him for three years.' He paused. 'A person can change a great deal in that time.'

'Not William.'

'And what of you? Are you the same young lady you were when Reverson proposed?'

'Of course.'

He stopped and turned to face her. 'Are you sure of that?'

Elyse frowned, angered that he should question her in this manner. Of course she had not changed. But when she looked up to tell him so the words died on her lips. He was looking down at her with a glinting smile that sent all thoughts of William out of her head. When their eyes locked she felt a tremor of something she did not understand run through her body. Heat pooled deep inside and her heart began to thud most uncomfortably in her chest. She felt suddenly breathless and wanted to look away from those disturbing blue eyes. They seemed to see into her very soul and read her most secret thoughts. Not only that, they encouraged new and uncomfortable ideas to form.

She dragged her eyes away but even then they only moved to his mouth and she found herself wondering what it would be like to be kissed by him. She did not doubt that he was very experienced and the thought made the heat deep in her belly curl even deeper. A little thrill of anticipation trembled through her, followed quickly by the knowledge that even thinking of such things was a betrayal of William. Heavens, how could she be so disloyal? In three years she had never before felt like this. She was shocked, and frightened.

Elyse pulled her hand from his arm and turned away, unnerved by his presence and even more so by her reaction. Northfield Square was in sight and she could see her aunt's house on the far side. She hurried towards it, not caring whether he accompanied her. In fact she would very much prefer it if he did not. She soon realised he was keeping pace with her but she refused to look at him and did not stop until she had reached the door of her aunt's house. Only then did she turn and force herself to confront him. There was no laughter in his eyes now when they regarded her, no mischievous glint, only a frowning look. She wondered if she had disappointed him and realised how much she did not want that to be the case.

'Of—of course I have changed,' she said defiantly. 'I am older and—and a woman. I am ready now for marriage.'

'You are certainly that, Miss Salforde,' he retorted. 'And I pity your husband.'

She stared at him, outraged that he should say such a thing, but without another word he swept off his hat, made her an elegant bow and strode away.

By the time Drew reached his lodgings his sudden flash of ill humour had abated. It was not the chit's fault that he found her so damned desirable. He had thought he had himself well under control. Granted he had teased her a little, just for the pleasure of it, but her forthcoming marriage to Reverson was no matter for levity. It was his responsibility as her guardian to look out for her. To warn her that people could change a great deal in three years.

He had tried to keep his tone light, but when she had fixed those huge brown eyes upon him he had felt again the stirring of desire, the urge to take her in his arms and make her forget all about William Reverson. He had tried to persuade himself that Harry's daughter was still a child but it was clear that she was not, and the more he saw of her the more his body told him she was every inch a woman, and a very desirable one. Gaining the seclusion of his room he tossed aside his hat and went over to the washstand. He poured some water into the basin and bathed his face, hoping the shock of it would restore his intellect. His anger was not aimed at Elyse, but at her ability to disconcert him and send all sensible thoughts flying from his head.

Drew was well aware that such a weakness could spell disaster for a man who lived by his wits, but after a period of cool reflection he could put the whole incident into perspective.

She was a pretty woman, he was a red-blooded male. Sparks were bound to fly when they were together. It was up to him to make sure it did not get out of hand.

By the time Drew made his way back towards Northfield Square later that day his good humour had returned and he found he was looking forward to dinner with Mrs Matthews and her niece. He had no doubt Elyse would still be at odds with him and who could blame her, when he had treated her so roughly? Perhaps he should not have questioned her about her betrothal to Reverson, but he had to be sure she was happy about it. He himself was uneasy about this whole business. Harry had not explained to his daughter why Lord Whittlewood had agreed to so unequal a match and Drew was convinced the viscount would not want the truth known.

Elyse and Reverson might have thought themselves in love during that brief, heady Season three years ago, but if they had been apart since then he suspected there could be little affection left, and although he thought Elyse a little spoiled he did not wish her to be hurt. He would have to be careful in his dealings with her. It had almost been his undoing when he had teased her, for he had been enjoying himself and relaxed his guard. Then she had turned those soft brown eyes to his and he had suffered a sudden rush of desire that had almost knocked him off his feet. It had driven all teasing thoughts from his head and he had wanted nothing more than to drag her into his arms.

Even worse, he suspected she had felt it too because she had pulled away from him and rushed off in a panic. But there was no harm done, he had been taken unawares, that was all. It would not happen again. And Elyse was obviously appalled by the attraction that had crackled between them, sharp as any electrical storm. Perhaps that little fright would do her good. She might now see the wisdom of keeping all men at a proper distance. He grinned, thinking again of the way she had ripped up at him. She undoubtedly had spirit and she was not unintelligent. He would do what he could to lay those ruffled feathers this evening and if he succeeded he thought she would prove entertaining company.

He arrived at Northfield Square at the appointed hour and was shown into an empty drawing room by a servant who was clearly distracted. However, Drew did not have long to wait before he discovered the cause. Miss Salforde came in and stood with her back to the door. She had not changed for dinner and was still dressed in her plain morning gown of black crepe, adorned only with a snowy apron. The simplicity of the homely garb only highlighted the delightful curves of her figure and he found himself once again indulging in highly inappropriate thoughts. However, when his eyes moved to her face he sobered immediately and his attention jumped back to the present, for her dark eyes were troubled.

'Sir, you must cancel your arrangements,' she said without preamble, clasping her hands at her breast. 'We cannot go to London tomorrow.'

'Is something amiss, Miss Salforde?' His brows snapped together. There was no sign of the confident, teasing miss he had seen last night, nor the haughty ice maiden of this afternoon. Instead she was very close to tears. In two strides he was at her side, taking her arm and gently drawing her to one of the sofas. Her silent compliance only confirmed to him how upset she was.

'Now,' he said when they were sitting down together. 'Tell me what has occurred.'

'M-My aunt has broken her arm. She has been hurrying hither and thither all day preparing for the journey and she tripped and fell on the stairs. If she had not been in such haste to make sure we did not keep you waiting—'

She broke off, hunting for her handkerchief. Drew gave her his own.

'Ah,' he murmured. 'So it is my fault. I should have known.'

She blew her nose and brushed away a rogue tear that had escaped on to her cheek.

'No, of course it was not your fault.'

'Very handsomely said, Miss Salforde.'

She gave a watery chuckle.

'Well, you cannot be blamed for the accident. Aunt should not have been carrying those bandboxes down from the attic, but Hoyle was busy packing the trunks and—'

'Hoyle?'

'Our maid. She is my aunt's dresser, really, but she has always looked after me, too. I have never required a maid of my own but with so much to be done in such a short time…'

'And where is your aunt now?'

'In her room. The doctor is with her, setting the bone. He says it is a simple break, but she is very shaken up and he will not hear of her leaving her bed for at least a se'ennight.' She sighed. 'So you see, Mr Bastion, we must cancel our journey to London.'

Drew's mind was racing. Mrs Matthews might be able to leave her room in a week but he doubted she would be fit to travel for several more—certainly not before Michaelmas. And those ominous words in Lord Whittlewood's letter were imprinted in his mind—if Miss Salforde was not delivered to him by Michaelmas then he would consider himself to have fulfilled his part of the contract, and the marriage would not go ahead.

'No, we will have to go on and your aunt will follow as soon as she is able.'

He found himself subjected to a disconcertingly direct gaze from those brown eyes.

'But that would be most irregular. I will not travel without my aunt.'

'I'm afraid you must. Lord Whittlewood is expecting you.'

'Then I shall write to him and explain, if you will not do so.'

'If I thought it worthwhile I *would* do so, willingly, but I do not think the viscount would consider your aunt's broken arm sufficient excuse to suspend his plans.' He could almost see the questions forming in her head and added quietly, 'Lord Whittlewood's instructions were very clear.'

'Do you mean, if I do not comply, there may be no wedding?'

'That is a distinct possibility, Miss Salforde.'

Elyse sat back. His words were like cold water, waking her from the nightmare of the past few hours into an even worse predicament. If she delayed, then she might lose William for ever. She had been seventeen when they had met, and William only a little older. There was no doubt that she had been dazzled to be singled out for attention by the son of a viscount. He was so handsome, too, everyone had said so. Was it any wonder that she had tumbled into love with him? Of course since then there had only been an occasional exchange of letters, but Elyse held his memory in her heart and longed for the day when he would claim her as his bride. Now the gentleman at her side was telling her that if she delayed that might never happen. She drew a deep, resolute breath.

'Then I shall have to go to William alone.'

A faint, glinting smile warmed his piercing blue eyes.

'Not quite alone, Miss Salforde. I shall be with you.'

Elyse found his words reassuring and that surprised her. Their encounters so far had been tempestuous, and occasionally disturbing, yet here she was preparing to travel to London and taking comfort from the fact that he would be with her. However, she had no time to consider such matters, especially since Aston was even now coming in to ask her what she wished to do about dinner.

'I do not know,' she said distractedly, putting one hand to her temple. 'I am not hungry.'

'Is it ready to be served?' Mr Bastion interjected, addressing the butler directly.

Aston bowed. 'Why yes, sir. It only needs a word and it can be on the table in a trice.'

'Then we should eat.'

Elyse bridled. At this juncture any man of sensibility would withdraw and leave the family in peace.

'I think not,' she contradicted him. 'I should go to Aunt Matthews.'

'The mistress is sleeping, miss,' said the butler, trying to be helpful. 'Hoyle says Dr Carstairs gave her some laudanum before he left and doesn't expect her to wake up for a couple of hours yet.'

There was no hint of triumph in the smile her guest bestowed upon her, but Elyse still ground her teeth when he said with maddening calm,

'Then we have plenty of time to dine and you can sit with your aunt afterwards.'

'I am not hungry.'

Elyse bit her lip. She sounded like a sulky child. What was it about Andrew Bastion that brought out the worst in her? She tried to be thankful that he appeared not to notice her bad manners.

He replied in soothing tones, 'Perhaps not, but it will do your aunt no good if you are fainting off from want of food.' He rose and pulled her to her feet, then he tucked her hand into the crook of his arm and patted it in an avuncular fashion.

'Aye, that's the ticket,' chuckled Aston, taking advantage of his position as an old family retainer. 'I'm sure you'll feel more the thing with some food inside you, miss, and I'll tell Hoyle to come and fetch you just as soon as the mistress wakes up.'

There was nothing to be done but to comply. Elyse had to admit that by the time she had partaken of several of the dishes displayed and enjoyed a glass of wine she was feeling much calmer. Her guest behaved impeccably during the meal, conversing on light, unexceptional topics that neither angered nor embarrassed her and she found herself relaxing. Her mind was occupied with the plight of poor Aunt Matthews and she could think of little else.

They had finished their meal when Hoyle came in to say that Mrs Matthews was awake and asking for her niece. Elyse went off immediately, following Hoyle through corridors littered with trunks and cases to her aunt's bedchamber. Aunt Matthews was propped up in the bed, one arm encased in plaster and resting on a mound of pillows. She was looking pale but composed in a nightgown and cap of frothy pink lace and when Elyse came in she held out her good hand, ignoring the maid who was fussing around her.

'Oh, my dear, what a silly thing for me to do, I am so sorry.'

'No, no, Aunt, you must not blame yourself. I am only relieved it is nothing worse. Dr Carstairs told me it would be a simple matter to set the arm and then you will be up and about again in no time.'

'Yes, but not by tomorrow morning. I will not be able to get up for *days*.'

Disregarding Hoyle's tut of disapproval, Elyse perched herself on the edge of the bed and took the proffered hand. 'You are not to worry about that. You can follow on as soon as you are well enough to travel.'

'You plan to go without me?'

'I must. Mr Bastion thinks the viscount would insist upon it.'

'Well, there is no doubt that these great men are used to having their own way,' agreed Aunt Matthews, sighing. 'And you have been waiting so long I am sure you must be eager to see your beau again.'

'I am of course.' Elyse replied quickly, although now the moment was approaching she felt more than a little apprehensive. 'But I would rather wait until you could come with me, Aunt.'

A knock made her turn and she saw Andrew Bastion standing in the doorway.

'I beg you will forgive the intrusion, ma'am?'

'Yes, yes, come in, sir. Do not stand on ceremony.' Mrs Matthews called to him, ignoring another disapproving sniff from Hoyle, who was tidying the pots and jars on the dressing table. 'We must decide what we are to do about getting Elyse to London.'

'My thoughts exactly, ma'am. I have hired a post-chaise to be here at nine o'clock tomorrow morning.'

'Could we not delay it a little?' said Elyse. 'I would like to know my aunt is improving before I leave Scarborough.'

'Oh, I shall go on well enough, my love, you need not worry over me,' said Aunt Matthews. 'And the roads being as they are you will want to have as much time as possible for your journey.'

This was very much what Andrew Bastion had told her, but it was no more palatable to hear it from her aunt.

'I am sure another week would not hurt.' Elyse fixed her eyes upon Mr Bastion. He met their challenge but would not capitulate and she felt her temper rising. 'Mr Reverson's letters tell me he is as eager as I am for us to be together, but if I explain everything I am sure he would understand if my arrival is a little delayed.'

'But his father would not.'

'Mr Bastion is right, my love. You must not give them any reason to reject you.'

'You think they would cry off, over such a little thing? But William and I love each other.' She reached into her pocket and pulled out a crumpled paper. 'Why, in his last letter to me he says he cannot wait for us to be united.'

'That may be so, but there is no doubt that while this is a brilliant match for you the viscount might have looked higher for a bride for his younger son.' Her aunt's gaze had become disconcertingly shrewd. 'If you want him, love, you must take him now, or it may be too late.' She squeezed Elyse's fingers, saying urgently, 'This is a wonderful opportunity for you, my love. You must grasp it with both hands.'

'I will, Aunt. I promise.'

'Good girl.' Aunt Matthews's eyes were suspiciously bright and she blinked a little before turning her attention to the gentleman standing at the end of the bed. 'My brother obviously thought a great deal of you, sir, to entrust you with the care of his only child.'

He bowed. 'I shall endeavour not to disappoint him, ma'am.'

'Good. Now, Elyse will be ready to go with you tomorrow morning. And Hoyle shall accompany her.'

There was a clatter as the maid dropped one of the hairbrushes.

'That I won't, ma'am. My place is here, with you.'

Aunt Matthews gave an exasperated sigh.

'Pray do not be tiresome, Hoyle. There is no one else to go with her.'

'That's as maybe, but I've been your maid for nigh on thirty years and I ain't about to leave you now, not when you needs me.'

'You'll do as you're told, Hoyle,' snapped her mistress. 'Or you can pack your bags and leave this minute.'

The maid did not look unduly worried by this threat. Drawing herself up she said with dignity, 'That's for you to decide, ma'am, but I ain't going.'

She stumped to the door, closing it behind her with a bang.

'Well,' Mrs Matthews stared after her. 'Of all the…she knows I won't turn her off, of course, but all the same.'

Elyse gave a little shrug. 'Hoyle has always been a little jealous of me. But even if she were not, you really cannot expect her to leave you now, Aunt, when you are confined to bed.'

'We must find some female to accompany you,' stated Mr Bastion.

Elyse was already smarting from Hoyle's rejection, and the note of impatience in the gentleman's voice only added to her hurt.

'Every other maid in the house would be more of a hindrance than a help,' declared Mrs

Matthews frankly. 'They would most likely fall into hysterics if I suggested they travel more than a mile out of Scarborough.'

He exhaled sharply. 'Then I shall have to hire someone. Though who I might find by nine o'clock tomorrow morning—'

'You need not trouble yourself on my account,' said Elyse, holding herself very stiff.

'You cannot travel alone,' he retorted.

'You are my guardian, are you not? There can be no impropriety in our travelling together.'

She glared at him. He was only trying to help, but suddenly the excitement of her forthcoming marriage was gone, replaced by a feeling that she was merely an inconvenience. It was not a pleasant thought. The gentleman regarded her in silence for a moment and when he spoke his tone was decisive.

'Very well. If there is someone from the household that you can persuade to go with you it would be an advantage, but as you say, it is not necessary. We can always arrange for a maid to attend you at the inns.' He turned to Aunt Matthews. 'I wish you a speedy recovery, ma'am.' His gaze flickered to Elyse and the indifference she saw in his eyes only added to her dismay.

'I shall call for you at nine o'clock sharp, Miss Salforde. Be sure you do not keep me waiting.'

Once more Drew walked away from Mrs Matthews' house with his mind in turmoil. He had been in England for less than a week and already what should have been a simple task of escorting a young lady to London was turning into a nightmare. First of all there was Lord Whittlewood's ultimatum, making it necessary to reach London with all speed; and now her aunt, the most proper person to act as a chaperon, could no longer travel with them. Such a trifle would not have worried him unduly, if it was not for the fact that his ward was no schoolroom miss but a very desirable young woman.

He recalled that immediate tug of attraction he had experienced the first time he had seen Elyse in her aunt's drawing room. In their subsequent meetings, even when she was at her most tiresome, it had only grown more powerful. Whenever their eyes locked he could feel the energy crackling between them, a pleasurable anticipation of what it would be like to pull her into his arms and kiss her, to unlock the passion he felt sure she possessed.

Impossible, of course. Not only was she a

gently reared young lady and the future wife of another man, she was also his ward, the daughter of his friend, and he was sworn to protect her. And if she was not his responsibility, and not another man's fiancée, what then? Would he seduce her? Of course not. Elyse Salforde was a gently reared young lady; he could not take her for his mistress. Yet what else had he to offer her? He was a rogue, a traitor. He had decided years ago that he could not ask any woman to share that burden.

He let his breath go with a hiss. This was not about his misfortunes. He must concentrate upon Elyse. She might be damned attractive but he would cope with that. He was her guardian, he would employ a maid at each inn to share her room at night and preserve her reputation. If she was happy to make the journey to London without a chaperon of any sort then so be it. He was damned if he would worry about it.

Yet worry he did. He had agreed to Harry's dying wish to take care of his daughter, and that would not include ravishing her before she could be delivered to her fiancé.

The next day dawned clear and bright, only a slight mist on the sea indicating that it was no longer high summer. Elyse donned her travelling dress, a riding habit of olive-green twill with a collar of buff velvet and small gilt buttons. She had added black ruffles at her neck and cuffs and a black lace veil was suspended from the rim of her bonnet. The veil was folded back at present but when it was pulled down it completely obscured her features. It was all very sober and no one, not even the infuriating Mr Andrew Bastion, could doubt she was in mourning.

Aston came to tell her that the carriage was at the door and once she had directed him to have her baggage taken out she went off to take leave of her aunt.

'I wish we could wait until you could come with us,' she said as she gave Mrs Matthews a final hug, taking good care to avoid her injured arm. 'I do not know how I shall go on without you.'

'You will do very well, my love, if you remember your manners.'

Elyse pulled a face. 'I am sure that will not be difficult when I am with Lord Whittlewood, but I am not looking forward to the journey with that man.'

'You mean Mr Bastion?' Aunt Matthews patted her cheek. 'Your father wrote in his final letter that he would trust Drew Bastion with his life. I have no doubt he will look after you, for Harry's sake. But …'

She paused, the restless fingers of her free hand pleating and re-pleating the edge of the sheet until Elyse felt compelled to prompt her.

'Yes, Aunt?'

'I beg you will be careful when you are with Mr Bastion, Elyse. He is not a man to be crossed. There is steel behind his charm.'

Elyse's solemn mood was routed by her aunt's last words. Her eyes twinkled and she gave a merry laugh.

'Charm? I have not seen any *charm*, Aunt. He is rude and overbearing.'

'Well, tread warily my love.'

'I will, I promise.' She leaned over the bed to give her aunt another kiss on the cheek. 'But what can he do, after all? He is only a man.'

With a cheery wave she sailed out of the room and her aunt listened to her dainty boots tapping down the stone stairs. She shook her head.

'Yes, he is a man, Elyse,' she murmured. 'And that is what worries me.'

Elyse was impressed with the elegant equipage at the door. It may only have been a hired post-chaise but it was freshly painted and had four spirited horses harnessed to it, under the care of two smart postilions. Mr Bastion was waiting to hand her in, his hat tucked under one arm. She noted his appearance with approval, the exquisitely tailored riding coat in dark-blue wool, the pale buckskins and shiny top-boots that covered his legs. They all fitted to perfection. The first time she had seen him he had appeared the perfect society gentleman, at home in any drawing room. Now he was dressed for travel, ready for action and adventure.

It flashed through her mind that a young lady might easily lose her heart to such a man and Elyse was relieved to think that her own heart was already engaged. It belonged to William and she was therefore in no danger. Yet she was troubled by a niggling thought that perhaps she was not being completely honest with herself.

Those disturbingly blue eyes glinted down at her and she wondered again if he was able to read her thoughts. She looked away and moved to the carriage, silently putting her hand into his as she prepared to climb in. Immediately she was aware of the strength in his lean fingers. Her mouth went dry. Neither of them had yet put on their gloves and Elyse realised that this was a mistake, because a bolt of excitement shot through her when skin touched skin. Her heart leapt into her mouth and then settled high in her chest, where it beat a rapid and irregular tattoo that disrupted her breathing. It reminded her of the thrill of receiving admiring glances, or allowing a gentleman to kiss her fingers. Only ten times more exciting.

And far more dangerous. Elyse realised that this was beyond anything she had experienced before. She was no fool, all her life she had been pampered and cossetted. She knew she had been protected from the harsher realities of life. Mr Scorton's attempts to kiss her should have warned her that the power she had so far enjoyed over the gentlemen of her acquaintance might not always be under her control. It was also daunting to know that she was just as vulnerable; she could not rely upon her own body to behave itself, as proven by the fact that she had to make a conscious effort before her hand would release those long, lean, masculine fingers.

Elyse sat down quickly, aware that Andrew Bastion was watching her but determined not to meet his eyes, lest he should see the consternation in her own. He jumped in after her, casting his hat upon the seat between them. Almost before the door had closed the chaise set off. Elyse had been so preoccupied she had not settled herself comfortably. Her skirts were tangled and without thinking she stood up to shake them out. At the same time the chaise lurched as it swung around the corner and out of the square. She lost her balance and collapsed back, directly into the lap of her companion.

Drew reacted instinctively and caught her in his arms, laughing. She was very light, a deliciously scented, complicated bundle of serviceable twill and frothy lace, but beneath it was the tantalising outline of her body, hinting at luscious curves beneath those layers of cloth. For a moment she remained gazing up at him, her shock quickly replaced by a twinkling look as if she, too, realised the absurdity of the situation.

'Well, this is an unexpected pleasure.'

Why the deuce did you say that?

The rakish response had been automatic and Drew cursed himself as the glow in her eyes fled, replaced by horror and alarm.

'Oh, I *do* beg your pardon.' Her voice was a little breathless as she struggled in his arms.

Quelling the desire to hold her even tighter, Drew helped her on to the seat.

'Pray do not make yourself uneasy,' he said,

leaning down to recover his hat, which had been knocked on to the carriage floor. 'I am quite aware that you did not fall upon me intentionally.'

He grinned at her and was pleased when she responded with a wary smile.

'Thank you.' She shifted her position to look out of the window. 'I was taken unawares by the speed of the carriage. Shall we travel like this all the way to London?'

'I have instructed the postilions to keep up a good pace, but it will be dictated by the state of the roads. The highways leading from Scarborough are in reasonable repair and as long as the weather remains dry we will make good time. I hope we need spend no more than three nights on the road. However, if it rains the track could turn into a quagmire and that could slow us down considerably. It might even take longer than a week to reach London.'

'Oh, good heavens,' she said, without turning around. 'I do hope that is not the case.'

'So too do I,' muttered Drew, regarding the delectable view she was presenting. She had her back to him, but her close-fitting jacket hugged her body, tapering in at her waist before flaring out again over her hips and the soft buttocks that moments earlier had been resting in his lap.

Drew settled himself into the corner of the carriage and closed his eyes, trying to ignore the way his blood was stirred at the sight of her. Even three days of this would tax his self-control to the limit.

They travelled long and fast, stopping only to change horses and swallow a mouthful of food and coffee before setting off again and at the end of the first day Elyse was so bone-weary she ate her dinner and retired, making no demur when her escort ordered a truckle bed to be made up in her room for a serving maid. The second day was better, she was anticipating the punishing pace and her youthful resilience made the journey much more enjoyable.

She gazed at the unfamiliar landscape flying by, trying to take in as much as possible. Her companion spent most of his time lounging in the far corner, his hat pulled low over his eyes. If he was tired then she had no wish to disturb him for he was decidedly out of humour. She had tried to talk to him but while he had been coolly polite and answered the questions she put to him, he made no effort to prolong the conversation and she had the distinct impression he was not enjoying the journey, or her company.

She thought ruefully that she could not blame him, for she had behaved very badly to him when he'd arrived in Scarborough. More like a spoiled schoolgirl than a young lady about to be married. And then the embarrassment of falling into his arms! It had been an unfortunate accident and she had been tempted to laugh it off until he had made the sarcastic remark that had filled her with shame and remorse. It did not matter that he had tried to recover the situation afterwards. The damage was done. One thing was certain; Mr Andrew Bastion was no gentleman.

By the time they reached the Three Bells where they were to put up for the night Elyse was not only ready for her dinner but also longing for a little conversation—even if it was only with the vexatious Mr Bastion. Really, it was no wonder that she was out of temper with the man since he had been ignoring her most of the day. She listened to him issuing his orders to the landlord, who fawned and bowed in the most sycophantic manner, and recalled her aunt's words, that Andrew Bastion was not a man to be crossed. Well, she did not wish to cross him. Elyse had by now recovered her natural sunny spirits and she hoped she might be able to charm him into a better mood.

The private parlour set aside for them was comfortable enough and the warm weather made the sluggish fire irrelevant, so when Drew glanced around with obvious distaste she gave a little laugh, determined to be cheerful.

'It is not palatial, but it will serve us for one night, sir.' She waved to a tray on the side table. 'May I pour you some wine?'

She met his frowning look with a smile and proceeded to fill two glasses. She held one out to him.

'We made a bad start, Mr Bastion, but I think we should put our differences behind us. After all, we have only each other's company for the next few days. Will you drink a toast with me? To new beginnings.'

'Trying to bamboozle me, Miss Salforde?'

The look in his eyes dared her to try and she had to resist the temptation to look away.

'Not at all, but surely the journey would pass much more quickly if we were not at odds with one another. Besides, it behoves me to be on good terms with my guardian.'

* * *

There was no guile in those velvet-brown eyes but Drew was cautious. He was too old and too experienced to be ensnared by a pretty face.

The devil of it was that Elyse Salforde was not just a pretty face. She was intelligent, too. And spirited. A damned attractive package that brought out the rake in him. He had feigned sleep for most of the day to avoid making any more remarks like the one that had slipped out at the start of their journey. It had upset her, and shown him what a dangerous line he was treading. But it now appeared that his attempts to keep the attraction at bay had resulted in her thinking he was angry with her. She was offering to make peace and he could not bring himself to snub her.

'I agree with you,' he said at last. 'It will make life much more comfortable for both of us.'

She handed him a glass and raised her own. 'I hope we can be friends from now on, sir.'

A scratching at the door announced dinner and he escorted Elyse to the little table where they took their places and waited while an array of dishes was spread before them. Drew had to admit that the food was good and the company even better. Elyse had been well educated and conversed easily on any number of subjects. Time passed quickly and he barely noticed the servant coming in to light the candles and build up the fire. He did notice, however, that unlike the previous evening, Elyse was in no hurry to dash off to her bed. When the covers had been removed and they had only their wine and a dish of sweetmeats on the table between them Drew sat back in his chair, smiling.

'I have enjoyed this evening, Miss Salforde, very much.'

'And do you still pity my husband?'

He laughed.

'So that rankled, did it?'

'Of course.' A rueful smile lit her eyes and hovered on her full lips. 'No woman likes to be thought unattractive.'

'I meant merely that your husband will need his wits about him, if you are not to lead him a merry dance.'

She looked down, the dark sweep of her lashes shielding her eyes but he heard the wistful note in her voice when she replied.

'I will have to learn to be a biddable, conformable wife.'

'That would be a pity.' Immediately her eyes

flew to his face and he added quickly, 'I am sure it was your liveliness that attracted Reverson in the first place.'

'Yes, but married ladies have to be much more responsible, do they not? And I mean to be a very good wife to William. I shall give him no cause to regret his choice.'

Her words and the look that accompanied them were very earnest. Drew did not doubt her sincerity but he could not help wondering about Reverson's intentions. From what she had told him he guessed the man was an infrequent correspondent and he could not discover that he had visited his fiancée at all in the past three years. To Drew's mind that did not augur well for their future happiness. But then, what did he know of such matters? He had reached six-and-twenty without ever once finding anyone he wished to marry. The unsettling thought occurred to him that he might have felt differently if he had not spent the past ten years living as an outcast with a price on his head. As such he was in no position to consider taking a wife. And never would be.

Elyse was watching him and Drew shifted in his chair. He had made his choice and he must take the consequences. No regrets. He filled the ensuing silence by recharging their glasses then he picked up his own and held it out.

'I shall give *you* a toast, now, Miss Salforde. To your future happiness.'

She looked a little surprised by the gesture, but followed his lead and raised her own glass, taking a little sip before placing it carefully back upon the table.

'Thank you.' She selected a sugared almond. 'Why did my father appoint you as my guardian?'

He did not reply immediately. What was it Harry had said?

I can rely on you to bring Whittlewood and his boy up to scratch.

'I suppose he thought you needed a man's protection until you married.'

'Odd that he should think that now.'

'It was very natural, since he would no longer be there to protect you.'

'My father was never there to protect me.'

The words were spoken thoughtfully, no hint of blame, but they made Drew raise his brows.

'He cared for you a great deal,' he said cautiously.

'Yes, but he was never *there*. He brought Mama to England soon after I was born and set her up in a little house near Dover, but he could not be still. At first he went off for only a few months at a time, but gradually his journeys became longer until he was only with us for a few weeks of the year. Mama said he was *bougeotte*—restless. She understood him and never complained. She died when I was eight years old and I was put into the care of Aunt Matthews. She was already a widow and I suppose Scarborough was even more difficult to reach than Dover, for I saw even less of Papa after that.'

'That does not mean he did not think of you,' said Drew. 'He spoke of you often. His reason for continuing with his way of life was to provide you with an inheritance.'

She gave him a straight look.

'Perhaps I would have preferred him to provide me with a father.' She bit her lip. 'I hardly knew him, you see. It could take months to receive a reply to my letters. That is why I wonder at his appointing you.'

'He thought I could ensure your safety on your journey to your new family.'

A shadow flickered over her face and he heard her sigh.

'I had hoped that William might come to

fetch me, but his last letter did say that his father keeps him very busy.'

'He writes to you regularly?'

'Oh, yes...Sometimes.' Again that hesitation, as if she were trying to convince herself. 'When he first left Scarborough he wrote to me often, but it is more than three years since we last met, so I suppose we have said all there is to say.'

Her unaccustomed air of sadness disturbed him and he said, trying to give her thoughts a happier turn, 'Tell me about Reverson. Where did you meet him?'

There was no doubt he had said the right thing. She smiled and the soft glow in her eyes winded him, like a blow to the body.

'At the assembly in Scarborough, just after my seventeenth birthday. Lord and Lady Whitlewood had come to take the waters and William was with them. It coincided with one of Papa's rare visits, which was most fortuitous, because he and Lord Whittlewood agreed the betrothal between them. No one was more surprised than I when William made me an offer. It was like a fairy tale. We had fallen head over heels in love, but I never imagined—' She broke off, blushing. 'It never occurred to me that the viscount would agree to it, and after so short a time, too, just a couple of months! I am very conscious of my good fortune.'

Good fortune indeed, to be marrying into a noble family. Drew sipped his wine and wondered if he should tell her that the marriage had been arranged in payment of a debt. Looking into Elyse's frank, shyly smiling eyes Drew could not bring himself to do so. But could the young couple be happy, could the pair of them really be in love? They had not seen each other for three years and it seemed unlikely that such a youthful infatuation could last. But perhaps he had grown too cynical. And there was no denying that Elyse Salforde was a most delightful companion. She would make any man a good wife.

'Now it is your turn.'

Her voice, rich with laughter, captured his attention.

'I beg your pardon?'

She was regarding him over the rim of her wineglass.

'So far we have only spoken about me. I am curious to learn about you, Mr Andrew Bastion.'

The ease that had been growing within him

withered. What should he tell her, that he was a soldier of fortune? A gambler? A traitor?

Drew was glad to be distracted by the opening of the door. A cheerful-looking maid with rosy cheeks came in and bobbed a curtsy.

'The master said I was to come and see you, sir, to accompany the young leddy up t'bed.'

He took out his pocket watch.

'I had not realised it was so late.' He bent a smile upon Elyse. 'We have another early start tomorrow.'

'Then I shall retire and save my questions for another night.'

He rose and walked with her to the door where she stopped. Only inches separated them, so close he could see how flawless her creamy skin was, smell the faint scent of summer blossoms that hung about her. He wanted to reach out and loosen her hair, watch it cascade in dark waves down her back. Then he would drive his hands into it and pull her close, breathing in that elusive flowery perfume…

He heard the soft, musical cadence of her voice and he blinked, bringing her face into focus. She was gazing up at him, smiling slightly.

'I really am very grateful to you, sir, for taking me to William.'

It took a moment for the words to register.

'Yes, well,' he said gruffly. 'I hope Reverson appreciates you.'

Chapter Three

Another long day's travel followed, but unlike the previous days Elyse found her companion was in a sociable mood. He no longer slept in the corner but engaged her in conversation. The topics were unexceptional, but he was well read and very knowledgeable. Elyse told him something of her life in Scarborough, but while he was happy to describe to her the cities he had visited, he refused to be drawn on his own history. She did not press him, for she did not want to risk damaging their burgeoning friendship.

Their conversation helped to pass the time but the pace was still gruelling. Elyse accepted it stoically, making no complaint at the brevity of the stops, but when her escort handed her down from the carriage late in the afternoon signs of her exhaustion must have been apparent in her face, for he ordered the landlord to show them into a private parlour. Elyse immediately protested, begging him not to prolong their journey for her sake.

'We are making good time,' he said, leading her into the inn. 'We can afford to take a little rest here and still reach St Neots this evening. After that it is but fifty miles to London and if the weather holds you will be with Lord Whittlewood by tomorrow night.'

The landlord escorted them to a comfortable room on the first floor and went off, promising to send up refreshments.

'Do you always travel at this breakneck speed?' asked Elyse, removing her cloak and bonnet. She eyed the cushion-strewn settle but did not sit down, her bones still protesting from the long hours sitting in the carriage.

'Only when it is necessary.'

She smiled. 'And you are anxious to be rid of your tiresome burden, is that it?'

'Do not be putting words into my mouth, Miss Salforde.'

She laughed at that. 'You could always disclaim and respond with some courteous remark, Mr Bastion.'

'What would you have me say, that I wish

the journey could go on for ever, solely for the pleasure of enjoying your company?'

She saw the humorous quirk to his lips and fluttered her eyelashes, murmuring, 'That is what many gentlemen of my acquaintance would tell me.'

He smiled and shook his head.

'Then they are nodcocks,' he said. 'To subject a lady to the rigours of a journey for any longer than necessary is not the way to win her favour. She would end up tired, cross and extremely bruised.'

A gurgle of laughter escaped her.

'I should take issue with you for disparaging my admirers in that way, but honesty compels me to agree, sir.' She put one hand on her back and rubbed it. 'I should not appreciate any gentlemen who prolonged this experience.'

'Has it been very trying? You have been very brave, enduring it all without a word.'

'No, no, it has not been so very bad.'

She broke in, flushing at this unexpected praise and moved towards the table as a serving maid entered at that moment with a laden tray. Elyse was surprised and unsettled by his approval and could not quite understand why. After all, other men paid her much more fulsome compliments and she took them in her stride.

The coffee was freshly brewed and Elyse was grateful to have time to appreciate it, and to enjoy a couple of the sweet biscuits that the maid told her the landlady had baked fresh that morning. Feeling much better for the rest she took advantage of the landlady's offer of a private room, where she might wash her face and hands and make use of the mirror to tidy her hair. When she returned the door of their private parlour was open and she could see the serving maid clearing the table. Drew Bastion was still in his seat, leaning back in his chair and idly watching the girl as she gathered the dishes on to a tray. His thoughts were clearly elsewhere and he did not appear to notice that the girl was flaunting herself before him. Elyse could see that the thin white edge of her chemise peeping above her bodice did little to hide her generous bosom as she leaned over to collect the final cup.

'Is there anythin' else I can do for you, sir?'

There was a blatant invitation in the maid's voice and in every line of her body as she straightened and stood for a moment, hands on hips. Neither of them had seen Elyse in the passage and she broke her stride, waiting for the gentleman's response. He glanced up at the maid, his thoughtful look replaced by a grin and a wicked look. Even from a distance Elyse could feel the power of his charm.

'No, thank you, Rose. That is all.'

Rose? Elyse blinked. She had only been away for five minutes. How had he discovered the maid's name so quickly? With a cough and a brisk step she carried on into the room. As she entered the maid picked up the tray, dropped a quick curtsy to her, cast a roguish glance towards Drew and went out, humming to herself. Elyse kept her lips firmly closed, torn between irritation that a servant should be so forward and a sneaking admiration at such cool composure.

Drew Bastion rose and pulled out his watch.

'Are you feeling better now? I think we should be moving on.'

'Already?'

It felt as if her body had only just recovered from the continual jolting of the carriage and Elyse had to steel herself not to beg for another ten minutes before they resumed their journey. Something of her struggle must have shown in her face, for as he placed her cloak about her shoulders he said,

'Chin up, my dear. There is not much further to go tonight.'

His gentle words, combined with the feel of his hands resting on her shoulders sent a wave of something she did not understand washing through her, from her head to the tips of her toes. She stood very still, wanting to make some laughing rejoinder but her wits had deserted her. She was all too aware of him standing behind her, could feel his strength enveloping her. She wanted to close her eyes and lean back against him, and she could only be thankful when he moved away to collect his hat and gloves before opening the door.

'Shall we go?'

Forcing a smile she preceded him out of the inn. She did not look up when he handed her into the chaise and busied herself with arranging her skirts until the door was shut and they were on their way. Then she sank back against the squabs and closed her eyes, taking time to consider just why she was so unsettled by that one small act of courtesy.

She thought back over the moment, remembering the profound comfort of Andrew Bastion's presence. She felt that it was not merely the cloak that he was wrapping around her, but his whole being, warm and dependable. To have someone to lean on, someone taking care of her, was an unfamiliar sensation.

Aunt Matthews was a kind and loving companion, but she had never instilled in Elyse the feeling of security that she now experienced. It was something that had been lacking for most of her life. From the moment Elyse had emerged from the schoolroom she had known that hers was the more forceful character. Aunt Matthews might suggest or advise, but she was happy to allow Elyse to go her own way. In a very short time Elyse had taken charge of the household, organising the menus, discussing budgets and staff changes with the housekeeper and deciding which parties they should attend.

In truth, it had been Elyse's idea not to cancel the soirée when they had been informed of Papa's sudden demise. Elyse had argued that there could be no impropriety in having guests, as long as they provided no entertainment. She had insisted that their friends would want to call and offer their sympathies. She had been right, of course, their drawing room had been full and no one had voiced disapproval until Andrew Bastion had appeared. And the fact that he had found her in the arms of one of her swains had made it very difficult for her to justify the decision.

Elyse had thought him rude and overbearing when he had first arrived, but she had to admit that there was something very pleasant about having someone else take responsibility for her comfort. Her eyes flew open. This would not do. She would not allow anyone to run her life—except her husband, of course. When she was married to William she would naturally love, honour and obey him. A tiny voice in her head whispered that she might not find it easy to acquiesce in all things, but William loved her, so she had no doubt that they would be able to resolve any little disputes quite amicably. After all, she considered herself to be quite an easy-going person and never fell out with anyone.

Except Mr Andrew Bastion. She stole a glance at him. He was staring out of the window, lost in thought. He had a very strong profile, she thought, observing his wide brow, the lean jaw, the set of his lips. Masterful.

She remembered his autocratic behaviour when they had first met. Surely it was not at all surprising that she was annoyed with him when he had appeared from nowhere and began to organise her life? No man had been her master, not since those far-off days as a very young child when Papa had been at home, looking after her and Mama, promising to take care of them for ever. So long ago, now, but no one would replace her papa. No one. Certainly not Andrew Bastion, even though he was her guardian.

She thought back a little wistfully to the past few heady years in Scarborough. She had learned that with a few smiles and pretty words she could wrap the men of her acquaintance around her little finger. She did not see why Andrew Bastion should be any different. She sat up a little straighter, a daring plan forming in her mind. He was already softening towards her; witness his behaviour in the coffee room. Perhaps, with a little more effort, he might become more amenable.

'Well, this is it, Miss Salforde. Our final night on the road. Tomorrow we shall be in London.'

Drew picked up his glass and regarded his dining companion over the rim. They were sitting at the dining table in a private parlour of the busy hostelry he had chosen for their last overnight sojourn. The dinner had been excellent, served by the landlady herself with the help of her son who, despite his best attempts, could not prevent himself from staring in silent admiration at Miss Salforde.

Drew had to admit that Elyse looked particularly enchanting. The light from the candles gave a golden sheen to her skin, rivalling the glow of the simple string of pearls she wore around her neck. Her dark hair was piled artlessly about her head with one glossy ringlet hanging down on to her shoulder, where it seemed to direct the eye to the soft mounds of her breasts rising from the neckline of her gown.

They were alone now, the covers had been removed and only the decanter and glasses were left on the table. Drew sipped thoughtfully at his wine. Elyse had obviously taken some care over her dress this evening, leaving off the travelling habit with its high-necked shirt in favour of an open robe of dove-grey silk over a white quilted petticoat. The sleeves of her gown ended in a flurry of silver lace ruffles that fell back to display her shapely arms. Her behaviour throughout dinner had been exemplary and she had treated him with a pretty deference—very much as one would treat an aged uncle, he thought, with an inward grin—but for all that he was on his guard, not quite believing the demure image she was presenting to him.

'And shall we be in time to call upon Lord Whittlewood tomorrow?' she asked him.

'I hope so, and I expect him to take you into his establishment immediately. I am happy to find lodgings for myself until everything is signed and sealed, but I am sure he would prefer to have you under his roof.'

She pouted prettily.

'You are mighty eager to be rid of me, sir.'

'Not at all, but I feel sure you will find a room in Lord Whittlewood's mansion far more comfortable than anything I can procure for you.'

'If it is a question of funds—'

'It is not. The viscount's letter indicated that he wishes to take you into his household at once.'

''But I have money, should I need it?

'Your father placed your not inconsiderable fortune under my control until Michaelmas,' said Drew. 'So yes, you have money.'

Elyse nodded and he wondered if it was a comfort to her to know she was not penniless, that she did not need to marry Reverson if she did not want to do so. And why should she not wish to marry him? he thought bitterly. It would give her status and entrée to the highest society. The very things he could not offer. He pushed aside such thoughts to concentrate upon her next remark.

'You and my father must have been great friends, for him to place so much trust in you.'

'We were.'

'Where did you meet?' When he hesitated she put up her hands. 'Please do not think you need to invent a history for me, Mr Bastion. I am well aware that my father was an adventurer and I promise you will not shock me if you tell me the truth.'

The naïvety of her statement made him smile, yet he decided to tell her as much as he dared.

'We met three years ago, in Vienna. Harry had just returned from England. We had much in common, a love of freedom and adventure, a penchant for gaming. We struck up a close friendship. I owe your father a great deal, Miss Salforde. When we met I didn't have two groats to rub together. He took me under his wing and we travelled Europe together.'

'Gambling?'

'Yes, amongst other things.' He hoped she would not ask him about the other things.

'You must have been very successful,' she remarked. 'My father regularly sent money back to England.'

'We were extremely successful, but always by fair play, and to the best of my knowledge it was always from those who could afford to lose. Harry was very conscious of his responsibilities, too, witness the sizeable sum you have inherited.'

'And did you, too, manage to put aside a fortune?'

Drew smiled. 'I am not a pauper, Miss Salforde.'

'I am relieved to hear it. And how did it end?'

'In Paris. At the gaming table of a rich nobleman.'

'So it was not footpads.'

He glanced up, an enquiry in his eyes. Too late did he remember the story he had told her in Scarborough. Elyse gave him a rueful smile.

'I suspect the French nobleman took exception to your winning.'

'Something of the sort.' He would not tell her that he and Harry had been manhandled out of Paris by the nobleman's lackeys, thrown out on to the filthy cobbles and kicked like curs.

'And was my father killed in a duel?'

'Nothing so honourable. Harry was a crack

shot and an excellent swordsman. If he had been challenged to a duel there is little doubt he would have won.'

He saw the consternation in her face, her eyes dark with anger.

'And did you exact revenge from the man who had done this?'

He shook his head. 'I had to return to England to carry out Harry's last wishes.'

Her dainty fingers curled like claws around the stem of her wineglass.

'I would have done so,' she declared. 'I would have found out this wicked Frenchman and made him pay.'

Drew shrugged. 'He was not so wicked. And in the *duc*'s defence the provocation was great. No, revenge was not your father's way. He took adversity in his stride, laughed at it, learned from it and bore no man ill will.'

'But this was more than mere gambling losses, this was my father's life! You should have revenged him.'

'Harry would not agree with you. He always maintained that revenge was a sword that cut both ways. He was more concerned for your welfare and insisted I should concentrate on looking after you.'

* * *

Elyse felt the sudden fizz of anger dying away. She should be grateful that Papa's last thoughts had been for her. She shook her head to dispel her melancholy thoughts and fixed her eyes upon the man sitting opposite.

'And what are your plans, sir, once you are free of your obligation to my father?'

'I shall go abroad again.'

'Would you not like to make your home in England?'

He did not move, but she was aware of a change, as if a shadow had fallen across his countenance. The blue eyes darkened and his mouth tightened to a thin line.

'England can never be my home.'

She wanted to ask him why, but some instinct warned her against it and when, a moment later, he began talking of something else she followed his lead. She had no intention of undoing the good work she had achieved so far this evening.

Elyse had set out to charm her escort into a good mood and she felt that she had succeeded reasonably well. When she had first put on the gown she had hesitated to leave off the lace neckerchief, but she knew from experience that gentlemen favoured a low neckline and enjoyed gazing upon a lady's bare neck and shoulders—witness her escort's wicked grin at Rose the serving maid! Elyse had to admit to a little twinge of displeasure at his reaction there and it had roused some hitherto dormant competitive spirit in her. She had been told by one of her beaux that her shoulders were particularly fine and she had therefore decided to leave them uncovered tonight.

She had noticed Mr Bastion's blue eyes resting upon her from time to time, and hoped he thought she made a pleasing picture. She sipped at her wine, aware that a pleasant lassitude had crept up on her. She felt distinctly light-headed and more than a little pleased with the success of her plan. Mr Bastion—Drew—was certainly more relaxed this evening, and she had even made him laugh on more than one occasion.

A distant clock chimed the hour and Drew took out his watch.

'Midnight.' He frowned. 'Your serving maid should have called by now.'

'I told her to go on to my room and wait for me there.' She added innocently, 'I thought you might escort me.'

'I suppose I shall have to do so.'

His tone was less grudging than the words,

but they still piqued her. In Scarborough her admirers would have been falling over themselves to escort her anywhere. He got up to pull out her chair and as they moved towards the door she put her hand on his arm.

'Would you like to kiss me goodnight?' She knew she was taking a great risk but he did not look outraged, nor did he admonish her for her forwardness. When he maintained his silence she added softly, 'You are a rake, are you not? And rakes always want to kiss a pretty girl.'

He stopped, frowning down at her fingers resting on his sleeve.

'You would not be wise to pursue this, Miss Salforde.'

A tiny *frisson* of excitement ran along her spine as she heard the warning note in his voice. She moved a little nearer.

'Surely it would not be improper for my guardian to call me Elyse?'

Her excitement intensified as his gaze moved to her face, so piercing that for a moment it took her breath away. She read danger in his look but the wine she had imbibed had given her courage and she felt emboldened by the challenge. She schooled her face into a picture of innocence, at the same time leaning closer so that the lace at her breast was almost touching his waistcoat. She saw his eyes darken and felt a flicker of satisfaction.

Usually by this point the object of her attentions would be panting slavishly, ready to promise anything if only she would grant him a kiss. However, so far she had only employed such methods with the young gentlemen of her acquaintance, and even then very rarely. Her guardian was some years older and clearly made of sterner stuff. She ran the tip of her tongue over her lips, wondering what to do next, but that slight, innocent gesture brought a flare of interest to his intense gaze. Triumph soared within her.

'You are playing a dangerous game, *Miss Salforde*.'

The wine had made her reckless and she opened her eyes wide at him.

'Will you not call me Elyse? I intend to call you Drew in—'

Her words were cut off. He dragged her into his arms and covered her mouth with his own. She had been expecting a tender embrace, a soft touching of the lips. Instead she found herself forcibly imprisoned against his rock-hard body. Her lips had parted in shock and now she found that his tongue was flickering and teasing, stirring up such sensations deep within her body that she thought she might swoon with the pleasure of it. She closed her eyes, senses reeling out of control. Her very bones had turned to water and she could only clutch at his coat as the hot blood pounded around her body. It seemed to be pooling deep between her thighs, where a hot, longing ache was growing. It was the most shocking, disturbing, exciting and exhilarating assault she had ever experienced.

The end came very suddenly. He released her and she staggered back, drawing her breath in ragged gasps and trying to calm the tumultuous pounding of her heart. When she raised her eyes to his face she realised with a shock that he was watching her, but not pleasantly. His eyes were like cold blue flames, burning into her as they roved over her body. His glance stripped her naked.

'Well, *Elyse*? You wanted me to kiss you. I hope it lived up to your expectations.'

Her face flamed. The surge of exhilaration she had felt was subsumed in shame. He had humiliated her. She put a hand up to her lips. They felt bruised and swollen. When she would have retreated his hand shot out and hooked around the back of her neck, drawing her closer. Her limbs would not work, she was transfixed and could not look away from his predatory gaze.

'No!' Her protest was no more than a whisper, for she was still unable to control her breathing. In response he bared his teeth in a humourless smile.

'Never trust a rake, my dear.'

He drew her to him for another bruising kiss and this time when he released her she did not hesitate. She threw herself at the door, scrabbled with the handle and fled to her bedchamber, his savage laughter echoing after her along the dim corridor.

Drew watched her fly along the passage and disappear into her bedroom, then he carefully closed the door and dropped back into his chair. Hopefully he had taught her a lesson she would never forget. He picked up the decanter and was surprised to see that his hand was shaking as he poured his wine. The encounter had cost him something, too, and it had taken all his iron will to break off that red-hot kiss. He had been unprepared for the urgent potency of the desire that had slammed through him when their lips met. By heaven she roused him!

But she was Harry's daughter and he had given his word to protect her. He put his head back and gazed at the ceiling, letting his breath go in a long sigh. The problem was that she was too innocent to realise the danger. All her flirtations so far had been undertaken under the watchful eye of her aunt and for all Mrs Matthews's seemingly easy nature she knew how to protect her own. If Elyse had tried such hoydenish tricks on any other man tonight then he doubted she would have escaped with her virtue intact.

Drew finished the wine and refilled his glass. Thank heaven they would be in London tomorrow and he could hand her over to her fiancé's family. There was only so much temptation human flesh could stand.

Elyse asked the maid to bring her breakfast in her room the following morning. Since she wanted only a cup of coffee and some bread and butter this was easily accommodated and she did not go downstairs until Drew sent word to say he was ready to depart. She hurried outside to find him waiting by the carriage. He was carrying a riding whip, an accessory that caused her to frown until she noticed the bay hack behind the chaise.

'You are riding?'

'I am.'

For a moment Elyse felt ludicrously disappointed and bereft, but then common sense reasserted itself. She was much better off travelling alone than shut up with in the chaise with him, where he might, if he so wished, berate her for her forwardness last night. Or—even worse—try to repeat his even more disgraceful behaviour.

She knew she had brought it on herself, but she had expected Drew to bestow a chaste kiss upon her, not sweep her into that passionate embrace. Why, he was every bit as bad as Mr Scorton. But here she found her conscience would not agree. Being kissed by Mr Scorton had been a thoroughly unpleasant experience, whereas when Drew had pulled her into his arms it had not been unpleasant at all. Shocking, yes, heart-stopping, definitely, but not unpleasant. And not frightening, either, save for her alarm at her own reactions.

She could not forget his cruel laughter as she ran away, and knowing that she was to blame had only heightened her distress and caused the hot angry tears to soak her pillow for most of the night. She settled back into the corner and closed her eyes. What was done was done, she must live with her embarrassment. It would fade, given time, but she did not think she would ever quite forget it.

London. Elyse gazed out of the window at the long, elegant terraces that lined the cobbled streets. She had not enjoyed this last stretch of the journey, her spirits weighed down by the events of the previous evening, but now the novelty of being in the capital distracted her from her melancholy thoughts. She would soon be reunited with William, and she would never again have to see the horrid man who was even now riding beside her carriage.

At last, after travelling for what seemed like hours through increasingly busy streets the carriage pulled up in front of an elegant town house in Grosvenor Square. Elyse felt suddenly very nervous and when Drew handed her down she clung to his fingers, fear of the unknown outweighing her memories of last evening's explosive confrontation.

The door was opened to them by a very superior butler and they were shown into a cold but elegant reception room. Elyse was tempted to turn and flee but the sounds of the servants bringing her baggage into the hallway reminded her that it was too late for second thoughts. She and Drew were alone in the room and she struggled to fill the uneasy silence.

'I suppose this is where we say goodbye, Mr Bastion—'

'Not quite. I remain your guardian until Michaelmas and there will be legal matters to attend to, regarding your forthcoming marriage.'

'Oh, yes, of course.' She swallowed. 'About last night—I owe you an apology. I am very sorry for the way I behaved.'

'I am glad to hear it. I hope you have learned your lesson and in future will behave with much more circumspection.'

Drew felt a twinge of pity as she bowed her head, meekly accepting his strictures. He had treated her abominably, but he hoped the experience might protect her in the future. Footsteps could be heard crossing the hall and Elyse raised her head. A stab of something he could not identify cut through him when he saw the hopeful look on her face. She was expecting to see William Reverson, but it did not take her hastily concealed disappointment to tell Drew that the fellow who came into the room was not her fiancé. He was a thin, soberly dressed individual and Drew guessed he was not a day under forty. The man made them a low bow.

'Good evening, sir, madam. I am Settle, the viscount's secretary. His lordship sends his apologies for not being here in person to greet you, Miss Salforde, but he and the family have been called away.'

Drew glanced around the cold, lifeless room and his brows snapped together.

'Do you mean they are no longer in London?' he demanded. 'But I have the viscount's letter saying he would be here.'

'A sudden bout of illness made it necessary for Lord Whittlewood to go to Bath without delay, sir, to take the waters.' Settle gave another small bow. 'He has instructed me to escort Miss Salforde there.'

'The devil he has!' exclaimed Drew.

'Oh.' Elyse sank down on to a chair, looking bewildered. 'And has Mr Reverson gone with him?'

'*All* the family are removed to Bath, miss.' Settle turned his attention to Drew. 'Our lawyers are expecting you tomorrow morning, Mr

Bastion. All the necessary papers have been drawn up and are waiting at their offices for you to sign in the morning. His lordship will assume responsibility for Miss Salforde from here.' He crossed the room and tugged at the bell-pull. 'A room had been prepared for you, miss, and dinner will be brought up to you—'

'One moment.' Drew put up his hand. Warning bells clamoured loudly in his head. Something wasn't right. 'So you are taking Miss Salforde to Bath.'

'That is correct, sir. We set out in the morning. I shall assign the second housemaid to accompany us, since I have ascertained that Miss Salforde has not brought her maid with her.'

His look and tone indicated severe disapproval at this lack of a personal maid, but Drew ignored it.

'I think I would prefer to take Miss Salforde there myself.' If truth be told he would prefer not to go within a hundred miles of the place, but he had promised Harry.

'There is no need for you to trouble yourself, sir. Lord Whittlewood is anxious that you are not inconvenienced any further in this matter. Miss Salforde will be perfectly safe in my care.'

'Nevertheless I mean to accompany her. I shall come with you.'

'But we leave at first light. There are papers to be signed—'

'I am sure you can arrange for them to be sent on to Bath, or new ones can be drawn up there. I am not prepared to leave Miss Salforde until I have at least seen the viscount.'

The merest flicker of annoyance crossed the secretary's face.

'If that is your wish, sir, you are welcome to come with us, but it will be very cramped.'

'Then leave the maid behind,' snapped Drew. 'Miss Salforde has managed perfectly well without one thus far.'

Settle's lips closed tightly for a moment while he regained his composure.

'Very well,' he said at last. 'We will be leaving here promptly at seven o'clock tomorrow morning. I am sure Miss Salforde is anxious to complete the journey and join her new family.'

The slight upward inflexion demanded a response from Elyse, who was still looking shocked.

'I am, of course,' she managed. 'But I should very much like my guardian to come with me.'

Drew gave a little bow. So she, too, was uneasy at this unexpected turn of events.

He was somewhat reassured by the homely, smiling countenance of the housekeeper who appeared in answer to the bell and requested that miss should follow her upstairs. Elyse rose and gave Drew her hand, accompanied by a tremulous little smile.

'Until tomorrow, then, Mr Bastion.'

'Until tomorrow.' He squeezed her fingers. 'I shall find myself lodgings for the night and send you word of where I shall be, in case you need me.'

'Thank you.'

He watched her follow the housekeeper out of the room, then turned back to the secretary.

'The viscount's departure is very sudden.'

Settle inclined his head.

'His lordship was most put out that he could not stay to welcome you.'

'I would have thought he might have spared one of his family to be here. Miss Salforde's fiancé, for instance.'

'Mr Reverson was desolated that he could not remain, but he has put his faith in me to bring his bride to him in time.'

'In time?'

Drew's eyes searched the man's face but the smooth mask did not slip for an instant.

'In *good* time, I should say, sir.'

Drew took his leave, his mind working on what possible motive the viscount could have had for leaving town so abruptly. The first one that came to mind was that he was trying to wriggle out of the marriage contract. After all, if Reverson cried off then the debt would have to paid, in full, but if Elyse failed to arrive… The viscount's letter had stipulated that Elyse should be delivered into his care by Michaelmas if the contract was to stand. But Michaelmas was almost two weeks away and Elyse would be in Bath in three days, five at most.

Unless something unfortunate occurred on the road.

Drew shook his head, laughing at himself.

'I am growing far too suspicious and seeing villains at every turn,' he muttered. 'This is nothing more than the precocious whim of a rich man.'

He knew the road to Bath well—too well—and had his own reasons for not wanting to go there, but he had promised Harry that he would see his daughter safely installed with her new family, and he would have to do so, whatever the consequences.

Drew arrived early at the Whittlewood mansion the following morning. There had been no opportunity to visit his bankers, but if he was travelling as Lord Whittlewood's guest then he should not require much money for this journey, and it would be easy enough to draw funds once he arrived in Bath. A travelling chaise was ready and waiting at the door when he arrived and at the stroke of seven he escorted Elyse from the house.

'I had the distinct impression Settle was disappointed to see me,' he murmured.

She showed none of her nervousness of the previous day and a sparkle of mischief lit her eyes.

'He said if you were late we would have to go without you.'

He raised one quizzical eyebrow.

'And would you have minded that? I thought you could not wait to see the back of me.'

'That is true, of course, but I have no doubt if we had set off you would have come after us, and that would not have improved your temper one jot!'

He laughed as he followed her into the carriage, glad she had recovered her spirits.

The first leg of the journey was accomplished in almost near silence. Elyse seemed preoccupied, possibly anxious about her reception at her new home, thought Drew, or perhaps it was merely the dour presence of Settle sitting opposite them. When they made the first stop to change horses Drew followed the secretary out of the coach and took the opportunity to stretch his legs. Knowing how quickly the ostlers could accomplish their task he merely walked a little way around the inn yard. As he made his way back to the carriage he noted that there was no crest upon the door. Settle was in earnest conversation with the coachman and instead of climbing aboard Drew waited for him.

'If I were Miss Salforde I might be aggrieved that the viscount has not put one of his own carriages at her disposal,' he remarked as Settle came up.

'The viscount keeps only one travelling carriage in town and he had need of that himself,' came the reply. 'I can assure you no slight is intended to Miss Salforde.'

'I hope not,' said Drew. 'I notice you have no outriders.'

The secretary spread his hands.

'Outriders are not necessary since we are travelling in an unmarked carriage.'

Drew's brows rose. 'The road to Bath must have improved considerably since the last time I travelled it.'

Settle's face remained a polite mask.

'I have no doubt it has, sir.'

Elyse watched the two men talking outside the carriage and was aware of her growing unease. She did not know what she had expected to happen when she arrived in London, but she had thought at least that Lord Whittlewood and his family would have been there to greet her. Settle was perfectly civil but she could not like him and was thankful that Drew had not washed his hands of her. The idea of travelling all the way to Bath in the company of the cheerless secretary had been very daunting indeed and after her disastrous attempts to flirt with Drew she was wary of showing too much friendliness to any man.

They set off again and were soon crossing the bleak expanse of Hounslow Heath. Mr Settle's observation that the guard sitting up beside the driver was armed with a blunderbuss gave her some reassurance, but she was relieved when they had left the infamous heath behind them.

She could not fault the inn chosen for their first overnight stop, but Drew took exception to the secretary's assertion that they need not bother with a private parlour.

'And where are we to dine?'

'When I made the arrangements I assumed Miss Salforde would take dinner in her room, since she was travelling alone and I would not presume—'

'No, I hope you would not,' retorted Drew. 'However, Miss Salforde is not travelling alone now, and she will dine with me.'

Elyse might think Drew far too autocratic but in this instance she was pleased that he had overridden the secretary's plans, as she told him when at last they were alone in the private parlour the landlord had found for them. She was very conscious of their previous dinner together and was anxious to make amends.

'I would have had a very miserable journey

if I had been obliged to travel alone with Mr Settle.'

'He is not the most stimulating company is he?' Drew grinned. 'I imagine he is enjoying a bowl of thin gruel in his room even as we speak.'

Elyse giggled. 'Poor man. I only hope he will not be in trouble with the viscount for this extra expenditure. I cannot think Lord Whittlewood meant any discourtesy, but if he has been taken ill then perhaps he was not thinking too clearly.'

'Perhaps not, but surely his family might be expected to consider your plight.'

She had been thinking the same thing and did not wish to dwell on it. She sought quickly for another subject.

'How long will it take us to reach Bath do you think?

'We should be there the day after tomorrow, travelling in easy stages.'

'You sound very confident of that, sir. Do you know this road well?'

'Well enough, although it is more than ten years since I travelled this way.'

'Was that the last time you were in England?'

'Yes.'

His short answer made her look searchingly

at him, but his impassive countenance had a hard, closed look that did not invite further enquiry. Since she had no wish to antagonise him again she introduced another topic of conversation and he obligingly followed her lead.

The evening continued thus until Elyse bade him goodnight and retired to her room, confident that although she and Andrew Bastion might never be the best of friends, they could at least be civil to one another.

The following morning she arrived downstairs to find a crowd gathered in the coffee room and at the centre of it was Mr Settle, perched on the edge of a chair with his arms wrapped about his stomach. Drew was standing beside him, his face thunderous.

The secretary addressed him in a querulous voice. 'I am very sorry, sir, but I dare not set out.'

'Come man, it is most likely wind,' snapped Drew. 'Take a little brandy and you will soon feel better.'

Settle began to rock back and forth on his chair, his face creased in pain.

'No, it is not wind, sir, I can assure you.'

'I have sent for the doctor,' put in the landlord, wiping his hands on his apron and gazing in consternation at the miserable figure hunched before him. 'He should be here within the hour.'

'Very well, we will wait and see what he says.'

'Yes, yes, we will see what he says,' repeated Settle. He waved to one of the footmen. 'You, come here and give me your arm. I must lie down upon my bed.'

With a great deal of puffing and panting and the occasional wince of pain Settle was helped to his feet and staggered out of the room. He was almost bent double and would not have paid any heed to Elyse if she had not addressed him.

'Why Mr Settle whatever is the matter?'

'Pains, Miss Salforde, agonising pains throughout my body. I fear I shall not be able to travel further with you.'

He hobbled away with the footman's help and Elyse approached Drew. He was still frowning, but when he saw her he took her into the private parlour, where a breakfast of rolls and cold meat was laid out in readiness for them.

'It would appear that whatever ailment has afflicted Lord Whittlewood's family has been passed on to his secretary.' He pulled out a chair for her. 'I only hope you do not contract it, having spent the night at the house.'

'I feel perfectly well,' she reassured him. 'But poor Mr Settle, I do hope it is nothing serious.'

'It is my opinion that the fellow is shamming.'

Elyse put down her knife and fork and stared at him.

'Why should he do that?'

He was looking very serious, but after a moment he shrugged and said lightly, 'Do not mind me, I am very impatient of illness.'

'But if it is serious we shall have to delay our journey.'

'Oh, I do not think it will come to that,' he said, filling their coffee cups. 'Let us wait and see what the doctor says.'

They were finishing their meal when the landlord came in to say that the doctor had arrived and was with Mr Settle.

'Very well,' said Drew grimly, 'Let us go and see what he has to say.'

He followed the landlord out of the room and Elyse was left alone to while away the time as best she might. It was some fifteen minutes before Drew returned.

'Well?' She went over to him immediately. 'How is Mr Settle?'

'The doctor is baffled, but agrees with Settle that he should travel no further until he feels better.'

'What? But how can that be?'

'Precisely.' Drew nodded, meeting her eyes with a sombre look in his own. 'He prodded and poked the fellow but has no idea what is the matter with him, and can only concur with Settle's own decision to keep to his bed.'

'Does that mean we cannot continue?' asked Elyse.

'Oh, no, I shall take you on to Bath alone.'

She gave a long sigh of relief. 'Oh, thank you, Mr Bastion. That is wonderful news.'

'Is it, though?'

She gave him a questioning look and his thoughtful mood vanished. He smiled at her.

'Go and finish packing up your things. We have already lost a couple of hours but I hope we can still reach Marlborough this evening.'

Elyse was afraid that being shut up in the carriage with Drew for hours on end would be difficult, but in fact Mr Settle's absence seemed to lessen the constraint. She remarked upon it as they bowled along, making good time on the excellent roads.

'There is no doubt about it, we go on much more comfortably without the secretary do we not, Mr Bastion?'

'I think so. And it's Drew.' He grinned. 'My friends call me Drew.'

She brightened immediately.

'Are we friends now?'

'I should very much like us to be.'

His words sent a rush of pleasure through her.

'Then you should call me Elyse.'

'Very well. Elyse.'

She laughed.

'If we are truly friends then you must tell me all about yourself.'

'If we are truly friends then I will not bore you with such trifles.'

'Then, will you please tell me about my father?' she asked, a little shyly.

She observed his hesitation, but he did not refuse and he whiled away the journey by telling her something of their adventures on the Continent.

'It all sounds very exciting,' she remarked, when he had finished. 'Papa's letters were so infrequent, you see. He told us almost nothing of his life abroad.'

'Perhaps he did not wish to make you anxious,' suggested Drew.

She chuckled. 'It is more likely that he thought we would be shocked if we knew how he lived. I suspect you have given me a heavily expurgated version of events, but I am glad to have any information of my father, however little.'

'Harry was very proud of you,' he told her.

'Was he?' Her smile was a little twisted. 'He was very pleased at my betrothal to a viscount's son.'

'Naturally he was happy to think your future was secured. I believe you were the reason he continued to haunt the gaming tables, so that he could leave you with an independence. You are a wealthy woman now, Elyse.'

'Am I?'

'Indeed you are. By the time he died Harry had amassed a small fortune, which I hold in trust until you attain your majority in a few days' time.'

Elyse forced herself to smile. It was comforting to have money, of course, but it could not compensate for the fact that she had not known her father, that all she had was the memory of his brief, infrequent visits and a few hastily scrawled letters. She shook off her depression and reminded herself how fortunate she was.

'I am glad to know that. Is Lord Whittlewood aware of my changed circumstances?'

Drew shook his head. 'I think not. The settlements were agreed at the time of the betrothal, when your father was much less wealthy. I only discovered the small fortune he had amassed after his death and I have not informed the viscount or his son.'

'Then I am sure they will be delighted to receive the news.'

She turned to gaze out of the window at the passing countryside feeling much more hopeful for the future. She was relieved to know that she would have more to offer William than just herself. His letters had never mentioned money and he had never indicated that the small amount settled upon her was insufficient, but she had felt the difference in their stations and had suspected it was the reason she had not seen William or his family for the past three years.

By the time they reached Marlborough it was late in the afternoon and she remarked that the town was surprisingly busy.

'Aye, which is unfortunate,' muttered her companion.

'But why? Mr Settle told us our rooms at the Castle were bespoke, so we should have no difficulty.'

'I was hoping we might find accommodation elsewhere.' When she looked askance at him he added, 'Getting to sleep in a busy coaching in can be the very devil.'

'We have managed very well so far,' she said as he handed her down. 'Do not fret, sir, I shall not plague you with my complaints.'

Determined to be cheerful, she followed him into the inn and was soon being escorted upstairs by the female servant appointed to act as her lady's maid for the duration of their stay. Drew remained below to explain to the landlord that the viscount's secretary had been detained and to confirm that a private parlour had been set aside for them.

'Aye, sir. Lord Whittlewood's orders have been followed to the letter.' The landlord replied with a genial smile, but there was a slight frown in his eyes as he regarded Drew. 'Beggin' your pardon, sir, but you looks very familiar. Have you stayed here before, perhaps?'

Drew shook his head and shifted his position so that the light was behind him.

'This is the first time I have enjoyed his lordship's hospitality.'

The landlord regarded him for a little longer before saying with a shrug and a smile.

'Strange, because I'm very good with faces.'

'You must see a great many, running such a busy house.'

'Aye, sir, that I do.' His host puffed out his chest, saying proudly, 'Been here for twenty-five years, man and boy.' He broke off, his head going up. 'Ah, there's another coach arriving. If you'll excuse me, sir, I'll have to go.'

Drew excused him gladly and ran up the stairs. The inn was full to overflowing and he had his own reasons for wanting to avoid the crowds, but he also wanted to warn Elyse to stay out of the public rooms. The serving maid was just setting off down the stairs with Elyse's travelling gown and when he knocked on the door Elyse answered it cautiously, opening it only a crack.

'Let me in,' he said tersely. 'I need to speak to you.'

It was only when he had entered and shut the door behind him did the reason for her caution become apparent. She was wearing a dressing gown. It covered her from neck to toe, but from her self-conscious look he guessed she was probably wearing very little beneath. For a moment he forgot what he had come for, distracted by the thought of the delectable figure beneath those folds of frothy lace. When her hand crept to her neck he realised he was staring. He cleared his throat and dragged his eyes to her face.

'I beg your pardon. I just came to warn you to keep to your room or to the private parlour while we are here. The inn is full tonight.'

'Yes, and I know why it is so busy,' she replied, instantly diverted. 'There is a masked ball at the Town Hall this evening. Would it not be entertaining to attend?'

'Not at all.'

She pouted.

'But I have been cooped up in the carriage for so long and I would love nothing better than to dance. It is not as if anyone here would know me, after all.'

He made a face.

'But this is merely a local assembly, mainly yokels and tradesmen.'

She looked a little surprised.

'I never thought you would be so top-lofty.'

'I am merely looking out for you. We shall be in Bath in a couple of days, I am sure you will have as much dancing as you wish then.'

'No, I won't,' she replied, sighing. 'I am still in mourning.'

'Of course you are.' He frowned, berating himself for having forgotten Harry so soon. 'So there is another reason why you cannot attend a ball.'

'But it is so *dull* to do nothing but travel and sleep,' she said. 'I do not see there could be any harm in it. I am a stranger here, and in a mask and domino no one would have the least guess who I might be. Oh, Drew, *do* say we can go, just for a little while. No one need ever know.'

She laid a hand on his arm and looked up at him with such an appeal shining in her dark eyes that for a moment he wished he could give in and take her. But it would not do, not only would it be highly improper for Elyse to attend, he dare not risk it. They were within a day's ride of Bath and he might be recognised.

'I am sorry, Elyse, but it is not possible. You need to rest. We have another full day's travel tomorrow.'

'But I can sleep in the chaise tomorrow. Oh,

please, Drew, let us look in, just for an hour. I will not dance, if you would rather not, but I should so much like to see everyone in costume and hear the music. Kitty, the serving maid, says the landlord can procure tickets for us.'

She had moved a step closer, eyes shining, her breast rising and falling beneath the soft folds of her the silk dressing gown. He could smell the light, flowery perfume, reminding him of warm summer days…and nights…

'No.' Hell and damnation it was all getting out of hand. He backed to the door. 'Not another word, Elyse. When your maid returns you will dress and join me for dinner, do you understand?'

He left her then, ignoring her look of burning reproach. He resolved to coax her out of the sullens when they met at dinner. He had some sympathy, for her lively nature must find life very dull, obliged to mourn for a father who had been little more than a stranger to her. Yet it must be done, and he would assure her that life would be infinitely more enjoyable once she was living in luxury in Lord Whittlewood's household.

Chapter Four

When Elysc joined Drew for dinner in the private parlour she had changed into an open robe of blue brocaded silk with a white quilted petticoat and white lace ruffles at her neck and sleeves. His eyes narrowed.

'Very becoming, but I am still not taking you to the masquerade.'

'I would not expect you to do so,' she told him equably. 'But I had to change into something, for my travelling dress is very dusty. Also, Kitty has taken away my ruffles to wash them ready for the morrow. Would you prefer me to sit here without any lace at all?'

Glancing at her, he thought the ruffles at her elbows might be dispensed with, but not the froth of lace around her shoulders. It covered the delightfully smooth skin of her neck and as his eyes shifted to where it was gathered and tucked into her embroidered stomacher he found himself thinking of the plump swell of her breasts concealed beneath the lace. With an effort he returned his gaze to her face and discovered she was watching him with a speculative look in her eyes. He grinned.

'Do you think to charm me into doing what you wish? You will be disappointed.'

He was pleased with the way she accepted this. No sulks, merely a smile to acknowledge that he had been right. He invited her to join him at the table and they sat down to dinner in genial accord. The easy companionship lasted throughout the meal and when the covers were removed Drew knew a moment's disappointment when Elyse said she would retire and leave him to enjoy his brandy alone.

'You do not need to run away,' he told her. 'I will gladly take coffee with you, if you would like that—or even tea.'

Smiling she shook her head.

'No indeed, sir, that is very kind of you but I find I am more fatigued than I had realised. I do not wish to meet my betrothed tomorrow with dark circles beneath my eyes. I shall take my leave of you, and will see you here in the morning for an early breakfast.'

* * *

She went out and he settled back in his chair to enjoy the surprisingly fine cognac that the landlord had supplied. This part of the journey was always going to be difficult, it was so close to his old home. He had known a moment's alarm when the landlord had almost recognised him. Thank heaven he was travelling as Mr Bastion, for his own name would have been instantly recognisable. After all, Castlemain was an uncommon name. He would have been revealed as Sir Edward's disgraced son, the rebel whose actions had dishonoured the family and caused his mother's death.

Restlessly he shifted in his seat. Enough of that. What was done was done, he would live with it, as he had done for the past ten years. Better to think of the task before him, getting Elyse safely to Bath.

Settle's sudden illness had struck him as odd and he had been on edge throughout their journey to Marlborough, but they had arrived without mishap. Yet tomorrow's journey, the last stage on the road to Bath was the most dangerous, or it had been when he had lived here. The secretary had told him things had changed and he sincerely hoped that was the case, and that he would be able to hand Elyse over to Lord Whittlewood tomorrow. After that he would remain just long enough to see Elyse settled and hope to heaven no one recognised him.

He went to the door to call for more brandy, and when the waiter returned with it he requested the fellow to send someone up to Miss Salforde's chamber and ask her if she had everything she needed for the night.

'She might like a cup of hot chocolate,' he added, recalling that there was no fire in her room. 'The lady is to have whatever she wants, make sure she knows that.'

The servant gave a little bow and withdrew, returning a few minutes later to inform him that Miss Salforde was asleep.

'Already?' Drew looked at his watch. It was close upon eleven, later than he had realised.

'Yes sir,' affirmed the waiter. 'I knocked quite loud, like, but there was no reply from the lady. Nor her maid. They must be sound asleep.'

'Really? Both of them?' Drew felt the first stirrings of unease.

'Aye, sir.' The waiter grinned. 'Kitty—the maid—must be fair tired out 'cos she ain't even snoring, which she usually does, enough to wake the dead. T'other maids is always complainin' of it!'

Drew was out of his seat even before the waiter had finished speaking and demanding that the landlord be fetched immediately, and that he bring his set of keys.

'It won't do no good sir,' protested his host, following him up the stairs a few minutes later. 'Not if the lady's shot the bolt.'

'If she has then we shall know she is safe inside,' retorted Drew.

It was the work of a moment to open the door. As he feared, the room was empty. One of Elyse's trunks had the lid thrown back and a jumble of clothes lay over every surface.

'My gawd, she's been robbed!' declared the landlord.

Drew's mouth thinned. 'No, I've been duped.'

Leaving the landlord gaping and with orders to lock up again, Drew went to his own room and hurriedly changed his dress. Then he set out for the Town Hall.

Prodigious amounts of arrack punch and strong ale had led to an excess of high spirits and the masked ball was becoming riotous. Elyse wondered if she had been wise to attend.

It was all very well having Kitty waiting downstairs for her, but here in the assembly room she was alone and unprotected.

She had quickly discovered that a public ball was a vastly different affair to the select private balls she had attended in Scarborough. She was thankful it was a masquerade, although her pink domino was not all-enveloping and hung open at the front to display her brocaded silk skirts. Her gown was as lavish as anything to be seen at this provincial assembly and she had attracted no little attention when she had come in. At first she had enjoyed dancing, secure behind the anonymity of the silk mask that covered her face. Everyone she met tried to guess her identity and she was amused by the idea that she might be Lady So-and-So's daughter, or Lord So-and-So's wife, but along with the deferential attentions of those who thought they might be acquainted she was subjected to the unpleasant sensation of being ogled by perfect strangers. She had been ogled before, of course, but in Scarborough she had known she was amongst friends, and her aunt was always there, in the background.

Here she knew no one. Many of the gentlemen were thinly disguised with no more than a strip of black silk across their eyes, but some were swathed from head to toe, like the tall figure in the black domino who swept her away just as she had been about to dance with a ruddy-faced gentleman that she suspected might be a local farmer.

'My dance, I think.'

His voice was scarcely more than a gravelly whisper as he led her to join a set that was forming. The flickering candles cast heavy shadows and his face was nothing more than a pale blur beneath the enveloping hood. It did not matter, it was only a country dance and her partner proved to be an excellent dancer. As the music ended he held on to her hand, his grip tightening when she tried to pull away.

'Two dances is the norm, I believe.'

Again that breathy murmur. She glanced down at his long fingers wrapped about her hand. Frothy lace ruffles covered his wrist and she noted the wide velvet cuff on his sleeve. No country tailor had made that coat. She tried a little smile.

'Thank you, good sir, but I think I would rather not.'

She gave a little tug but his grip was like iron.

'Two dances, madam.'

The voice was faint but implacable. The musicians were striking up again. He would have to release her at some point in the dance, but to run off then would only bring the sort of attention she needed to avoid if she was to maintain her anonymity. With a little shrug she gave herself up to the dance, but as they skipped and turned she kept glancing up into the darkness of that hood, trying to see the face beneath. As last she was rewarded as a movement of the dance coincided with a flare of candlelight that pierced the black shadows, but it only showed her that he was wearing a Venetian mask, white and featureless.

Quickly Elyse averted her eyes. She wished now she had never looked at him, for the mask covered his whole face save for the eyes, which gleamed out at her in a manner she could only describe as predatory. She missed her step and he caught her around the waist, pulling her to him when she would have fallen. He was solid as a rock. She should have been grateful that he had supported her, instead she felt an uncomfortable sense of danger in being so close to this stranger. The crowd around them roared their approval and Elyse's face flamed. She tried not to listen to the bawdy remarks, nor to notice the lewd winks and grins of the men.

Silently her partner set her back in her place and they finished the dance. This time she was ready. Even before the last note faded she snatched her hand away, made him a hasty curtsy and slipped off into the crowd.

She thought she might leave, but too many people barred her way, too many gentlemen wanted to dance with her. As the evening progressed Elyse became more uneasy. Her partners began to squeeze her fingers, leaning closer until their wine-sodden breath could not be avoided and placing their hands on her back as they danced. And all the time she was aware of the figure in the black domino. Whenever she looked up he was there, watching the dancers. He seemed to be shadowing her. She had the irrational thought that he was like some bird of prey, waiting to strike. Her only recourse was to keep dancing.

That was not difficult, for there was no lack of partners, but the company was becoming ever more rowdy and the gentlemen much more free with their lascivious comments. Some were even inclined to follow her off the floor so that she was obliged to accept another invitation to dance, just to avoid them. This worked for a while, until her partner refused to give her up to the next gentleman. From their loud, indecorous language she feared both gentlemen had imbibed far too freely of the wine. Her partner tightened his grip.

'No, no, sir, the lady is promised to me for a second dance, is that not so, madam?'

He clung to her fingers with one hand while the other clasped her around the waist in a very proprietorial manner.

'Damn your eyes, sir, I say she will dance with me!' declared his rival in a bluff, angry voice. 'Come, madam.'

The man grabbed her free hand. She noticed that his short, stubby fingers were brown with snuff stains and his ragged fingernails rimed with dirt. Elyse was beginning to feel seriously alarmed, especially since no one seemed to be taking any noticc of what was going on. Certainly no one was coming to her aid.

She managed to say with a fair assumption of amusement, 'La, sirs, I beg you will both unhand me, or I fear you will pull me in two.'

Her protest was ignored as the two men glared at each other.

'Let her go, sirrah, she is mine!' cried the man with dirty fingernails.

'Never!' declared his rival, his arm tightening around Elyse. 'She will dance with me!'

'I fear you are both to be disappointed, gentlemen. The lady is promised to me.'

The two men looked up, surprised outrage on both their faces. The words were spoken in a soft drawl, the tone slightly bored, but with sufficient steel in it to give them pause. Looking over her shoulder, Elyse's alarm increased when she saw the black domino close behind her. She was not at all surprised to find herself released by her tormentors. They backed away, scowling, and Elyse was left with only the black domino at her side. He took her hand and drew her closer. Suddenly she felt very tired and she could no longer subdue her panic. She gave a little sob.

'Oh, no more, sir, I beg of you.'

'I thought you loved nothing better than to dance.'

The words were spoken softly, but in a very different voice. She looked up quickly.

'D-Drew?'

Elyse did not know whether to smile in relief or shrink away from him, for his voice was chill and he towered over her in a very menacing way.

'Of course. Now, do you want to dance?'

She shook her head, saying meekly, 'If you please, I think I have had enough dancing for one evening.'

'Then we shall go.'

He pulled her fingers on to his sleeve and escorted her from the ballroom. They abandoned their masks in the lobby, Elyse called to Kitty to follow them and they made their way in silence back across the wide market street to the inn. They were greeted by a sleepy waiter who asked if they required any refreshment.

'Brandy and ratafia, in our private parlour.' Drew rapped out the order then turned to Elyse. 'From what I saw of your room it will need to be cleared before you can go to bed. Give your key to the maid and she can tidy it while you take a glass of wine with me.'

Elyse did as he bade her, then she followed him into the private parlour, pushing back her hood and saying as the door closed, 'You have every right to be cross with me, Drew, I—'

'You little fool.' He rounded on her, his eyes blazing with cold blue fire. 'Did you not realise where your recklessness might lead? You are a child playing a woman's games. To attend a country dance, unchaperoned—by heaven, it could only end one way, with your ruin.'

'Then I am *truly* grateful to you for coming to my rescue.'

'I should have left you to your fate.'

He broke off as the waiter came in and placed a tray upon the table. Elyse turned away, struggling with the knotted strings of her domino. It did not help that her eyes were full of tears. She heard the waiter go out again but she did not turn around. A rogue tear spilled over and she dashed it away.

'To have abandoned me would have been no more than I deserved,' she said in a small voice. 'I should not have disobeyed you and gone out. I am sorry I am such a burden to you.'

Drew sighed and closed his eyes. All the angry words he had conjured when he had found her missing faded from his mind when he heard the humble note of contrition in her voice. She had her back to him, but he saw her hand brush her cheek and guessed she was crying.

'Your father left you to my care. Once I knew where you had gone I had to come after you.'

He stepped closer and held out his handkerchief. 'Here.'

She wiped her eyes. 'I thought taking Kitty with me would be sufficient protection.'

'That shows how little you know about the world. It is full of villains and adventurers.'

'Such as yourself?'

He stiffened immediately, but felt a wry smile tugging at his mouth. She could not resist challenging him, even now.

'Such as myself.' As if determined not to look at him, she fumbled again with the ties of her domino. He reached out to her. 'Let me.'

Elyse quickly stepped away.

'No.' If he touched her she would fall to pieces. 'I—I think I shall keep it on, after all.'

'Are you cold, shall I rekindle the fire?'

'Can you do so?' she asked, momentarily diverted.

'An adventurer has to turn his hand to many things, Miss Salforde.'

'I suppose he does.' She gave a sigh. 'But to answer your question, no, I am not cold, not really.'

'Then what is it?'

'I deserve that you should give me the most tremendous scold.'

'You do, but I am not going to scold you any more than I have done already.' He handed her a glass of ratafia. 'I hope you have learned a valuable lesson.'

'Oh?'

He went back to the table to pour himself a glass of brandy, saying over his shoulder, 'That a pretty young lady should never venture into society without someone to look out for her.'

Elyse sipped at the ratafia and its sweet warmth put heart into her. She felt confident enough to dispute this.

'But they could not know whether I was pretty, for I was hidden beneath the domino and the mask.'

He turned and Elyse tried and failed to meet his glance, her fragile spirit shying away from the disapproval she feared she would see there.

'Do you think any gentleman of experience would be fooled by such a disguise?' He put down his glass and came closer. 'To begin with, your hood had slipped back a little to reveal dark curls.' He caught one between his fingers. 'They are so glossy and luxurious they could only belong to a young woman. Then there is your figure. Since the domino is only fastened by a string at the neck it falls open to show the creamy smooth skin above the lace at your breast—another sign of a woman in high bloom. And your tiny waist is perfectly obvious, too. Then, of course, your neat ankles are displayed to great advantage when you skip through a dance.'

She was listening, spellbound, to this catalogue of evidence and hardly noticed when he stepped closer. He took her chin between his finger and thumb. Her head came up under the gentle pressure of his hand and she was obliged at last to meet his eyes.

'The mask you wore only enhanced the dainty line of your jaw and those full, cherry-red lips. And as for your eyes, they sparkled so enchantingly through the slits of the mask that I am surprised any man could resist them.'

He was holding her gaze and she saw the look in his eyes change, darken. She was drawn deeper into the spell he was creating around them, his words spinning a web as fine as gossamer, as strong as steel. She felt quite dizzy and her hands clenched around the now empty glass as she resisted the temptation to clutch at his coat and hold on to him. He ran his thumb lightly across her lower lip and her eyelids fluttered.

She almost moaned with the sensual longing that seemed to melt her inside. She wanted to kiss him. The ache was so strong that it took all her will-power not to reach up and pull his head down so that she could do so. She knew such behaviour would be considered wanton, and it was only the fear that he would pull away from her in disgust that kept her motionless, even though her body was screaming for release. Her breasts felt so full and tender she thought they might burst through the bone and silk of her bodice.

These sensations were so new and frightening that her body trembled. Heady anticipation began to bubble up inside as her body answered to the siren song of his presence. Could he not feel it? Hope soared for an instant, only to be dashed and replaced by a searing disappointment when Drew released her.

'So,' he said lightly, taking the glass from her nerveless fingers. 'Now you know why it is important that you have a chaperon to accompany you when you go into society. To protect you from the bad men.'

Elyse knew the danger had passed. She

should be relieved, but instead she felt unaccountably bereft and close to tears. She must not show it, however, and forced a little smile as she tried to concentrate upon his words.

'And do you count yourself a bad man, Drew?'

'Of course.' A shadow crossed his face. 'I am an adventurer, and they are the very worst kind.'

She heard the bitterness in his voice and her heart contracted, as if a vice was squeezing it dry. If only she could take his face in her hands and kiss away the pain she saw in his eyes but that was impossible. What had he called her? *A child playing a woman's games.* He did not see her as anything but a nuisance. She must not embarrass him further with her impetuous actions.

Besides, kisses were for brothers and fathers. For husbands and lovers. Drew was not, could never be, any of those and it was not her place to comfort him. The distant chiming of the church bell announced the hour.

'It is late,' he said, his tone matter of fact. 'I will give orders that breakfast is to be put back in the morning. We are less than forty miles from Bath and there is no need for a very early start.'

'Thank you.' Elyse clasped her hands together to disguise the fact that she was shaking from the chill of unhappiness that had penetrated her very bones. 'I must go to bed.'

'I will escort you, it would be most improper for you to be wandering alone around the inn at this hour.'

Improper, Drew, but not so dangerous as being alone with you.

Silently she accompanied him through the dimly lit passages of the inn to the door of her room, where he stopped. He reached out and took her hand, lifting it to his lips.

'Goodnight, Elyse Salforde.'

She gripped his fingers and said urgently, 'You are not a bad man, Drew. I will never believe that.'

The flickering candles in their wall sconces sent the shadows dancing across his face, almost as if he had suffered a sudden spasm of pain.

'You do not know me.'

You do not know me.

Drew's parting words echoed through Elyse's head far into the night, and they were still there when they resumed their journey. When they had met at breakfast he had been polite but distant. By tacit consent they went back to addressing each other formally, and when she had tried to apologise again for slipping off to the ball he stopped her, saying it was best forgotten. But she did not want to forget. Not everything. The noise and excitement of the ball had set her pulse racing and although she had not enjoyed being pawed and ogled by the drunken men, she had experienced a fierce pleasure when she'd recognised Drew and realised he had been watching over her. She had put that down to her relief at being rescued from unwanted attentions in the ballroom, but when they had been alone at the inn and he had moved so close she had felt a breathless, heart-thudding exhilaration.

That Drew had not taken advantage of her she knew was solely because of his strength of character. He had desired her, she had seen it in his eyes and her own body had felt the tug of mutual attraction. He thought her too young, too innocent, but Elyse was beginning to recognise her own feelings and she knew that if he had taken her in his arms at that moment she could not have resisted.

She remembered the first time he had kissed her, to teach her a lesson. She had been ashamed, yes, and humiliated, which had been his intention, but she could still recall the leap of excitement she had felt at his touch, the way his body had called to hers. It was a dangerous, forbidden desire and Elyse could only be thankful that Drew had not acted upon it. He might be an adventurer and a self-confessed rake but he had a strong sense of honour. Papa had charged him with delivering her safe to her fiancé and she knew Drew would do everything in his power to fulfil his obligation.

Elyse turned her head slightly so that she could watch him as the coach rattled on towards Bath. He was lounging back in the corner, one hand pushed into the pocket of his frock-coat and his hat pulled low over his eyes. Only the lower part of his face was visible to her and she took the opportunity to study him, the lean cheeks and strong jaw, the mouth that even in repose had a slight upward tilt at the corners, as if he was always on the verge of laughter. Very rakish. Very attractive. She caught herself up on the thought. Drew was her guardian and he was going out of his way to escort her to her fiancé. Whatever he was, whatever his past, she should be grateful for that.

* * *

When they stopped at Calne to change horses Drew did not move, but Elyse knew he wasn't sleeping.

'Do you not wish to get out and stretch your legs, sir?'

'No.'

'Why, are you hiding, perhaps?'

He pushed his hat up and looked at her.

'Why should I do that?'

'I am not sure,' she said slowly, considering the matter. 'Perhaps you are afraid of being recognised.'

'What a foolish notion.' He refuted the idea coolly and pulled his hat low again, leaving Elyse once again to the enjoyment of her own company. She did not object, for there was so much to see and once they had left the bustling inn she settled back to watch changing scenery outside the window. She did not know whether it was the new horses or the terrain that made their progress slower, but she was too diverted by the unfamiliar landscape to worry. A layer of heavy grey cloud covered the sky but even so she was entranced by the view.

Rolling hills and verdant woodland stretched away on either side, interspersed with hedged fields and small, picturesque villages. At every bend there was something new to observe, a pretty group of cottages or a grand manor house nestling amongst the trees and instead of the grey stone of the north the buildings here were built of wood or a warm, honey-coloured stone. She became aware that her companion was stirring and was about to remark upon the delightful countryside when she heard him mutter angrily under his breath. By the time she turned to face him he had let down the window and was shouting to the coachman to stop.

'What is it?' she asked. 'What is the matter?'

He did not reply, but jumped out as the carriage slowed and she heard him addressing the coachman.

'Why are we going this way? The road via Box is much the quickest route.'

'I've got me orders, sir.'

'Wait—you are not the driver who brought us to Marlborough.'

'No sir, we comed from Bath—me an' the guard—to bring you in from there, since we knows the road better.'

'If that is so then you know I am right, the road through Box would be quicker.'

'Blocked, sir, so we've had to come by way o' Biddestone.'

The route meant nothing to Elyse, but when Drew climbed back into the carriage and they set off again she quickly asked him to explain.

'We have taken a more northerly road and will enter Bath via Batheaston.'

'Is it not a good road?' she asked, observing his frowning countenance.

'Perfectly good,' he replied, 'but one would normally take the more direct route. However, if it's blocked there's no help for it. 'Tis awash, I suppose. It was always prone to flooding.'

'You must be very familiar with this area, sir, to know that.'

'I am.'

Elyse frowned over this as Drew sat back in his corner, his eyes fixed on the passing landscape. The rolling hills were lost to sight as the road descended through an area of thick woodland, robbing the carriage of even more light and plunging them into gloomy shadow.

'I think you would not have come here again, out of choice,' she ventured, watching him carefully. 'I think you are afraid that someone will recognise you.'

He looked at her, his eyes shuttered and wary.

'Why do you say that?'

She gave a little shrug.

'For several reasons. You remained in the carriage when we stopped to change horses, the landlord at Marlborough thought you looked familiar, and your knowledge of the route we are now taking.'

'You are very observant, Miss Salforde.'

'I like to think I am not quite a fool.'

She saw a wry smile tugging at one side of his mouth.

'No, you are not that.' He looked out of the window once more. 'I have not travelled this road since I was a boy and would not be here now, if I had not made a promise to your father.'

So he had not come this far for her sake. She knew that, of course, but he need not have expressed it so baldly. Elyse hid her wounded spirit with a show of defiance.

'You did not have to come. The viscount had made arrangements to convey me—'

'And look what happened to his secretary! You would not even have reached Marlborough yet.'

'And if I had not? It would not be any of your concern.'

'Oh, yes, it would,' he said grimly, 'I am your guardian until Michaelmas.'

'I am sure Papa would be content that you had escorted me to the viscount's London home.'

'I have a duty to deliver you into the viscount's personal care and I shall do so, even if it means risking—'

He broke off, but she pounced on his words.

'Risking what, Mr Bastion? Being recognised?'

Drew cursed himself for his slip of the tongue and tried to appear nonchalant.

'Do not be absurd.'

'I do not think I am being absurd,' she said slowly, a faint crease puckering her brow. 'You arrive from France, a self-confessed adventurer and you said you left England ten years ago. That would be 'forty-five. The time of the troubles—'

She broke off as the coach lurched suddenly. It came to a halt amid shouts from outside and the sudden explosion of the guard's blunderbuss. Drew quickly pulled Elyse away from the window.

'Get back!'

He looked out. A group of horsemen stood across the road in front of the post-chaise, their faces shrouded in black mufflers and each one of them brandishing a long-nosed pistol. Two of the men rode up to the door, one calling out in a rough voice, 'Ho, you there! Step out where we can see you. And be quick about it.'

Drew weighed up the odds and decided there was nothing to do but obey. With a curt word to Elyse to remain in the coach he opened the door and jumped down. He could see only four horse-riders. A glance at the box showed that the coachman and guard were sitting with their hands clapped to their heads. Of the blunderbuss there was no sign, but since it had already been discharged he could look for no assistance there. Drew was wearing his sword and had his own pistol in his pocket, but the riders were all armed and one bullet against four—the odds were too great. As least for the moment.

He heard a rustle of skirts and Elyse was beside him. Confound it, why had she not stayed in the carriage out of sight? Quickly he addressed the rider nearest to him, the one who had ordered them out of the carriage.

'My purse is a fat one. Take it and leave us to continue on our way.'

'Your purse?' the fellow seemed a little nonplussed by Drew's words, then he gave a laugh.

'Ah, of course, yes, I want yer purse, master. Throw it over, but carefully. The others are watching ye, so no tricks!'

Slowly Drew reached into his pocket and pulled out his purse. It was galling to give away his money and if he had been alone he might have put up a fight, but with Elyse at his side he dare not take the risk. He tossed the purse at the rider, who caught it deftly and stowed it away inside his coat.

'That is all we have,' said Drew. 'Kindly let us resume our journey.'

'Not so fast, sirrah. The lady can return to the carriage, but you will stay where you are.'

Elyse stepped a little closer to Drew.

'I'll not go without you,' she muttered.

The man brought his horse even closer and waved his pistol.

'Get in the carriage, mistress, if you know what's good for you.'

'No.'

Her resolute refusal seemed to throw him. His hands tightened on the reins and his horse jibbed and sidled restlessly.

'Get in or by heaven I'll put you in myself,' he blustered.

Drew stepped in front of Elyse.

'I don't think so,' he said, pulling out his own pistol. 'Keep your distance!'

Then everything happened at once.

The fellow raised his arm to fire but Drew was quicker.

The man yelped as Drew's bullet grazed his hand and he dropped his weapon, exclaiming in an altered voice, 'Devil take it, he's winged me.'

From the corner of her eye Elyse saw the carriage jerk forward as the horses shied at the sudden noise. The coachman cried out in alarm.

'No pops—you promised there'd be no shooting.'

Even as he spoke a second retort sounded and Elyse saw the flash of the explosion. It came from a pistol carried by one of the men blocking the road. Drew staggered back against her and she screamed. She took his arm and began to back away, thinking to drag him into the carriage. The horses were moving restlessly as they approached but instead of reining them in the coachman whipped them up and drove off, unhindered by his erstwhile assailants. Elyse was so shocked that for a moment she could not move but stared in dismay as the coach disappeared around a bend in the road.

'Oh, d-devil t-t-take it, the fat's in the fire now!' cried one of the riders.

They appeared as stunned as Elyse by the events and were grouped together, circling uncertainly. Drew caught her hand and began to run towards the trees.

'Quickly, this way!'

They plunged into the undergrowth. Elyse tried desperately to hold her skirts away from the brambles that snatched at them as they pushed their way between the bushes. The road was soon lost to sight. The trees grew thickly all around them, their branches and leaves matted overhead to form a thick roof so that they were moving through semi-darkness. Elyse was so frightened she could hear nothing but her own heart thudding and the crash and rustle of their flight.

At last Drew stopped.

'Listen,' he gasped, 'can you hear anything? Are we being followed?'

She strained her ears, listening for the sound of pursuit, but all she could hear was her own and Drew's ragged breathing.

'No I think not.'

He sank down against a tree trunk and Elyse

gave a soft gasp. 'Drew, your arm! You are wounded.'

He looked down at the dark stain spreading over his sleeve.

'No time for that now, let us move on.'

He tried to rise but Elyse pushed him back again.

'We are not going anywhere until I see how badly you are hurt.'

She dropped down beside him and began to remove his coat, ignoring his protests.

'Damme, woman, are you trying to kill me?'

'I am very sorry if it hurts,' she said contritely. 'I am being as gentle as I can.'

She eased his coat off the injured arm to reveal the bloodied shirtsleeve. Elyse bit her lip. This was no time for missish nerves, she must work quickly. She tore away the sleeve and used it to wipe off the blood as best she could, then she pulled off her muslin neckerchief and folded it into a pad that she pressed against the wound.

'I th-think the bullet must still be in there,' she told him. 'If you can hold this in place I will find something to bind it up until we can find a surgeon.'

He did as she bade him, saying with a faint

laugh, 'How do you know so much about doctoring?'

'One of our footmen was involved in a brawl and the doctor needed assistance. Excuse me.' She turned away from him.

'What are you doing?'

'Removing one of my petticoats.'

With her back to Drew she lifted her skirts and tugged at one of the sets of strings beneath. The layer that came away was her newest embroidered underskirt but it could not be helped. She stepped out of it and began to tear it into strips. It took all her effort to rip the fine linen but fear gave her an added strength. When she turned back she noted that although Drew still held the pad in place, his eyes were closed and he was alarmingly pale. Silently she knelt beside him and began to wrap the bandage around his arm, noting when he removed his fingers that tiny red stains were already blooming on the pad. She bound it tightly, praying that it would be enough to prevent him losing too much more blood.

At last it was done and she sat back, regarding him anxiously. She was somewhat reassured when he opened his eyes.

'Are you badly hurt, Drew?' she asked him. 'I will try to fetch some help—'

'No, you cannot go alone. Stay with me, I can walk.' He struggled to his feet and she helped him to put his undamaged arm into the sleeve of his coat, pulling it loosely over his other shoulder and trying not to look at the black stain on the empty sleeve. When it was done he leaned against the tree trunk.

'If only I wasn't so dashed dizzy.'

'You will have to lean on me,' she said. 'I only hope we do not have to go too far, for the daylight is fading very quickly.'

'No, there is a house very close.' He nodded. 'This way.'

'But there is no path—'

'There is, trust me.'

He took her hand and began to push through the dense undergrowth. They had only gone a few yards when they reached a path. Drew staggered and Elyse quickly moved beside him, pulling his good arm across her shoulders.

'Which way?' she asked.

They set off in the direction of his nod. The track was just wide enough for the two of them, although Drew's unsteady steps made their progress erratic. It was growing dark when the path brought them out on a leafy carriageway and a short distance ahead Elyse could see a pair or ornate metal gates set into a high stone wall.

'Thank heaven,' She glanced at Drew, aware that his arm across her shoulders felt considerably heavier. 'You know this house?'

'Yes, it is Hartcombe.'

She helped him to the gates. They were closed and stiff with lack of use but she managed to push one open sufficiently for them to slip inside. The gravel drive was strewn with weeds and the bushes rearing up on either side looked formless and overgrown in the gathering dusk. However, ahead of them she could see the outline of a low, rambling building and a dim glow of light shone from the windows. Two shallow steps led up to a solid door. She grasped the knocker and rapped loudly.

There was no immediate response and she was about to knock again when she heard the faint sounds of movement within. There was the scrape of bolts, the door opened and an old man appeared bearing a lantern in one gnarled hand. Elyse almost collapsed under the weight of Drew's arm as he pushed himself a little more upright.

'Good evening, Father.'

Chapter Five

The old man stood in the doorway and raised the lantern. Its rays illuminated his face and Elyse thought she could see a vague resemblance to Drew in his hawk-like features. A thick mane of white hair hung like a ghostly halo about his head. Not by the flicker of an eyelid did he show he had heard Drew's greeting. He glowered at them.

'What do you mean, bothering good men like this? Go knock at the back door and the cook might find some scraps for thee.'

He thinks we are beggars.

Elyse could not blame him. In the gloom he would not see Drew's injury, only their dishevelled appearance. Drew gave a short, ragged laugh.

'A poor welcome for your son.'

Only then did Elyse see a shadow cross the old man's face. Pain? Sorrow? Revulsion?

'I have no son. Get thee gone from here.'

'Please,' Elyse begged him. 'He has been shot. We cannot go any further.'

The old man stared at her for a long, agonising moment, then with a shrug he stood aside for them to enter.

'Very well, bind him up then be on your way.'

It was dark inside the house for no lights burned other than the lamp carried by their host, but when her eyes had grown accustomed to the gloom Elyse could see that they were in a large hall. There was no fire burning in the huge fireplace but at least they were out of the damp night air. With no guidance from their host and Drew leaning heavily against her, Elyse had no idea if more comfortable rooms lay beyond the hall so she guided Drew across to an armchair beside the empty fireplace. He sank into the chair and put his head back, eyes closed. Even in the dim light of the lantern she could see that the binding she had tied around his arm was now dark with blood.

'He needs a doctor,' she said. 'Can you summon one?'

'No.' Her shocked gaze made the old man explain, albeit reluctantly. 'There is only Mrs Parfitt in the kitchens and my manservant has gone out and taken the only horse.'

Elyse wanted to scream at his lack of co-operation but that would not help Drew. If no one else would take charge, then it was up to her to do so. Resolutely she removed her cloak and looked about her.

'Then we must do what we can.' She dragged a small table across and placed it beside Drew's chair. 'I need more light, and water and cloths.' When he did not respond she said sharply, 'Can you ask your serving woman to fetch them, or must I seek them out myself?'

After placing his lantern on the table the old man went off and Elyse set about unwrapping the sodden bandages from Drew's arm. His eyes flickered open.

'You show scant respect for my parent, my dear.'

'Is he your parent? If so, he is a most unnatural one.'

'He has cause.' He raised his head and looked past her at the sound of hasty footsteps approaching. A large woman came into the room carrying a bowl and jug.

'Sir Edward said there was a gennleman here needin' attention.' She bustled up to the table, casting one searching look at Drew before putting down the bowl and proceeding to fill it with water from the jug. 'Here.' She pulled the cloth from her shoulder and handed it to Elyse. 'Let me fetch more light and then I will help you.'

Elyse felt her fear and anxiety easing at the sound of a friendly voice. The woman moved with surprising speed and efficiency, bringing a lighted candelabra to the table and fetching cloths and bandages. Between them they cleaned Drew's arm and dressed it, then the woman went off to prepare bedrooms, but not before she had provided a glass of brandy for Drew and a cup of fruit cordial for Elyse.

'Thank heavens Mrs Parfitt was here,' murmured Drew, fortified by the brandy. 'I feared we should be sleeping under the stars tonight.'

'We may still be,' murmured Elyse as the sound of raised voices came floating into the hall.

She put down her glass as the old man stormed back into the hall, Mrs Parfitt following behind him, puffing hard but addressing her master.

'Sir Edward, he has a bullet in his arm. We

must send Jed to fetch Dr Hall in the morning. I pray you do not be too hasty—'

'Hasty? I vowed I would never have that traitor in my house again.' Sir Edward surged forwards, glaring at Drew. 'Well, sirrah? I have done my Christian duty and dressed your wounds but you shall not sleep under my roof again, by God, sir, you shall not.'

Elyse moved closer to Drew's chair as if to protect him but that only brought her to the old man's attention.

'You and your doxy can leave my house this minute.'

Elyse reeled from the fury she heard in those words, but Drew put out his good hand and caught her fingers, steadying her. He said coldly, 'This lady is my ward, sir. I will thank you to remember that. We were attacked on the road nearby and only the direst necessity brought me to your door.'

'I can believe that,' stormed Sir Edward. 'But I care not what has happened to you, nor who this woman might be. I want you both gone, immediately.'

Elyse almost quailed beneath the violence of his attack, and if she had been alone she would have fled the house and braved the terrors of thc darkness outside, but one glance at Drew's pale and haggard face gave her the courage to speak up.

'Mr Bastion needs a surgeon to remove the bullet from his arm.'

The old man's lip curled. 'Bastion is it? More like Bast—'

'Sir Edward!' The housekeeper's shocked interjection cut him off.

'I could hardly travel under my real name,' said Drew bitterly.

'Well, you will find Dr Hall in the village, where he has always been.'

Mrs Parfitt threw up her hands.

'Good heavens, Sir Edward, that's two miles hence. You surely wouldn't expect him to walk there tonight?'

'I expect him to leave my house, and take the woman with him.'

Drew dropped Elyse's hand so he could push himself to his feet.

He said coldly, 'Send me away if you must, sir, but I am under an obligation to deliver this young lady to her fiancé. With a bullet in my arm, my purse gone and our carriage stolen I cannot now fulfil that task. I beg you, as a gentleman, to offer protection to the lady and see her safe to Bath.'

'I'll be damned if I will—' the old man declared wrathfully.

'Drew!' Elyse cried out as he swayed and fell back into his chair.

'Oh dear, oh Lord.' Mrs Parfitt came bustling up. 'He has fainted clean away. P'raps it's for the best, for we can get him into bed without causing him any more pain.' She ignored the growl of protest from her master. 'I've prepared a bed for him just across the passage, so the best thing would be to carry him in the chair. Pity there ain't more staff to help us but we'll have to manage. Sir Edward, now, if you will take the legs, then I am sure the young lady and I can manage to carry the top, if we tip it back like so...'

Elyse wondered how the master of the house would respond to being ordered about by his housekeeper, but she could only be thankful when he merely followed instructions. It was impossible to tell from his scowling countenance if he was at all concerned for his son.

It was a struggle, because both the chair and Drew were heavy, but somehow they carried their burden across the hall and through the passage to the small chamber where Mrs Parfitt had made up thc bed. By the time they had lifted Drew on to the mattress they were all puffing heavily.

'Well, that's a good job jobbed,' panted Mrs Parfitt. 'I thank 'ee, Sir Edward. If you'd like to go and sit down in the parlour I'll be bringing your supper for you in a trice. Now miss.' She turned back to Elyse. 'You and I had better get the young master out of his clothes before he comes to his senses.'

Elyse swallowed. She had never undressed a man before and was sure Aunt Matthews would consider it most improper. But there was no one else to do it, and she could not leave the housekeeper to manage alone. She moved to the head of the bed and began to untie Drew's neckcloth.

The old man stood watching her but she ignored him and after a moment he went out, closing the door behind him with a snap.

'You mustn't mind the master, my dear,' said Mrs Parfitt. 'He has very few visitors nowadays and has forgotten how to go on.'

Elyse considered the old man's behaviour sprang more from animosity than a lack of manners, but she thought it best not to say so. She also made a decision at that moment. She would not leave Drew alone in this house. It was inconceivable she would abandon him to such an unnatural parent. She realised no one at Hartcombe knew her name and resolved that she would keep her identity a secret. That way Sir Edward would not be able to force her to leave, unless he cast her out on to the street, and somehow she did not think he would go quite that far. She hoped he would not.

Elyse cleared her throat and asked the housekeeper if she had known Sir Edward a long time.

'Oh, that I have, my dear. I started as a maid when Sir Edward's father was alive and worked my way up to housekeeper. They was happy days, and I had a house full of staff, too. Now I'm cook, housekeeper and maid of all work, but I couldn't leave. I've been part o' this family for nigh on forty year and as long as Sir Edward needs me I'll be here.'

'And is he really Mr Bastion's—this man's father? I am sorry, that is the only name I have for him.'

'Castlemain,' said the housekeeper. 'That's his real name.' She smiled fondly at the unconscious figure on the bed. 'Andrew Castlemain, and wasn't he always a rascal? Oh dear, oh Lord, yes. I saw 'twas Master Andrew as soon as I comed in, for all the master said it was merely *some gennleman* with a bullet in his arm. And Dr Hall will recognise him, too, as like as not, since he has known the young master since he was a boy, but we need not worry about that, for *he* won't tell anyone.'

'And does that matter?' asked Elyse. She had unbuttoned Drew's shirt and was busy easing him out of it, trying not to notice the hard contours of his chest nor the crisp dark hairs that shadowed it. This was no time to be distracted.

Mrs Parfitt stood back and placed her hands on her hips.

'Matter? Of course it matters, my dear. Why, if he's discovered he'll be dragged off to Lunnon and hanged as a traitor.'

'Oh.' Elyse leaned against the bed as the room began to swim. She stared down at Drew, studying his lean, handsome face. She could believe him an adventurer, even a rake, but a traitor? 'Surely not.'

'Aye, 'tis all too true, my dear,' affirmed Mrs Parfitt as she rolled down Drew's stockings. 'He got himself mixed up in the 'forty-five and ended up with a price on his head.'

Elyse pressed her hands together. How much he had risked to come to England. And how much more so to escort her to Bath, so close to his old home. What if he were recognised and arrested? Suddenly it was not an unconscious man lying before her on the bed, but a corpse.

'He must not die because of me,' she whispered.

Mrs Parfitt chuckled, misunderstanding. 'Oh, Lord, no, he won't *die*. Strong as an ox, is Master Andrew. Dr Hall will have the bullet out in a trice in the morning, then a few days' rest and he will be right as a trivet. Now, if you'll give me a hand to get him out of his breeches we can tuck him up in bed...'

'There, all done now.'

Mrs Parfitt gave the bedcovers a final twitch.

'He looks peaceful enough, so now, miss, I'll take you to the parlour and you can dine with the master.'

'I would rather sit here with Mr Bas—Mr Castlemain.'

Recalling Sir Edward's harsh words, Elyse had no wish to dine with her host. Mrs Parfitt was reluctant to leave her, saying that she would come and sit with the young master once she had finished in the kitchen, but Elyse was adamant and at last the housekeeper went off, promising to bring her a tray when dinner was ready.

'And I'll make up a bed next door for you tonight, rather than one of the guest chambers. Then you can lie down when you wish and won't need me to show you to your room.'

The housekeeper hurried away and Elyse was alone with Drew. Calm settled over her, it felt like the first chance she had had to rest since they had left Marlborough. It was very quiet, the stillness almost unnatural as she pottered about. She collected up the clothes that were scattered over the floor and tidied the room, sending frequent, anxious looks towards the patient, who continued to sleep peacefully. Mrs Parfitt brought her dinner on a tray and came back some time later to collect the empty dishes. She glanced at the still form lying in the bed, touched his skin to ascertain there was no fever and after uttering a few reassuring words to Elyse she departed, promising to look in once more before she retired.

Alone again, Elyse pulled up a chair beside the bed and sat down, resting her arms on the edge of the bed and staring at Drew.

He was propped up on a mountain of pillows, still and unmoving save for the regular rise and fall of his chest. The bare skin of his head and shoulders looked dark against the white linen and he looked particularly boyish with his long dark hair flopping over his brow. But there was nothing boyish about his body. She had tried not to stare as she helped Mrs Parfitt to strip him, but it had been impossible to ignore the muscled limbs, broad shoulders and the flat, hard stomach. There were scars, too. Vivid lines inflicted by a sword or knife, and when she had lifted him she had felt ridged welts across his shoulders. From a flogging, perhaps? She looked now at his smooth, unlined face. What had he done for the past ten years, how had he lived?

You do not know me.

His words came back to her now as the shadows closed in and the candles guttered in their holders. She did not know him, but even if his heart was as black as sin and he had committed endless evil deeds, in his dealings with her he had been honest and honourable. He had risked his life for her sake.

Drew stirred and she was immediately alert. She placed the back of her hand on his brow and uttered up a little prayer of thanks when she found it was not fevered. He did not open his eyes, but he batted her hand away, as if it was some irritating insect. She fetched the horn beaker and held it to his lips.

'Here, drink this. It is barley water and will refresh you.' She wished it had been laudanum, but Mrs Parfitt had told her there was none in the house.

He raised his head and took a few sips, his eyes remaining closed as if in exhaustion, then he sank back against the pillows. Elyse returned the cup to the table and sat down on her chair again. There was nothing to be done until the doctor arrived.

'Elyse.'

He barely breathed the word. She could not even be sure she had heard him correctly.

'I am here.' She reached out and clasped his good hand. 'We are safe.'

He squeezed her fingers. It was the faintest pressure, but somehow infinitely reassuring.

Elyse woke to find the morning sun pouring into the room and bathing everything in a golden light. She was slumped over the bed, her hand still holding Drew's. She sat up stiffly, blinking in the light. As she tried to pull her fingers away Drew's grip tightened. He was awake and watching her.

'Have you been here all night?'

'I fell asleep.' His gaze was oddly disconcerting and she felt the hot blush rising through her body to be so close, to be holding his hand as if they were…friends. Lovers.

Drew was aware of the nagging pain in his left arm. He had only the vaguest idea of what had happened last night. He remembered the explosion of pain as the bullet hit his shoulder, the struggle through the trees and the look of horror on his father's face. Everything else was a confusion of pain and oblivion.

Until now. Now he was lying in a familiar room and Elyse was holding his hand. Her fingers were nestled beneath his and for some unfathomable reason he felt it was imperative that he did not let her go. He heard the door open and Elyse rose from her chair beside the bed. Reluctantly Drew released her hand as a familiar, cheerful voice addressed him, taking him back to his childhood.

'Now then, Master Andrew, here's Dr Hall come to see you.'

Mrs Parfitt came into the room with a rustle of black skirts, as large and cheerful as ever. Save for a few more grey hairs she looked no different than when she had waved him off from Hartcombe all those years ago. She had expected him back within a month, but it had been a decade, and he should not be here. His father did not want him here.

Pushing aside the unpleasant thought he raised his eyes to the tall, bewhiskered man in a black frock-coat and wide-brimmed hat following in her wake. The doctor had known him all his life, had treated him for his childhood illnesses and accidents and the housekeeper had wisely not tried to keep his identity a secret. Neither of them would betray him, Drew was sure of that, but what sort of reception could he expect from the good doctor? Drew waited warily for Dr Hall to speak.

'Well, you young scamp, what have you done now?'

Immediately Drew was twelve years old again, having fallen out of a tree and broken his leg. His relaxed and managed a grin.

'I've got you out of your bed at an unholy hour, sir, that's for sure.'

'I sent Jed off to summon Dr Hall the moment he got back,' put in Mrs Parfitt, clasping her hands across her snowy apron. 'Not that the doctor needed any second bidding when Jed told him who it was lying here with a bullet in his arm. And you're not to be worryin' that anyone else'll learn your identity, Master Andrew, for neither me nor Jed would mention it to another soul outside this house.'

Their loyalty moved Drew so much that he was unable to speak. Silently he returned his attention to Dr Hall, who was already removing his coat.

'So it's a bullet this time, is it? Well, let me have a look at you, then we had best get it out.'

'I shall assist you,' said Elyse.

'You will not.' Drew glowered at her. 'You will go and get some rest.'

'Well, I shall need someone to help me,' declared the doctor, rolling up his sleeves, 'And Mrs Parfitt has never been very good with the sight of blood.'

'That's true, sir,' affirmed the housekeeper. 'Preparing a rabbit or pheasant for dinner is about as much as I can manage, but when it comes to people—' she shuddered.

'And Sir Edward will be wanting his breakfast very soon,' said Dr Hall, adding cheerfully, 'So off you go, Mrs Parfitt, and leave this to me. Now, miss, we'll need some hot water and clean bandages—oh, and brandy, I think, for the patient. And something for him to bite upon.'

* * *

For the next hour Elyse followed the doctor's directions. She dared not look when he set to work to remove the bullet and could not be sorry when Drew fainted off, for the sight of his pain-racked face made her want to cry out in sympathy. While Dr Hall bandaged up the arm again she busied herself clearing everything away. She was thankful that Mrs Parfitt had suggested Drew should remain in a room on the ground floor, for with no one to help her she had to make constant journeys to and from the kitchen for fresh water. There was no sign of Jed, the manservant, and she guessed he was catching up on his sleep, while Mrs Parfitt was busy looking after Sir Edward, whose deep voice she could hear whenever she passed the small dining room.

The housekeeper looked into the sickroom just as Dr Hall was putting on his coat.

'Ah, Mrs Parfitt, would Sir Edward like me to report to him before I leave?'

For the first time since she had arrived at Hartcombe Elyse saw the older woman looking uncomfortable. She would not meet the doctor's eyes and twisted her hands in her apron as she replied.

'The master is too busy to see you today, sir, but I'll pass on any message to him later.'

'Too busy, eh?' Dr Hall frowned a little, then shrugged. 'Well, I have done all I can. The bullet is out and I have cleaned the wound but only time will tell how it will heal. I shall leave you some laudanum to help with the pain. He may become a little feverish for a few days but you'll know how to deal with that.'

'Oh, yes, Doctor.' The housekeeper was looking more cheerful again. 'Now you's wrapped up that wound I shan't mind nursing Master Andrew.'

'Good. And I've shown this young lady how to bandage him up again, if that should be necessary, is that not so, Miss...?'

'You have, and I shall be glad to help,' Elyse affirmed, smiling and ignoring his attempt to learn her name.

'Capital, capital.' He picked up his bag. 'I shall call again in a couple of days to check on his progress. No need to see me out, I know my way.'

With another cheerful smile he was gone, and the two women were left staring at the unmoving figure in the bed.

'He is very pale,' offered Elyse.

'Only to be expected.' Mrs Parfitt bustled about, straightening the bedcovers and tidying the room. 'I doubt he will wake for a while yet, so you should go and get some sleep, dearie. Unless you would prefer to come to the kitchen and I'll find you something to eat?'

Elyse yawned. 'Sleep, I think.'

'Well, I have prepared a guest room for you upstairs Miss, so I'll show you the way—'

'If you please,' Elyse hung back. 'I would prefer to sleep on the truckle bed you made up for me last night,' she said. 'Then if Dre—if Mr Castlemain does wake up I shall hear him.'

'But I don't mind popping in every now and again—'

'But you have your own work to do and I should not sleep half so well if I was too far away.'

Elyse's gentle determination won the day and she settled down to sleep in the little room next door, but her rest did not last long. When the brandy wore off Drew became restless. His mutterings roused her and she was already at his bedside when his restive tossing caused him to move his injured arm and he cried out in pain.

She forced a little laudanum between his dry

lips, then bathed his brow with the lavender water thoughtfully provided by the housekeeper. His temperature was rising, and by the evening she was obliged to call Mrs Parfitt to help her as he was growing increasingly agitated.

Throughout the night they took it in turns to remain at his side and it was only the older woman's experience that prevented Elyse from seeking out Jed and begging him to ride for the doctor once more. Mrs Parfitt assured her that there was nothing to fear, that the fever was mild and would run its course. Elyse could not be easy, but by the morning Drew did indeed appear a little calmer. His restlessness had set the wound bleeding again during the night and she was left wondering anxiously just how much blood he could afford to lose.

She spent the day sitting by his bed, wiping his brow and forcing small amounts of water between his lips. Mrs Parfitt did not even suggest that she should leave him and once again brought her dinner to her on a tray. Elyse thanked her and consumed her meal in the sick-room. As the evening wore on Drew did indeed seem to be sleeping peacefully, so Elyse slipped out to take thc cmpty dishes to the kitchen rather than add to the housekeeper's workload.

'Why thank you, my dear.' Mrs Parfitt was busy at the kitchen table, a large bowl before her and her arms white with flour up to the elbows. 'I'm just making bread for the morning, so take the plates through to the scullery, if you would. Jed will deal with them later.'

'It is such a big house, do you have no one else to help you?' Elyse looked around her. There were signs of neglect throughout the building and even here in the kitchen, the copper pans on the higher shelves did not look as if they had been touched for years.

The housekeeper gave her a wry smile.

'We manage. Times have been hard for the master and he has become something of a recluse in recent years, especially since Master Simon's death.'

'Simon?'

'His oldest son—Master Andrew's brother. He died in a riding accident two years ago. After that the master shut up most of the house and turned off the staff. He never entertains, so mostly Jed and me manage to look after him well enough.' She smiled cheerfully and went back to her bread-making, leaving Elyse to make her way back through the dim corridors.

The door of the dining room was open and she glanced in. Sir Edward was sitting in lonely state at the head of the table. The covers had been removed and the light from a branched candelabra illuminated the decanter and wine-glass before him. Elyse paused, then knocked softly on the open door.

'I thought you might like to know how your son goes on.'

He looked up at her soft words.

'I have no son.'

'Very well, then, the sick man you have allowed to shelter in your house. He had been very feverish, since Dr Hall removed the bullet, but I am sure you will be relieved to know that he seems a little more comfortable this evening.'

The shadows were too deep for her to read his expression but he did not move and after a few moments she gave a tiny shrug she turned away.

'Thank you.'

Elyse glanced back, wondering if she had imagined his reply. Sir Edward was refilling his glass, his hand not quite steady.

'Tell Parfitt she may summon Hall again as

she sees fit. And she can tell him I'll pay whatever is needed.'

Elyse did not know whether to show gratitude for his generosity, or outrage that he should be so uncaring of his son. In the end she merely nodded and began to walk away.

'Before you go,' She turned back to find Sir Edward regarding her. 'You have not told me your name.'

She looked at him for a long moment. Despite his assurances that he would pay the doctor's bills she still did not trust him to look after Drew. She gave a faint smile.

'No,' she said quietly. 'I have not.'

And with a slight curtsy she left him.

The first thing Drew was aware of when he awoke was that the light no longer hurt his eyes. The next thing was that he was at Hartcombe, but not in his own bedchamber. He recognised the room as one of the small guest chambers on the ground floor, but what in heaven's name was he doing here?

He was still trying to answer that question when the door opened and Mrs Parfitt came in.

'Well, now, Master Andrew, so you are awake

at last. That is good news. Would you like a little food, perhaps?'

'Not hungry,' he managed, frowning with the effort. 'Thirsty.'

She came over to the bed.

'Take a little water, then I will find you something more nourishing. A mug of ale, perhaps.'

'Splendid idea.' He winced a little as she helped him to sit up and pushed another pillow behind his shoulders.

He sipped at the cup she held to his lips. The cool water soothed his parched throat and helped him to collect his scattered wits.

'How long have I been unconscious?'

'Lord bless you, Master Andrew, nearly all the time since Dr Hall took the bullet from your arm, so that's four full days.'

'The devil it is!' He struggled to hold on to the returning memories. 'And the lady who came with me—is she gone to Bath?'

'Heavens, no, sir. She's been nursing you night and day. She'd be here now if I hadn't insisted that she take a turn around the gardens. Very reluctant to leave you, she was, but I told her it would do you no good if she was to become ill, too, so I sent her out to get some fresh air. But you need not fret, she won't be away from you any longer than she can help, I'm sure.'

'She has been nursing me?' He rubbed his good hand over his chin. 'Has she been shaving me, too?'

'No, not that she wouldn't have tried, but she persuaded Stinchcombe to do that.' Mrs Parfitt gave a cheerful laugh. 'Quite adept she is at getting her own way.'

He frowned.

'She is a lady. She should not be looking after me.'

The housekeeper directed an arch look at him.

'And who else is to nurse you, pray? I have done what I can, but a body's only got one pair of hands and mine have been busy running this house and looking after Sir Edward, and since the master refuses to take on anyone else I'm very thankful to the young lady for knuckling down to work with me.'

'Yes, of course. I beg your pardon, Mrs Parfitt. My coming here has placed an added burden upon you.'

'Now you are not to be thinking like that, Master Andrew. Where should you come, when you're in need, but to your old home?' She put down the cup and straightened, beaming at him. 'Now, I shall be off to get your breakfast and I'll be back just as soon as ever I can.'

She hurried away and Drew was left alone once more. He put back his head and closed his eyes, trying to recall the events leading up to his coming to Hartcombe, but the harder he tried to think the more confused he became. He heard the door opening again and looked towards it, expecting to see Elyse come in. Instead he was surprised to see his father standing in the threshold.

He had some memory of seeing him at the door when he and Elyse had arrived. His thoughts were confused, hazy and he recalled only the vague image of a stooping figure with white hair. Now he took the opportunity to study his father and he suffered a severe shock at how much he had aged. Ten years ago Sir Edward had stood tall, a proud man in the prime of life. Today his face was lined and his back hunched, as if he had suffered much. He had always worn a powdered wig over his shaved pate but now he stood before Drew with his white hair flowing untidily around his head.

This is all my doing.

'Parfitt said you were awake.' Sir Edward took a few steps into the room. 'How are you?'

It was a cold, grudging enquiry. Drew thought bitterly that he would be a fool to expect anything different.

'Damned weak,' Drew said shortly. 'What date is it?'

'The twenty-sixth.'

'So late?' Drew sat up, then fell back again as the pain shot through his injured arm. 'And Elyse has nursed me all that time?'

'Is that her name?' Sir Edward's shaggy brows rose a little. 'Aye. She's looked after you. Waited on you constantly.'

'But she is not a servant,' exclaimed Drew. 'You should not have allowed it.'

'You both arrived without attendants and without baggage, how was I to know she was anything other than your—' Sir Edward broke off, flushing a little when he met Drew's angry look. He said defensively, 'There was no one else to nurse you. Parfitt did what she could but she was not able to sit with you day and night.'

'Then I should have been left alone,' snapped Drew. 'The lady should never have been allowed to remain here.'

'Oh, and what do you think I should have

done with her?' demanded Sir Edward, his colour rising. 'She refused to leave your side.'

'I told you I was taking her to Bath, you should have packed her off there and placed her in the care of her fiancé's family.'

'She has refused to leave until she knows you are out of danger.'

Drew snorted angrily.

'You could have made her go.'

Sir Edward cursed roundly.

'Since she would not divulge her name, nor that of her betrothed, what would you have me do, abandon her at the doors of Bath Abbey?' he stormed. 'Dashed cantankerous woman has had us all at sixes and sevens.'

He glowered at Drew, who felt his lips twitch and after a brief struggle he burst out laughing.

'Aye,' he grinned. 'She has a rare talent for that, I admit.'

'It's all very well for you to laugh,' growled his father. 'You have no conception of the trouble you have caused.'

The black cloud descended over Drew's spirits once more, stifling all desire to laugh.

'Oh, I think I have, sir. I—'

He broke off when he heard someone hurrying along the passage towards the open door.

The next moment Elyse came in, the jacket of her travelling gown unbuttoned, her curls disordered and a becoming flush mantling her cheeks. At the sight of Sir Edward she stopped.

'Oh, I beg your pardon.' She sank into a hasty curtsy. 'I heard a noise and feared—'

'You thought your patient delirious?' Sir Edward barked at her. 'No, he is conscious at last, and I hope to heaven you will soon be able to remove him from this house.'

With that he stalked out, leaving Elyse to stare uncertainly at Drew.

'I beg your pardon,' she said again. 'I am sorry if I interrupted you—'

He put up his hand.

'You interrupted nothing save possibly a quarrel,' he said shortly. 'It has always been thus between us.'

'He did not turn you away from Hartcombe.'

'I have no doubt he would have done so, and he could.'

'He is an old man, Drew, and he is suffering a great deal.'

'And I am not?' he bit back at her. He let his breath go with a hiss and raised his hand. 'I should not have spoken so, forgive me.'

'Willingly.' She came closer, her dark eyes

fixed anxiously on his face. 'Did you know about your brother?' she said gently. 'Did you know he had died?'

'Simon? No, I did not.' The news was like a blow to the stomach. He stared her, the gut-wrenching pain making his head spin. 'When was this?'

'Two years since. A riding accident. Mrs Parfitt told me.'

He closed his eyes, his good hand gripping the bedclothes until his knuckles gleamed white.

'No, I did not know,' he said again, adding bitterly, 'I have had no communication from Hartcombe for years.'

'I am very sorry.' She covered his hand with her own. 'Perhaps you understand now some of your father's unhappiness.'

Oh, yes. He understood it. He had been the cause of most of it. He had hoped at some point that he might at least make his peace with Simon, but now that would never happen. With an effort he brought his mind back to the present and opened his eyes again.

'There was no need for you to stay here.' He pulled his hand from beneath hers and had to steel himself against the feeling of loss. 'You should have asked my father to convey you to Lord Whittlewood in Bath.'

'How could I leave when there was no one to look after you?'

'Easily. It was not your place to be nursing me.'

'Someone had to do it, and to help Mrs Parfitt get you into bed. I helped to wash you and put you in a nightgown, too, although I decided not to try shaving you.'

The twinkle in her eyes and the mischievous smile playing around her lips succeeded in putting to flight his morbid thoughts, at least for a while. He grinned.

'I dread to think what you would have done with a razor in your hand. My father's valet did that service for me, I believe.'

'Yes. Sir Edward was a little reluctant to allow it at first, but when he realised that I was prepared to shave you myself he relented and ordered Stinchcombe to assist me.'

'Thank heaven for that!'

'I know.' She giggled. 'I think he feared I should cut your throat, which is very likely, of course, because I have never shaved a man before.'

'You should not have had to do *anything* for

me.' He frowned at the seriousness of her situation. 'We have only three days to get you to Lord Whittlewood. If I am not well enough then you will have to go alone. We can find a village maid to accompany you, and I will write a letter to explain—'

'Is that necessary?' she asked him, startled. 'Could we not write to the viscount now, telling him that we will be delayed?'

Drew shook his head. 'Lord Whittlewood's letter was most specific. You are to be delivered into his care by Michaelmas. If not, the marriage agreement is null and void.'

He saw the colour leave her cheeks and was sorry for it, but it was only right that she should know the truth. She clasped and unclasped her hands for a moment, mulling over his words.

'You said as much before,' she said at last. 'Do—do you think Lord Whittlewood would rather I did not marry William?'

'I fear so.'

'And is that the reason the family was not in London when we arrived? The viscount hoped I might not continue the journey?'

Drew was convinced of it, but he did not say so. Instead he watched the play of emotions over her face. Eventually he said gently, 'Elyse, are you sure you want to marry young Reverson?'

'But of course,' she replied immediately. 'And he wants to marry *me*. I have his letters. He loves me.'

'You have not seen each other for three years.'

'And we have neither of us wavered,' she said simply. 'It proves the strength of our affections, does it not?'

Drew regarded her in silence, debating whether to suggest it proved nothing of the sort, but as Mrs Parfitt came in at that moment with his breakfast he decided to keep his own counsel. After all, Harry had arranged this match, and he was merely carrying out his friend's wishes. It really was none of his business. But as he settled down to enjoy his first meal in days Drew was aware of a little worm of unease gnawing away at his conscience.

Chapter Six

A visit from Dr Hall confirmed that Drew's recovery was well under way. He was allowed to leave his bed for a few hours that day and the following morning he announced his intention of joining Elyse and his father for dinner. He refused to let Elyse help him with his clothes, pointing out that since his father's valet came in every morning to shave him he could dress him, too. Stinchcombe surprised Drew by putting up no resistance to the suggestion and even admitted that Sir Edward had ordered him to offer any assistance he could.

Thus, late in the afternoon, Drew eventually left his bedchamber. Mrs Parfitt had cleaned his coat as best she could and stitched up the bullet hole, but the bandaging on Drew's arm was too thick to allow him to wear it, so he appeared in his waistcoat and the borrowed shirt Stinchcombe had found for him, his injured arm resting in a sling. Since this was his first outing the valet insisted upon accompanying him to the parlour. Sir Edward was already there, seated on one side of the fire. Drew entered and heard the soft click as Stinchcombe shut the door behind him. He was alone with his father.

'So you are on your feet at last.'

A cold greeting, but no more than Drew expected.

'Yes. And in a few more days I shall be out of your house.'

The old man said nothing. He got up and walked to the sideboard and poured wine into two glasses.

'I will arrange a carriage for you, but nothing more.'

'I expect nothing more from you. Once I am in Bath I shall be able to draw on my own funds.' He added bitterly, 'Don't worry, my bankers know me by the name of Bastion, there is no risk of anyone knowing my connection to you.'

'That is none of my concern.'

He handed Drew a glass of wine and returned to his seat, staring moodily into the fire. Drew watched him for a few moments, then shook his head.

'Oh, what the devil!' He raised his glass. 'I wish you good health, sir.'

The old man stared at him. 'Do you expect me to reciprocate?'

'No. But I am grateful for your hospitality.'

The old man scowled into his glass.

'You cost me dear,' he muttered. 'The fines, the confiscated lands, the disgrace to the family. Even your mother's death.'

'Do you not think I know it?' Drew retorted, regret, bitter as gall, filling his gut.

'She never forgave herself for sending you to stay with her brother. She was convinced it was all his doing, that he persuaded you, but I know differently. You were always the wild one.'

'I was *fifteen*. Wild, yes, but still a boy, Father.'

Sir Edward turned on him with a snarl.

'Do not call me that! I will not recognise you as my son.'

Drew's lips thinned as the words cut deep. After a moment he said quietly, 'I am very sorry for it.'

Sir Edward hunched a shoulder and turned back towards the fire, and thus they sat in silence until the door opened again and Elyse appeared in a rustle of silk. The two men rose immediately, but Drew's first glance turned into an outright stare. Gone was the olive-green travelling gown; she was wearing an open robe of jonquil satin over a white skirt of quilted Marseille work and she looked quite breathtaking.

'You are wondering how I come to have another gown, when the carriage and all our baggage was stolen,' she said, correctly interpreting his curious look. 'Sir Edward gave permission for Mrs Parfitt to look out a gown of your mama's for me to wear.' She smiled shyly. 'Altering it to fit gave me something to occupy my time while I was at your bedside.'

'It becomes you very well,' replied Drew, hoping his face did not betray the desire he felt for the beautiful creature he saw before him.

She wore no kerchief about her shoulders but a demure flounce of blond lace edged the low neckline. The candlelight gleamed on her dusky curls and one wayward ringlet hung down to her shoulder, accentuating the flawless creamy skin. The embroidered stomacher drew his eye to her dainty waist and he imagined himself putting his hands around it and drawing her close. She would laugh up at him and he would bend to steal a kiss from those cherry-red lips. He had tasted them before and remembered how sweet they would be…

Quickly suppressing the thought he turned to his father.

'I can now make up for my previous lack of manners and formally introduce you. Sir, may I present Miss Elyse Salforde to you? Miss Salforde is the daughter of a good friend of mine. When he died he left her to my care.'

Elyse sank into a graceful curtsy, deep and respectful.

'I hope, Sir Edward, that you will forgive me for withholding my name from you for so long.'

'You had your reasons, I am sure,' he said shortly. He set a chair for her and the three of them sat around the fire in an awkward silence. Sir Edward cleared his throat. 'Did you enjoy your walk this morning, Miss Salforde?'

'I did, sir, thank you.'

'The pleasure gardens are very overgrown now. That was my wife's domain and I have not bothered with them since her demise. There has been no money for such luxuries'

His angry glance flickered to Drew, who felt its sting and could not resist raising a grievance of his own.

'Why did you not inform me of Simon's death?'

'I did not think it concerned you.'

'Concerned me? For Gad, he was my brother!'

'Aye, pity you didn't think of that before you turned traitor and put his inheritance at risk.'

Drew clamped his jaws together, determined not to respond and into the breach stepped Elyse. She turned in her seat and addressed Sir Edward.

'You must miss him greatly, sir. Mrs Parfitt said it was a riding accident.'

Drew braced himself, ready to fly to her defence if his father should snap at her, but it was not necessary.

'Yes, it was,' Sir Edward replied. 'It happened two years ago, at this very season. Simon had bought a new horse, handsome brute but with a vicious streak.' He glanced at Drew. 'He never did have your way with horses. He thought to school the animal, but he rushed it, took him out too soon to follow the hounds. The horse threw him at the first fence. Broke his neck.'

'I am so sorry,' Elyse said softly. 'And you have lived here alone since then?'

The old man looked up, saying defiantly, 'I

am content with my own company.' He rose. 'Dinner should be ready by now. Let us go in.'

The atmosphere in the dining room was distinctly chilly, but it had nothing to do with the weather, which was very mild, even balmy, and Elyse had no need of the shawl she had brought with her. The windows were thrown wide to allow in the late September sunshine and she was thankful to hear the cheerful birdsong from the gardens, for it gave her something to think of other than the strained silence. When the meal was over she rose to leave the gentlemen but Drew stood, too and suggested they might take a turn about the gardens together. Elyse was surprised, but pleased to accept. As they crossed the hall he disclosed his reasons for his invitation.

'I will not endure his disapproval another moment,' he muttered. 'He has not mellowed one jot. I have no doubt he would put Simon's accident at my door, an he could.' He stopped and rubbed his eyes. 'Forgive me, Elyse. I will not inflict my ill humour on you, but I needed an excuse to leave him to his own devices. I will retire—'

'No.' She caught his good arm. 'It is not late

and it will do you good to step outside for a little while. Do come with me, we can watch the sunset from the gardens.'

She thought at first he would refuse, but with a shrug he went outside with her. The shrubbery was so overgrown that it was impossible to walk there, but Elyse followed the route she had taken earlier in the day, descending the terrace steps to a series of wide gravel walks that were not yet impassable. They strolled together, not touching, but Elyse was very conscious of the man at her side. She could almost feel the tension in him, his anger ready to boil over.

'This would be so pretty, with a little management,' she remarked, in an effort to distract him. 'I believe there is only the one gardener now, and he spends all his time looking after the orchards and the kitchen garden.'

'Yes.'

She glanced up. His face was set, the eyes shuttered.

'Do you take the blame for that, too?'

'Of course.'

'Why should you do that?'

'My actions led to most of my father's estate being seized by the Crown. There would have been fines to pay, too, as well as the ignominy of having a rebel in the family. My father paid dear for my treachery. It would have been necessary to retrench.'

Elyse tucked her hand into his arm and gave it a little squeeze.

She said gently, 'Will you not tell me what happened?'

'There is nothing to tell. I allied myself with the Pretender in 'forty-five. He was defeated and thus all his supporters are traitors. The family was fortunate not to lose everything because of me.'

'But you were no more than a boy.'

'I was deemed old enough to know my own mind. To join forces with the rebels in an effort to force King George from the English throne. It is treason.'

They descended a flight of shallow steps to another weed-strewn gravel path. Elyse looked back, they were well away from the house now.

'I would like to hear your story.' When he hesitated she added with a smile, 'My father must have thought there was some good in you, to make you my guardian.'

'He was the only one to think so.'

They walked on and Elyse maintained her

silence. After a while she was rewarded when he began to speak.

'I had just reached my fifteenth birthday and went north to stay with my uncle, my mother's brother, in Strathmore. It was meant to be a short visit, a month at the most, then I would return to my schooling, but while I was there news came that the Prince had landed in Scotland. My uncle had always been a Jacobite, the family had been involved in the uprising in 'fifteen when they had lost all their titles and only narrowly escaped with their lives.

'That was a hard time for Mama's family. She was sent to live with friends in York, where it was hoped she might avoid the taint of belonging to a family of traitors. That is where she met my father and they fell in love. He married her and brought her here to Hartcombe, his family home. Despite my father's disapproval Mama kept in touch with her family, and even persuaded him to allow Simon and me to visit them occasionally. She thought there could be no harm, she had no Jacobite leanings herself and did not think we were in any danger that we would be persuaded by her brother's fanatical ravings for what she considered a lost cause. She was only half-right. Simon was the studious one, sensible and home-loving. I was always more restless, seeking adventure and impatient of books and learning.' He stopped, momentarily diverted. 'How could he have been so cork-brained as to take out a half-trained horse?'

'Sir Edward said he did not have your way with animals.'

'But all the same—he was meant to be the clever one.'

'Were you very close?'

'Close enough, until I went to Scotland that last time. After that I never heard from him again.' His lip curled. 'After I was declared a traitor my father sent a message to say he had forbidden any contact with me. I was cast off, no longer considered a member of his family. I never quite believed it. I was constantly on the move but I wrote to Hartcombe when I could, to let the family know where I could be reached. I only ever received one letter. That was from my father, four years ago, informing me that my mother had died. That I had killed her.'

She stopped. 'Oh, Drew.'

'Do not waste your pity on me, madam, remember that I am a traitor.'

He had thrown off her hand and was standing stiff and rigid as stone. His face was a cold mask

Elyse shivered, not knowing how to reach him. After a few moments she spoke, saying gently,

'We should walk on if we are not to become chilled.'

'Yes, of course.'

They walked on, the shadows lengthening around them as the sun dropped towards the horizon.

'How did she die?' asked Elyse.

'I broke her heart.'

'I do not believe that.'

He shrugged.

'My father told me she was struck down when the news arrived that there was a price on my head. She never recovered.'

Not knowing the words to comfort him, Elyse took his arm again.

'I would like to know what happened to you in the 'forty-five, Drew, if you can bear to tell me.'

He waved his hand dismissively.

'You cannot really wish to hear such an unedifying tale.'

'I do,' she assured him. 'And sometimes talking about things helps to heal old wounds.'

'Not mine.'

'I would still like to hear your story.'

'Very well.' He paused, as if deciding where to begin. 'The summer of 'forty-five, Simon was preparing to go to Oxford so I went to Strathmore alone. I should explain; the Jacobite leanings of my mother's family were never mentioned at Hartcombe. She had quite given up the cause, and my father was a staunch Hanoverian. It says something for the strength of his love for Mama that he allowed us to visit Strathmore. Whenever we went there my uncle was more than willing to entertain us with stories of the daring escapades of his ancestors, and of their loyalty to the Stuarts. They were tales of honour and the fight for a noble cause, just the sort of thing to catch the imagination of a boy longing for adventure. When the Prince landed in Scotland and my uncle rode off to join him, I went with him.'

A tiny cloud passed across the setting sun and there was a momentary dimming of the light. Elyse pulled her shawl a little closer and patiently waited for Drew to continue.

'The reality of the uprising was very different from the noble enterprise I had dreamed of. Oh, there was plenty of bravery and displays of courage, especially in those early days when success came easily, but I also saw crass mismanagement and self-serving advancement amongst the Prince's followers. Things went from bad to worse once the army turned back at Derby. There were minor skirmishes on the way north, and the odd victory, but the men were disheartened and demoralised. I was wounded at Falkirk Muir and didn't follow the Prince back to Culloden, which is where my uncle died, along with so many others. It was a bloody, bitter defeat and the government determined to crush the rebels completely.

'I had acquitted myself well in previous battles, but that worked against me and I found myself with a price on my head. I went into hiding and eventually my mother's family smuggled me across to the Continent.' When he paused she glanced up and saw that his lips had thinned to a bloodless line. 'Charles and his supporters had returned to France by then, but any thoughts I had of being welcomed into their ranks were quickly dashed. I was a poor wretch, disowned by my father: the last word I had from him before I fled Scotland was that my actions had laid my mother so low she was not expected to live. So I arrived in France without connections or money—just another burden. I was not yet sixteen, alone and far from home. I changed my name and did what I could to survive.'

He stopped. Elyse could only guess at the black days that followed. She thought of the scars and wheals she had seen on his body and shuddered.

'You became a mercenary.'

'Yes.'

'You were lucky to escape with your life.' She added quickly, 'You may not agree, but *I* am very thankful for it. You were a true friend to my father; you have proved as much by your behaviour towards me.'

'Do not make a hero of me, Elyse, I am nothing of the sort.'

She returned his troubled gaze frankly and with a warm smile.

'I know that, silly, but I also know I can trust you to keep me safe.'

'Only until Michaelmas, my dear. After that…'

Something flared in his eyes, causing the breath to catch in her throat.

She stopped and prompted him. 'After that?'

Elyse watched as the fire died from his gaze. He gave a bitter laugh, patted her hand and obliged her to walk on beside him.

'After that,' he said lightly, 'you are no longer my concern.'

Elyse accompanied him in silence. That is not what he had meant, she was sure of it. That look in his eyes hinted at something quite different. She had found it unsettling and even a little frightening. Surely the sudden heat that flooded her body, the way she wanted to cling to him, such were the feelings one should have for one's husband. One's lover.

She gave herself a little inward shake. Such thoughts had only occurred because she was lonely and missing William, but that would not be for much longer. They would be together soon. At Michaelmas. A few more days and then she would never see Drew again. But she had always known that, had she not? And not so long ago she had thought the day could not come soon enough. She had changed and suddenly Elyse was afraid to consider just how much.

'Well, naturally,' she said, forcing herself to speak calmly. 'After that you will not need to look after me, will you? I shall have William to do that.'

There was the briefest of pauses before he replied.

'Of course.' They resumed their walk. 'I propose that we journey to Bath tomorrow.'

'Dr Hall said you must rest for a few more days.'

'We have been here long enough.'

'But you have not left your room until today. You are not strong enough for another journey yet.'

'I thought you would be eager to reach your new family,' he challenged her.

'I am.' The words came quickly and she refused to think deeply about the matter. She was only concerned for his well-being, wasn't she? 'But surely we can spare one more day for your recovery?'

'My father would not think so. He would not spare me one hour, if he had his way.'

Her heart went out to him when she heard the bitterness in his voice.

'That is not true,' she told him. 'Sir Edward insisted that Dr Hall should be called to attend you as often as was necessary.'

'Only because he does not want the embarrassment of my dying here.'

'Drew!'

'Do not sound so outraged, my dear, I expected nothing else. If it were not for you he would have thrown me out already.'

'I do not believe that. Whatever you have done you are still his son.'

'Has he said so?'

'Well, no, but—'

He stopped her with a wave of his hand, saying impatiently, 'You cannot mend everything, Elyse. Do not forget there is a price on my head. I should not even be in England.'

'Then I should go on to Bath alone, as we discussed.'

'No, we discussed it when I thought I would be too ill to come with you. That is no longer the case. I promised your father I would see you safely delivered to the viscount. Besides, I want to assure myself that the marriage settlements are in order.'

'But after Michaelmas you will no longer be my guardian. I could do that myself.'

'You could, of course, but I wish to look them over carefully.'

'Do you not trust Lord Whittlewood?'

'I am acting on your father's behalf. He would want me to make sure everything was arranged to your advantage. After all, you will now be taking to your new husband a considerable fortune.'

His remarks barely registered with her. She

said, 'But will it not be dangerous for you, to be in Bath?'

'Not really, unless you disclose my real name.'

She squeezed his arm.

'I would never betray you, Drew.'

He covered her fingers, where they rested on the sleeve of his borrowed shirt.

'No, I do not think you would, but you must see that the sooner I get you to Bath the better.'

She did see it, but the thought of the momentous change that was about to take place in her life was also a little daunting.

'I still believe you should rest as long as possible, and we can spare another twenty-four hours. If we leave early on Michaelmas morning we can still be in Bath before noon. Pray, sir, humour me in this.'

He sighed. 'Very well, one more day, but we dare not leave it any longer.'

'Dare not?' She cast a glance at him. 'Do you truly believe that if I am not delivered to the viscount by Michaelmas he will call off the wedding?'

'I do.'

'And...do you think that the viscount might

be so opposed to the match that he would deliberately try to stop my getting to Bath?'

'What makes you say that?'

She did not answer immediately.

'I have been thinking,' she said at last. 'About the wording of Lord Whittlewood's letter, and the fact that the family had left London before we arrived. Also, there are the circumstances of the attack upon our carriage.'

'We were travelling a road that is notorious for its footpads and brigands.'

His reply was guarded and she guessed that he, too, was suspicious. She continued thoughtfully, 'Does it not seem odd to you that Mr Settle should be taken ill and leave us to travel on alone?'

'Yes, that was a little odd, but it proves nothing.'

'But there is more, Drew. "Pops" is a slang word for firearms, is it not? I thought I heard the coachman cry out "No pops!" after you had fired at the robbers.'

'I daresay he did. It is a common enough expression.'

'But you do not understand. He then said,' she wrinkled her brow trying to recall the sequence of events. 'He shouted out, "You said there'd be no shooting." Or something of that sort. Did you not hear him?'

'No, you imagined it.'

'I did not, I promise you. I have been thinking and thinking about it. At first it made no sense, but then I remembered that the coachman and his guard had been sent out from Bath to meet us, and when you told me the viscount had given you an ultimatum, I thought, perhaps, he had arranged for the coach to be held up.'

'That is merely fanciful nonsense.'

'If that is so, then why was the coachman allowed to drive off unmolested?'

Drew frowned. 'Did he do so? I had taken the bullet in my arm by then and confess I did not notice much at all.'

Elyse nodded. 'Yes, he did. And the robbers seemed quite startled by your shooting at them.'

'Not too startled to shoot back.'

'I realise that but what if,' she moistened her lips. 'What if Mr Settle was a party to the deed? What if, when you decided to accompany me to Bath, Mr Settle panicked and feigned illness rather than be found out?' She saw Drew's black frown and added quickly, 'Oh, I do not think they intended to murder me. Perhaps they merely wanted to frighten me into returning to Scarborough.'

'It sounds very far-fetched, Elyse.'

'I know, but we are agreed the viscount does not want me to marry his son.'

'Perhaps not, but—'

'It is possible, isn't it?'

'Yes, it's possible. '

'Oh, how can he be so cruel, when it is what William wants, as much as I?'

'Are you *sure* it is what Reverson wants, Elyse?'

'Of course.' She turned her dark eyes up to meet his. 'I have his letters, telling me so.'

Drew did not answer immediately. If Elyse had heard the coachman correctly then there was some mystery here, but he was not as convinced as Elyse that William Reverson was completely innocent. And if not, then what harm might come of forcing the marriage?

Quickly Drew put aside such thoughts. Harry was no fool; he must have been assured of his daughter's happiness when he arranged this union. And it was a chance in a lifetime for her, she would marry into the nobility and never want for anything again.

Still, he determined to meet the viscount and make up his own mind before he abandoned Elyse to her fate.

The light was fading fast when they returned to the house and Elyse needed her bedroom candle to light her way to her room. She did not go to bed immediately but took out the letters William had written to her. Thank goodness she had put them in the large pockets beneath her travelling gown when she had set out, rather than packing them in her trunk, which had been stolen along with the carriage and all her other belongings.

She untied the green ribbon that she had fastened around the bundle. There were barely a dozen letters, far less than she had written to him, but William had told her he was no letter-writer. She read through them all again now. They were not fulsome, but neither was there anything in them to make her think that he had changed his mind about marrying her. With a sigh she closed her eyes and clutched the letters against her heart. The viscount might be doing his best to keep them apart, but she was convinced that William was sincere.

She tried to conjure his image, but it was impossible. Instead all she could see was Drew's darkly brooding countenance. But that was understandable, thought Elyse. It did not mean that she loved William any less, only that she was concerned for Drew. She wished that he and his father would make up their differences. Slowly she began to pack the letters away. Drew had said to her that she could not mend everything, but she could at least try.

Elyse found Sir Edward in the little parlour, his chair pulled close to the dying fire and a decanter and wineglass on a small table at his elbow. He glanced up as she entered and pushed himself out of his chair.

'Miss Salforde. Is anything amiss?'

'No, sir, I came to speak with you.'

He waved her to the chair on the opposite side of the fire.

'What is it you wish to say to me?'

'It concerns Andrew. Please, hear me out.' She put up her hand as he made to rise from his chair again. 'Do you know anything of his life these past ten years?'

'No.' He sank back, frowning. 'And I do not want to know.'

'He was very young when he left Hartcombe, sir.'

'He made his choice. He must take the consequences.'

'And he has done so. After he fled to France he had no money, no friends, so he became a mercenary, fighting for foreign armies. Then he met my father and they made their money at the gaming tables of Europe.'

'Hah!' His white brows snapped together. 'Scoundrels, then, the pair of 'em.'

She shrugged. 'Quite possibly, but Andrew assures me they won by fair means, and took care not to ruin anyone.'

'You may believe that if you like, madam, although I take leave to doubt it. Yet it does not alter the fact that he was a traitor to his country.'

'He was a *boy*, young and impressionable, who was caught up in events beyond his understanding.'

'Did he send you to me to plead his cause?'

'He does not know I am here, Sir Edward. He thinks you can never be reconciled.'

'And he is right.'

She smiled. 'If that were so, why did you take him in and allow Mrs Parfitt to nurse him?'

'Any Christian would do as much.'

'Would they? I think it was more the action of a man who still cares for his son.'

He glared at her. 'You would be advised to keep out of what does not concern you.'

'But it *does* concern me, Sir Edward. My father made Drew my guardian, because he knew him to be a true and honest friend. And so he has proved himself to be. He has risked arrest to come to England and take me to Lord Whittlewood. He was wounded protecting me from highway robbers. It is only right that I should try in return to help him. We have one more day here, then he plans to leave Hartcombe and never return. I would beg you to make your peace with him.'

'Never.'

'Sir Edward—'

'No!' He swung around in his chair, turning away from her. 'If that is all you have to say then you had best leave, madam, for I shall not change my mind. Go. Go, damn you!'

Elyse rose.

'I know Drew to be an honourable man, Sir Edward. You should be proud to have such a son. It would mean a great deal to him if you could acknowledge him.' When he did not speak she continued quietly, 'My father was a restless man who travelled Europe, living on his wits. When he died he left me with money, but very few memories of him. He provided handsomely for me and my mother, while she was alive, but he rarely visited us. My biggest regret is that I never really knew my father. You have a chance to make peace with Andrew, I beg that you do so, sir, and make the most of the time you have left together.' She walked to the door, where she turned, speaking to his rigid, unmoving back. 'I pray you, sir, do not leave it too late.'

Drew's bedroom candle guttered and he threw aside his book. He should be asleep, but he was too restless. He eased himself off the bed and fetched a fresh candle, lighting it from the stub of the old one before pushing it into the candlestick. His thoughts turned constantly to Elyse Salforde. He wanted her, he could not deny it. She bewitched him and not just with her beauty. She had the power to soothe away his anger. Walking with her in the gardens, having her beside him, had eased the pain of the memories he had recounted, memories he had shared with no one, not even Harry. And she was not indifferent to him, he would swear it, but that made it even more important that he did nothing to hurt her.

He could offer her nothing save a tainted name and a life of constant wanderings. He could not even claim any burning zeal to return the Stuarts to the throne. He had followed his uncle into battle in a spirit of youthful adventure but he had never been truly wedded to the Stuart cause, which made his actions all the more disreputable. He had dragged his family through so much for nothing more than a youthful indiscretion. He turned restlessly in his bed. He could do nothing about the past, but he could discharge his promise to Harry honourably. He would make sure Elyse reached her future husband safely.

The thought of the marriage contract made him frown. It was watertight, he knew that, and biased heavily in Elyse's favour. He would ensure the terms had not been changed before he relinquished his guardianship. Harry had done his best to ensure his only daughter's happiness, but even with a measure of independence she would still be wed to William Reverson and would that really make her happy? Drew pondered the question and was surprised to realise just how much Elyse's happiness meant to him.

A gentle scratching at the door caught his attention.

'Stinchcombe! What are you doing here?'

His father's valet stood in the doorway, a pile of white linen in his hands.

'Sir Edward thought you might need your dressing changed, sir.'

'But it's near midnight.' Drew swung himself off the bed. 'Well, now you are here you had best come in. It will save you doing it in the morning.'

The valet waited patiently while Drew stripped off his shirt then got to work removing the old dressing.

'Sir Edward is not sleeping well, Master Andrew.'

'Well, what of it?'

Drew tensed as the bandage came away, but there was very little pain. The wound was clean and healing well.

'If you wrap it lightly I will be able to wear my coat tomorrow,' he told the valet.

'Yes sir.' A fresh dressing was wound around the arm. 'But if I might suggest, Master Andrew…'

'Well?'

'Sir Edward is not abed yet. When I left him he was pacing up and down his room.'

Drew gave a bark of hollow laughter. 'He would hardly thank me for disturbing him then.'

Stinchcombe stood back, surveying his handiwork.

'That's the point, sir. I think he *would* like to see you.'

Drew frowned.

'He would?'

Stinchcombe reached out and tidied away a loose end, never meeting Drew's eyes.

'I think he would, Master Andrew. I think something's troubling him.'

Drew put his shirt back on and allowed the servant to re-tie his sling before he dismissed him. He scowled. He was damned if he'd go to the old man. It could only result in another roasting. There was too much bad blood between them. Too much that could not be forgiven. He prowled about the room, picked up his book and climbed back on to the bed, but the words swam before his eyes and made no sense.

'Hell and confound it.'

Stinchcombe would not have come to him if he had not been seriously worried about his master. Drew swung himself off the bed again, pushed his feet into his boots and went out.

A thin line of light shone beneath Sir Edward's door. Drew knocked and received a curt invitation to enter. His father was sitting by the fire, a single candle burning on the mantelshelf.

'What in hell's name brings you here?'

The greeting was every bit as unwelcoming as Drew had expected. He bit back an equally curt retort.

'I saw your light under the door.'

'What of it? Can't a man sit in his own room now without being disturbed?'

'Is anything amiss, sir? Can I help?'

With a curse the old man pushed himself up out of his chair.

'Of course there is something amiss and no, you cannot help, since you are the cause of it.' Drew waited silently while Sir Edward strode over to the window. 'I was thinking of your mother,' he said at last, gazing out into the darkness. 'And Simon. Both gone.'

'I am very sorry, Fa—sir.'

'And so you should be.'

Drew's jaw clenched hard. He should not have come, but now he was here he would have his say.

'I do not see any reason why you should believe me, but I deeply regret what I did in 'forty-five. If I had not been so young, so foolish, I would have come back to England, discussed it with you before I took such a reckless step.'

'You know I would have forbidden you to join the rebels and you, like as not, would have run counter to my commands, as always.'

'There is always the possibility that I might have heeded you.'

The old man gave a scornful laugh.

'It would have been the first time.'

A long silence followed. Drew heard the crackle of the fire as a burning log collapsed into the embers. The timbers of the old house creaked, settling for the night. He should not have come. He was about to bid his father good-night when the old man spoke again.

'You are hot-headed, like me. Your mother always said so. Stubborn, too.'

'Another trait I inherited from my sire.'

Sir Edward turned with a snarl. 'Do not blame me for your misfortunes.'

'I do not,' Drew flashed back. 'I blame no one but myself.' He turned away with an exasperated sigh. 'I was a fool to come here tonight. What is broken cannot be mended.' He strode to the door. 'One more day, sir, then you will be bothered with my presence no more.'

He left the room and closed the door behind

him, hoping but not expecting his father to call him back.

There was only silence.

Chapter Seven

Drew was relieved when the first grey fingers of dawn crept into the room and he could get up. He had not slept well; his rest had been disturbed by dreams. After making a few tentative moves with his arm he decided to leave off the sling. The new dressing Stinchcombe had put on was much less bulky, and his frock-coat slid easily over his shirtsleeve. The dark stain was still visible on the sleeve of his coat. It would have to do until he reached Bath. He would buy himself some new clothes there before he returned to France.

And what then? He stood before the mirror, staring at his reflection. He had been a fool to come to England, it had set him yearning for a life he could not have.

'Why not?' he asked himself aloud. 'I could live in England as Andrew Bastion. Buy a little property away from here. In the north, perhaps, where no one knows me.'

The thought was pleasing, but it did not last long. Such a life would give him no rest. He would always be wary of being recognised, nervous of every knock at the door. No, he would return to the Continent. Perhaps not Paris, but there were other cities, fortunes to be won, ladies to be wooed.

Suddenly the life he had known with Harry did not appeal to him any longer.

'Well, that is unfortunate, sir,' he told himself savagely. He shook out his ruffles and made a final adjustment to the lace at his neck and stared hard into the glass. 'Because it is the only life you have now.'

With that he turned and strode to the door, determined to walk off his restless energy.

The sun peeping over the window ledge woke Elyse. She stretched and lay still for a few moments, wondering why her spirits should feel so depressed. Something weighed on her heart, a heavy problem that she had pondered long into the night. The morning light brought no relief. She slipped out of bed and dressed herself in the yellow morning gown that had belonged to Drew's mama.

Drew. He was part of her problem. William was the other part.

Elyse began to pace up and down the floor but it did not help. Her head felt it might burst with the thoughts that crowded in on her. In Scarborough she would have taken a walk along the cliff to clear her head but there was no convenient coastline here. She glanced out of the window. The neglected garden was the next best thing. Picking up her shawl she made her way outside.

Hartcombe's grounds were extensive. She saw Jed working in the kitchen garden and quickly turned the other way, going past the overgrown shrubbery and into what had once been a rose garden. The plants had not been tended for years, they rioted over the walls and were thickly entwined in the hedges. Only the very widest path was still passable and she picked her way along it, holding her skirts close to avoid the snatching thorns. Squeezing between two overgrown bushes she found herself at the western end of the garden. The high outer wall was ahead of her and beyond that the trees of the neighbouring woodland grew thick and tall. However, standing against the wall a short distance away was a small pavilion built in the style of a Palladian temple with a series of fluted columns supporting a pedimented roof.

The morning sun was already high enough to shine on to the building. It showed that the stucco was cracked and peeling in places, but it had a sad sort of elegance that appealed to Elyse in her present mood. She moved closer to investigate. It was quite a shallow structure, enclosed on three sides and it was bare of ornament save a wide marble bench placed against the back wall. Elyse sank down on the seat and gazed out. In more affluent times she thought the prospect must have been quite beautiful, but the box hedges had grown quite out of control and the shrubs and plants that had once flourished between the hedges had been ousted by weeds.

It looked very sad, but incredibly peaceful and she gave herself up to the thoughts that had been troubling her throughout the night. She closed her eyes and tried once again to summon up William's face, but it would not come. She remembered she had thought him extremely handsome, with his classical features, gently curving brows and soft brown eyes that she thought were quite the most beautiful she had ever seen. But now the only image that she could conjure was Drew's lean face with its straight dark brows and piercing eyes, the deep blue of a summer sky.

She knew she loved William but he had become a distant, shadowy figure, whereas Drew was such a vital, masculine presence that even now her body almost trembled at the thought of him. When he was near she wanted to reach out and touch him, to have him kiss her again and relive those exhilarating sensations that had made her feel so alive. She crossed her arms and hugged herself.

Would William affect me in the same way if he was here? In the years we have been apart I have become a woman.

Her arms tightened as she remembered Drew's cutting words the night she had attended the masquerade. Perhaps she was too innocent for him, but he was a rake and accustomed to amusing himself with women of experience. William would not see her thus. A tremor of doubt shook her. Perhaps he would. After all he, too, would have changed in the past three years.

She heard a sound, a rustle of leaves, a faint

step, and opened her eyes. Her heart gave a little leap when she saw Drew standing before her.

'Oh—I,' she stumbled over the words. 'I came out for a little air. I hope you do not mind...'

'No, why should I? I myself have been walking in the woods.' He gave her a searching look. 'Is anything wrong?'

'N-No, not exactly.'

He sat down on the bench and her eyes were drawn to the muscular thigh encased in buckskin that was so close to her own. Only inches separated them and she felt her mouth go dry.

'Tell me,' he said gently.

When she did not reply he reached out and took her hand.

'You were kind enough to listen to me yesterday. The least I can do is the same for you, when you look so troubled.' Her hand fluttered in his grasp and he continued, 'Tell me what is wrong, Elyse. I am not only your guardian, but your friend, too, you know.'

A friend? Yes, she did believe that, and he understood her, more so than anyone else she had ever met.

'I am afraid,' she said at last. 'William and I have not seen each other for so many years. What if he does not like me?'

'He cannot fail to like you.'

'You said I was a child, playing a woman's games. What if,' she felt the colour mounting in her cheeks. 'What if William expects—wants—a woman? What if I disappoint him?' She lifted her eyes to his face. 'This must seem very foolish to you—'

He put his fingers on her lips.

'Not foolish at all,' he said gravely.

His eyes had darkened to azure, drawing her in. With a sigh she leaned against him.

'Oh, Drew, how should I behave towards him?'

'You must be yourself, Elyse. He will be captivated, believe me.'

His words were so soft that she tilted her head up, leaning even closer to catch them. A delicious languor was spreading through her body. It was so comfortable sitting here with Drew, yet his words did not totally reassure her.

'But you are not,' she whispered unable to look away from his dark entrancing gaze. 'I have not captivated you.'

'Have you not?'

She could not move. She was staring up at him, her lips slightly parted and all she could do was to run her tongue around them. She saw his eyes widen and something flared in their depths, a look that sent a sudden shock of anticipation slamming through her even as he put his hand on her cheek and captured her mouth with his own.

Elyse closed her eyes. His kiss was infinitely gentle but it held her motionless while her senses reeled. He shifted his position, put his good arm around her and deepened the kiss. Elyse could not prevent the little moan of pleasure deep in her throat. Her arms crept around his neck and suddenly she was kissing him back. When his tongue tangled with hers a hot excitement exploded inside. She pressed her body against him and did not resist when he pushed her down on to the bench. She could feel his hard, masculine, body lying heavily against her. He continued to kiss her while his hand slipped beneath the lace fichu to caress her throat and the soft swell of her breasts. They strained against his fingers as if begging for more and he obliged, gently easing them out from the loosely tied stays and circling first one hard nipple then the other until she was almost swooning with the pleasure of it. When at last he released her from his scorching kiss she threw back her head, arching her body, offering it up to him. His mouth moved down over her throat and on to cover the hard nub of one aching breast while his fingers circled the other, drawing up the most delightful sensations from deep within her. She gasped and gave a little cry, but the pleasure had only just begun. His lips found hers again and he eased his body to one side, measuring his length beside her while his hand gathered up her skirts. She felt his fingers on the bare skin of her leg, circling, caressing, moving upwards, slowly, gently, until he reached the apex of her thighs. The blood was pounding through her body, she felt as if her bones were melting beneath his touch. She was like a flower, unfurling for him. A hot aching desire uncurled from her core, tugging at her thighs so that they opened for him, her hips tilting as she offered up her very soul.

She gasped aloud as his fingers slipped inside, startled by the shock of pleasure that rippled outwards at his touch. His hand was gripping her and she pushed against it, felt herself pulsing as her body was racked by spasms that robbed her of all control. She clung to Drew, eyes tightly closed as his fingers continued their magic, stroking and caressing, taking her higher, as if she was being carried on some giant wave. She knew it must soon crest and just when she thought she might faint from the sheer delight he was inflicting upon her, the wave finally broke.

Drew held her tightly, his elation soaring as he brought her pleasure to its height. Her head went back and she cried his name, clinging to him for a moment of shuddering ecstasy before the rigidity left her and she collapsed beneath him. A slight pain in his left arm reminded him of the bullet wound and he laughed to himself. He had been so intent upon pleasuring Elyse that he had quite forgotten about that. Had forgotten everything when she turned those dark, soulful eyes to him, inviting him to show her just what it felt like to be loved. He was hard as a rock and had been from the start, but he was a master of his art and she was a virgin, he wanted to make sure she was relaxed and ready for him. Her passion fired his own, but he would not rush her.

'Oh, Drew, I did not know, I never dreamed—'

He laughed softly and kissed her again. He could not remember the last time a woman had affected him like this. His arms tightened as he was suddenly overwhelmed by his emotions, not only desire but a fierce instinct to love and protect Elyse for the rest of his days. He held her close, knowing that in a few moments he would be able to rouse her again and this time he would take her. He would make her his own. By heaven he would make her his wife.

She is not yours and never can be!

The voice in his head was loud and full of reproof, bringing him back to reality with a jolt. What right had he to entice her away from her fiancé when he had nothing to offer her? If he made her his wife she would be condemned to wander through Europe with him. Or he might set her up in a house here in England, as Harry had done with her mother, but then their children—a surge of longing ripped through him at the thought of Elyse having his child!—their children would have no more memories of their father than she had of Harry. But that was not the worst of it. Harry had been an adventurer: Drew was charged with a much more despicable offence. He was branded a traitor and any woman who allied herself to him would be reviled, an outcast.

Only for an instant had he considered moving to some quiet corner of the country and setting up home under an assumed name. Bad enough for him to be constantly looking over his shoulder. He could not inflict that upon Elyse, too. And in the fleeting time it took for these thoughts to flash through his mind, Drew knew he could not condemn Elyse to such a life. He must stop. Now.

Summoning every ounce of will-power he forced himself to roll away from her, forced his hard, aroused body back under control.

'Drew?'

He heard the uncertainty in her voice and almost flinched when she touched his shoulder. His arm had begun to ache. He would be well served if it started to bleed again. A demon whispered to him to take her and to hell with the consequcnces. After all, she was willing.

Willing, yes, but innocent. It was up to him to protect her from a lifetime of regret.

Keeping his back to her he said politely, 'I am glad I pleased you, ma'am. You have some notion now of the happiness to be found in your husband's arms.'

'I—I do not understand you.'

'You were concerned Reverson would be disappointed in you.' He closed his eyes, he must speak coolly, rationally. 'We have just shown that your nature is passionate enough for any man.'

Her sigh nearly broke his resolve.

'I do not want any other man, not now. Drew—'

He jumped up and went to stand between the columns, leaning against one in what he hoped looked like a nonchalant fashion. He dare not turn and face her. Not yet.

'Do not be tiresome, Elyse. You know there can never be anything between us. You are going to marry William Reverson and I shall return to the Continent.'

'But I am not sure I want to marry William.'

'You think there may be some reluctance upon his family's part to accept you?' he said, wilfully misunderstanding her. 'As your guardian I shall discuss the matter thoroughly with Lord Whittlewood and do everything in my power to ensure your happiness before I consign you to his care.'

'Is that what it is?' He heard the hopeful note in her voice. 'You think that as my guardian you should not be here with me? Tomorrow is Michaelmas. After that your guardianship is over.'

'Yes, thank heaven, and I can resume my life.' He gazed out over the wild and neglected garden, thinking it looked as bleak and unwelcoming as the existence he envisaged for himself. For an instant he weakened, needing to explain. 'I am not free to settle down. I must travel constantly. It is not a life that would suit you, my dear.'

'What you mean is that it would not suit you to make me a part of it.'

'If you prefer to phrase it in that way.' He infused a note of boredom into his voice.

'I am not asking you to l-love me in return—'

Dear heaven, he could not bear much more of this. He turned, bracing himself to face her.

'Of course not. Absurd.' He kept on, inexorably cutting a chasm between them, too deep to cross. 'There is no knowing how soon I should be bored with you. There have been many women in my life, Elyse. As Harry's daughter you are very special, of course, but…'

'But not special enough.'

Dear heaven, if only she knew!

'I told you once before, my dear, you should never trust a rake.'

She was staring at him, tears coursing down her cheeks and Drew looked away, unable to bear the sadness in her eyes. It reproached him, but not as much as he reproached himself for letting it go this far. He concentrated on brushing the dust from his breeches as he said with studied indifference,

'Be thankful I left you a virgin. The delight of changing that state is something you can share with your husband.'

Almost before he had finished Elyse gave a low, shuddering sob and fled.

Chapter Eight

Drew did not move until the sound of her footsteps on the gravel had died away and stillness had fallen over the garden again. He swayed a little and put his good hand against the nearest column to steady himself. His arm was hurting like the devil but it was nothing to the pain he felt inside. With a growl he turned and banged his fist against the column.

'Oh, Harry why did I let you talk me into this?'

Only silence answered him. He waited a few more minutes and then made his way slowly back to the house. Tomorrow his guardianship would come to an end. He would escort Elyse to Bath and if he judged the viscount to be an honourable man he would put her into his care, if not he would hire a post-chaise and pack her off back to her aunt in Scarborough. Either way he would not see Elyse Salforde again.

After striding around the gardens while he cleared his head and regained some measure of control, Drew made his way back to the house. As he reached the terrace he heard someone call his name and turned to see Jed hurrying around the side of the house towards him

'Master Drew, Sir Edward was looking for you, sir. He is in his study and said to send you to him as soon as you could be found.'

'Very well, Jed. I will go to him directly.'

Drew's spirits sank even lower as he made his way through the house. What was it now? Did his father want to ring another peal over him? Possibly for disturbing his peace last night. Squaring his shoulders he knocked on the study door and went in. Sir Edward was working at his desk but he rose as Drew entered. His brows were knitted and the frowning look in his eyes did not augur well. Drew's nerves, already raw, stretched to breaking point. He said tersely,

'If you sent for me to enquire how much longer you must endure my company, I told you last night. We leave here in the morning. It was Miss Salforde who insisted we must wait for one more day. If it had been left to me I would have quit Hartcombe by now.'

'There is nothing wrong with my memory, damn you. I am well aware of your plans. I wanted to see you.' Sir Edward broke off as if startled by his choice of words. He went to the fire and added another log to the flames. 'There is something I need to tell you.' He straightened and turned back, saying testily, 'Don't stand there glowering at me, boy, sit down. But before you do you may pour us both a glass of claret. We may need it before this is finished.'

Drew wondered if he had heard these last, mumbled words correctly but he said nothing, merely walked to the sideboard where a decanter and glasses stood in readiness. He filled two glasses and carried them back across the room.

'Well?'

Drew handed one glass to his father and lowered himself into a chair. For a moment Sir Edward hesitated and half-turned, as if considering returning to his desk. Then with a sigh he sat down opposite Drew, sipping his wine and watching him over the rim of his glass.

'You have grown a great deal since I last saw you.'

This was so unexpected Drew almost laughed.

'I was fifteen when I left Hartcombe. A boy. Now I am six-and-twenty.'

'And just as hot-headed.'

Drew shook off the sudden spurt of irritation.

'Believe me, sir, I am not the reckless, impetuous youth who left here over ten years ago. That is something else I told you last night. I very much regret what I did.'

'And I regret that I did not come to fetch you home as soon as I heard the Pretender was in Scotland.'

This admission surprised Drew and he could not think of a suitable reply. Silence fell over the room.

'It was madness,' said Sir Edward at last, 'to throw your lot in with the Stuart.'

'I did not follow him to Paris. I wrote to tell you—'

'I burned your letters.' Sir Edward interrupted him. 'Never read them. I gave orders that your name was never to be mentioned again in this house. You were no longer a son of mine. I cut you out of my will.'

'I was amply punished, then, for my folly.'

Sir Edward continued as if he had not spoken. 'But I could not remove you from the entail. Now Simon is dead you will inherit Hartcombe when I die.'

'Ha, much good it will do me, since I cannot return to England under my own name.'

'That is not true.'

'Of course it is,' Drew retorted bitterly. 'Have you forgotten that I am traitor with a price on my head?'

'I have forgotten nothing!' Sir Edward pushed himself out of his chair and stalked over to the sideboard. He carried the decanter to Drew and refilled his glass before charging his own.

'She never gave up.' He resumed his seat and wrapped his fingers round his glass, holding it up so that he could stare into the blood-red depths. 'Your mother. It was the only time she ever disobeyed me. She sold her jewels to hire lawyers to plead for you. Up until her death she wrote to everyone of influence, bought favours, petitioned anyone who might be able to help.'

'I thought she was seriously ill.'

'Not then. You were her son and she would not abandon you.' The faded blue eyes flickered over Drew and away again. 'We never told you or Simon, but your mother had a weak heart. The news from Scotland distressed her, of course, but not as badly as I told you at the time. I wrote to you in anger. I wanted you to suffer, to believe she had collapsed because of your actions, but that was not the case. She was too intent upon obtaining a pardon for you to give in, at least for a long time. She fought hard for you, but it took its toll. By the time the letter arrived, the notice that you had been pardoned, she was dying. I read it out to her and by the end of the day she was dead.'

Drew sat very still.

'Why did I not hear of this pardon?'

'I loved her, yet it was only you she cared for.'

'So you did not tell me.'

The old man bowed his head. Drew watched him, so many emotions rioting inside that it was impossible to make sense of them.

'You did not tell me,' he said again, his voice deadly quiet. 'I was pardoned four years ago and you did not tell me. I might have returned to England, taken up my life again. And you let me think her death was my fault.'

'It *was* your doing. She fought for years, only waiting to know that you were safe, then she released her hold on life.'

Drew frowned. 'But Mrs Parfitt—Jed—they still think I am in danger.'

'I told no one. The letter came, I told your mother but no one else. It made her so happy.' His face contorted with pain. 'How I envied you.'

Drew stared at him

'You were jealous? Of me?'

The old man dropped his head in his hands.

'*Yes!* Oh, she loved me, too, and Simon, of course, but she showed such devotion to your cause.' Sir Edward slumped a little lower in his chair. He gave a long sigh. 'Perhaps I should not blame you for that. It might well have been fighting for you that kept her with me for as long as it did.'

'I am sure she would have done the same for any one of us,' said Drew slowly, his mind going over all he had learned. 'But why did I not hear of it? There must have been some announcement.'

'Possibly in London, but I made no effort to publicise your pardon, I put nothing in the local newspaper, hired no crier, posted no bills in the village square. All that mattered to me was the fact that my wife was dead.'

'But Jenkins, our lawyer, surely he—'

'Yes, he knew, but I forbade him to write to you. He has instructions not to contact you until I am dead.'

Drew was silent for a long moment. He said at last, 'You must hate me very much.'

Sir Edward raised his head and for the first time Drew saw the haunting sadness in his eyes.

'I did at that time. I blamed you for taking her away from me.'

'I know. You wrote to tell me as much.' Drew held his breath. 'And now?'

'Now? I do not know. You are heir to Hartcombe, or what is left of it.'

Silence filled the study. Sir Edward sat up straight in his chair and pushed one hand through the white mane of hair. Slowly he rose and turned to face Drew.

'If it is not too late,' he said, 'I want to tell you I regret keeping the truth from you and—to ask if you can forgive me.'

Drew stood up. When he had left Hartcombe ten years ago he had been a head shorter than his father. Now they were of a height and he looked straight into his father's eyes, blue, like his own, but faded by age. He saw no anger in them, only pain, sorrow and anguish. And, underlying all the rest, loneliness.

His own bitterness melted away.

'Can you forgive *me*, Father, for bringing such hardship to the family? If so, I would like to come home. I would like to help you rebuild Hartcombe.'

Sir Edward's eyes misted. He put out his hand.

'Come home, and welcome, my boy.'

They gripped hands and moved closer to embrace each other briefly. Drew found his throat constricting. Home. He could return to Hartcombe as its heir, invest the fortune he had made in the estate, perhaps buy back some of the land they had lost.

'You will need to see the accounts,' said Sir Edward, as if reading his mind. 'We must sit down together and discuss what needs to be done.'

'Of course. We will do so as soon as I return from Bath.'

'Ah yes. Miss Salforde must be delivered to her fiancé.'

Must she? Drew remembered how passionately she had succumbed to his kiss, how right she had felt in his arms. He had hurt her, pushed her away but if he explained that he had been trying to protect her…

'Delightful lady, Miss Salforde.' Sir Edward was refilling their glasses. 'She upbraided me for cutting you out, showed me what I was giving up for the sake of stubborn pride.'

Drew looked up. 'Does she know, then?'

'That you are pardoned? No, her concern was that we should not lose one another.' The old man smiled. 'We owe her a great deal.'

Drew nodded. A plan was forming in his mind. Perhaps it was not too late. They must go to Bath, of course, but he could tell her that now there was an alternative, if she found she did not love William Reverson, after all.

Finishing his wine Drew excused himself and set off in search of Elyse. He went first to her bedchamber, but there was no answer when he knocked on the door. Quickly he ran back down the stairs. Could she still be outside, wandering the grounds, distraught? What a devil he was to cause her such pain, even if he had thought it was right to protect her, to put himself beyond reach. He must find her, quickly, and repair the damage. If he could!

He saw Jed coming in from the garden and asked him if he had seen Miss Salforde in the grounds.

'No, Master Drew, she be in the kitchen with Mrs Parfitt.'

Drew made his way towards the kitchen. The door was open and light spilled out into the dim passage, along with the sound of voices. And laughter. He stopped and drew back into the shadows. Surely that was Elyse laughing, a clear, joyous sound as if she had not a care in the world.

The meeting with Drew in the pavilion left Elyse confused and distraught. She fled from his presence, tears streaming down her face. The gardens were so overgrown that everywhere was a wilderness and she had no idea where she was going, merely following any path that was still passable. Eventually she found herself in a small walled enclosure that might once have been a flower garden. It was wildly overgrown but she picked her way to a wooden bench in one corner and sank down to give way to her distress.

Drew had roused such wonderful feelings in her, brought her body alive. It had positively thrummed with passion and, yes, with love. She had come very close to saying *I love you* as he kissed and caressed her, at least until she had become incapable of saying anything or controlling the waves of giddy exhilaration that had rolled over her, leaving her shocked and drained and not a little frightened by the experience.

Then Drew had destroyed the new-found wonder in a stroke.

He had not kissed her out of love, but lust. He had told her so. He was so well practised she had not known the difference and had responded, surrendering herself fully, prepared to give him her heart and her body, but it seemed he wanted neither. And he expected her to thank him for the consideration he had shown in leaving her a maid.

She searched for her handkerchief and mopped her eyes. So this was how it felt to be seduced by a rake. Oh, he might not have completely taken her virtue but he had totally destroyed her happiness. How could she now give herself to any other man?

'Oh, do not be so *weak*.' She blew her nose defiantly. 'You still have William and if you go to him a little older and a little wiser, surely that can only be a good thing?'

She remembered Drew's arms drawing her close, his lips on hers, and hungry desire leapt again, tearing at her insides. How could she endure another man's touch now?

Angrily she thrust aside the thought and drew on her pride. She was no milk-and-water miss to sink into a decline. Papa had been an adventurer, loving and leaving her while he went off to pursue his own life. What was it Drew had said of him? He had laughed at adversity. Well, she would do the same. Not laugh, perhaps, but she would not cry any more.

'You must pull yourself together, Elyse Salforde.' She rose and shook out her heavy skirts, straightened the fichu over her shoulders. 'You are not the first maid to be seduced by a rake and you will not be the last.'

She made her way to the house and slipped in through the garden entrance. As she passed the kitchen she paused, gazing in through the open door. Mrs Parfitt was sitting at the kitchen table, an array of vegetables spread out before her.

'Oh, pray do not get up,' said Elyse quickly, when the housekeeper saw her. 'I have just realised I have not yet broken my fast and—'

'Well, here's a to-do! If you goes on in to the little dining room, my dear I'll put something together for you now and bring it through.'

'Oh, no, I would rather not sit at the breakfast table.' She wiped away a stray tear. 'I am feeling a little sorry for myself and would rather not see Sir Edward…'

'Lord, you won't do that, miss. He broke his fast about an hour ago, he did, and has gone into his study. Sent Jed off to find Master Andrew, too, so you needn't worry about seein' anyone.'

'All I really want is a cup of tea and perhaps a piece of bread and butter.' Elyse stepped into the kitchen. 'Pray do not stop your work for me. If you tell me where I may find everything I can see to it myself. Indeed, I should like that, and,' she added, having no wish to run the risk of bumping into Drew or Sir Edward at that moment, 'I would very much like to sit here with you, if I may.'

'Well, it that's what you wants, dearie, then do stay, by all means. I'd be glad o' the company.' Mrs Parfitt beamed at her.

Under the housekeeper's instruction Elyse pottered about, swinging the kettle over the coals, fetching the silver teapot and bringing the tea caddy to the table for Mrs Parfitt to unlock with one of the keys dangling from the chain at her waist.

'And will you drink a dish of tea with me, Mrs Parfitt?'

'Thank you kindly, Miss Salforde, I'd be delighted to join you, as long as you don't mind me carrying on with these vegetables in between? Quite like old times it will be, Miss, for when the mistress was alive we often took tea together. Not here, of course, but in her private sitting room. We had plenty of staff then and she would invite me to join her while we discussed menus and flowers for the house and all the other day-to-day little things that were required. Everything changed, of course, when the Stuart landed in Scotland. The mistress was heartbroken when Master Andrew was forced to fly the country. She left the running of the household to me after that. Too busy with her other concerns then, she was.'

'I thought she was taken ill when, when Mr Castlemain left England?'

'Lord, no, miss, not then. She was laid low for a few days, of course, but after that she spent her days helping Sir Edward. They lost some of the estates, you see, and had to sell others to pay the fines. Dark times, they was, but the mistress never gave in. We had to cut back, of course, but we managed, and my lady was always writing letters, always hopeful that she would be able to bring Master Andrew home. But it was not to be, and then of course she got so ill, and when she died, well, Sir Edward and Master Simon were happy for me to run the place as I saw fit. Which I did, and not so badly, even if I do say so myself.'

'But surely you had more help then?'

'Aye, 'twas only when Master Simon died that Sir Edward shut himself away. Turned off all the staff save Jed, Stinchcombe and me. I think he'd have sent us off, too, if he could, but as I said to him at the time, "Where is we to go, at our time o' life?" so he let us stay.' She broke off while Elyse went off to fetch the bread. 'Sir Edward might grumble but we all rubs along pretty well now.'

Elyse prepared the tea and poured two cups, one of which she placed beside Mrs Parfitt before taking her own cup and a slice of bread and butter to the far end of the table, where she could sit and talk to the housekeeper without getting in her way.

Elyse sipped at her tea. The kitchen was warm and Mrs Parfitt such a motherly soul that Elyse began to relax and the leaden misery around her heart eased, just a little.

'No doubt you're all excited at the thought of

seeing your beau again,' said the housekeeper, watching her crumble the bread upon her plate.

'Yes.'

Excited was not the word to describe her feelings, but she did not want to think about that.

'He's the son of a viscount, is he not?' asked Mrs Parfitt, continuing to prepare the vegetables, peeling, chopping and slicing with the dexterity born of years of practice. 'If you forgive me for asking?'

Elyse realised that the question was not posed out of rampant curiosity; the kindly woman was trying to cheer her up by giving her thoughts a happier turn. Without quite understanding how it happened, Elyse found herself telling her all about her engagement to William.

'He must love me very much, do you not think?' she mused, when she had finished. 'It could not have been easy for him to persuade his father to accept me as his wife. After all, when the arrangements were made I was not at all rich, and although my birth is respectable I am sure the viscount would prefer to ally his son to another grand family.'

She thought again of the attack on their carriage. Would a respected peer of the realm go so far to prevent a marriage? The idea had been a minor concern, while she considered Drew as her friend. Now, knowing him for the rake he undoubtedly was, she felt very much more vulnerable.

'The young man must be head over heels,' said Mrs Parfitt in her comfortable tone. 'But you say you haven't seen him for years?

'No, that is his father's doing, I fear.' Elyse paused. 'He may prefer us not to marry, but if William is still willing, then I think we should do so, do not you?'

The last of the vegetables were swept into a large pan and the housekeeper began to clear the table.

'Of course you should, if you loves each other.' Mrs Parfitt stopped to dab at her eyes with the edge of her apron. 'Oh, how romantic it all sounds. I vow, when you turned up here with young Master Andrew t'other day I did think that the two of you would make a lovely couple, but—'

'Oh, goodness me, no.'

Elyse forced herself to laugh at such a ridiculous idea. Nerves and unhappiness combined to make it louder than she had intended and it echoed around the lofty kitchen.

There, you are your father's daughter. You can laugh at adversity.

'Mr Castlemain is merely acting as my guardian. My father arranged my marriage years ago and it is a brilliant match for me.' She hesitated then added, trying to convince herself, 'The marriage settlements are very advantageous, I believe.'

And it will be better to have a husband who loves me, rather than one who cannot return my affection.

Elyse stared into her cup. Drew had made it very clear that he did not love her but she would not repine. At least, not openly. No one must ever know that she had lost her heart to a rake. She would leave Hartcombe in the morning with her head held high.

With this noble resolve in mind she said brightly, 'So you see, Mrs Parfitt, I am really looking forward to reaching Bath tomorrow and seeing dear William. I mean to make him the best, most loving wife there ever was.'

The words floated out to Drew as he stood in the shadowed passage. That she could laugh so gaily, speak so cheerfully—obviously his kisses had not meant as much to her as he had supposed. And why should they? When he had first seen her she had been flirting shamelessly. So like her father, quick to love, but equally quick to forget. His fists clenched at his sides as he fought down a wave of bitter disappointment.

He leaned back against the wall, feeling suddenly tired and dispirited. His eyes moved around the dingy passage, taking in the signs of neglect, the cracked plaster on the ceiling and worn flags beneath his feet. He should be glad she was taking it so well. After all, what could he offer her? Even though he could now resume life and was heir to Hartcombe, the house and estate were so run down it would take all his money and many years to make it viable. Nothing to compare with the life she would have as daughter-in-law to a viscount.

But he could not forget the pain he had seen in her face when she had fled from the pavilion. Perhaps he *had* touched her heart and she was trying to be brave. If so then what right had he to turn her world upside down again? And even if she could forgive his crass behaviour, if he could persuade her he was sincere, what might be the outcome, should she choose to throw in her lot with him? Years of hard work to put Hartcombe in order. He remembered something Harry had once said to him: 'Nothing like drudgery to destroy love. The ladies like a romance, my boy, not real life.'

Slowly Drew made his way back to the study. His father was still there, sitting behind his desk, writing, but there was something different about him. He sat a little straighter, there was an air of purpose about him and when he looked up the sombre shadow was gone from his eyes. Drew went in and closed the door carefully behind him.

'Have you told anyone here about the pardon, sir?'

'Not yet, but I am writing to Jenkins now.'

'I would rather we did not make any announcement until I return from Bath.'

Sir Edward put down his pen.

'I would have thought you would want the world and his wife to know as soon as possible. Especially Miss Salforde, since she is already aware of your true identity.'

Drew could not meet his father's questioning gaze. He turned his eyes to the window, watching the grey clouds scud across the sky.

'It can make no difference to her. Tomorrow she comes of age. She will no longer be my concern.'

'And you are happy for her to marry Reverson?'

'If that is her choice.'

'Do you think it would still be her choice if she knew you were a free man? Oh, do not frown at me, my boy. I have seen the way she looks at you. She is more than half in love with you already.'

'She deserves better.'

'Is that not for the lady to decide?'

Drew began to pace up and down the room. He pushed his fingers through his hair.

'She has grown up cossetted and petted and with such high expectations. For the past three years she has been engaged to Reverson, a brilliant match. She will move in court circles, the very highest society and she will shine there, the brightest star. What am I, compared to a viscount's son? How long would she be content to be the wife of a mere baronet, going to town once a year—twice perhaps, when funds allow.'

A wry smile put Sir Edward's serious look to flight.

'Do you think your fortune will weigh with her, any more than your past? From what I have seen of the lady she is quite capable of knowing what will make her happy.'

'No.' Drew shook his head. 'If she decides not to marry Reverson it must be a clear, logical decision. She must not be swayed by any foolish romantic notions.'

'And if she decides not to marry him? Will you then offer for her?'

The vision of Elyse's stricken countenance flashed into his mind again. He had put an unbridgeable chasm between them. The brief burst of elation he had experienced when his father had told him of the pardon had gone and with it the short-lived optimism that he might just be able to win the lady back.

'Andrew?' Sir Edward persisted, 'Surely you will not let pass this chance of happiness.'

'I am concerned with the lady's happiness, not mine.'

He met his father's gaze steadily. At length the old man sighed.

'Very well, we will keep your secret another day, if it is what you wish.'

Elyse left Mrs Parfitt to her baking and retired to her room. Once she had quit the warmth and comfort of the kitchen misery engulfed her again and she threw herself on to her bed to indulge in a hearty bout of tears. Eventually she fell asleep and did not wake until late in the afternoon. She lay still for a while, deciding what she should do. Part of her wanted to go to Bath immediately and throw herself on the mercy of William's family but she knew that was not possible. However much she wanted to avoid seeing Drew ever again he was her guardian, at least for one more day. She sat up and addressed the empty room.

'He shall fulfil his obligations and escort me to Bath, but once he has signed over my inheritance he can quit the city, quit England, and I am sure I shall not care.'

She kept to her room until the dinner hour, when she made her way downstairs, dressed in the borrowed evening gown and with her hair pulled back into a simple knot. Sir Edward was waiting in the parlour. She noted that he was looking smarter than she had ever seen him in a suit of cut brown velvet and his white hair had been tamed and was confined at the nape with a ribbon. He rose as she entered.

'My son has not long gone upstairs to prepare himself for dinner, Miss Salforde. I hope you are content to take a glass of wine with me while we wait for him?'

'Of course sir, and...you said *my son,* does that mean you are reconciled?'

He smiled and for the first time she saw the resemblance between him and Drew. It tore at her heart and she had to fight to prevent her own calm demeanour from breaking down. Instead she forced herself to smile back.

'I am very pleased for you, truly,' she told him.

'And I have you to thank for it, Miss Salforde.' He raised his glass to her. 'You persuaded a stubborn old man to face the truth. My dear, about Andrew. He too can be very stubborn—'

'Oh, pray do not let us talk about him,' she interrupted him, pinning on a cheerful smile. 'Let us instead talk of Bath. I am very much looking forward to seeing it. I believe you have arranged for a carriage to take us there early tomorrow morning?'

'Yes. I understand there is much business to attend to.'

'I believe there will be papers to sign and then we must find Lord Whittlewood and his family, but I do not anticipate that will be difficult.'

'No, if he is in Bath then Nash will know of it, although I do not think the Beau commands the respect he once did. I have not been there for several years but I believe Nash is much altered. Why, he must be eighty if he is a day. A subscription was started for him last year, for a history of Bath that no one expects him to write, but I do not think it raised much income for him.' He shook his head. 'A sad end for the man who has done so much for the city. Ah, there you are, Andrew.'

'Good evening, Father. Miss Salforde.'

Elyse kept her eyes averted and acknowledged him with the merest inclination of her head. If he noticed her coolness he did not show it but engaged his father in conversation. She sat up very straight, chin raised and full of steely resolve to show him that she, too, could act as if their encounter in the pavilion had never occurred. The mask slipped only once. Sir Edward went out and they were left alone. Elyse remained statue-like in her seat, staring straight ahead of her.

''Elyse, I—'

'Pray do not speak to me, Mr Castlemain. I do not wish to acknowledge you.'

'And how the devil are we to travel to Bath together?' he demanded.

She said icily, 'You should have thought of

that before you treated me so abominably this morning.'

'Then let me apologise—'

'No. I want nothing else from you, ever, save my freedom.' She summoned up a look that would cut through stone. 'Please do not address me further. Once you have done your duty tomorrow, I never want to see you again.'

She hunched a shoulder at him as Sir Edward returned to the room and any hasty retort Drew might have made remained unsaid. How little he must care, if he would make not the slightest protest. Burying her hurt and anger, she began conversing with her host as if she had not a care in the world.

Chapter Nine

Despite a certain lack of finesse in the presentation and the fact that food was served by the housekeeper, the meal that evening was the very essence of civilised dining. The diners talked of unexceptional topics and Elyse played her part with all the ease and gaiety of a consummate actress. She addressed all her remarks to Sir Edward and avoided looking at Drew but she was very much aware of him, felt his presence like a magnet, a force that she had to resist constantly. Her emotions were deeply conflicted, one part of her was glad she had helped to bring about a reconciliation between Drew and his father, but it angered her that he could apparently enjoy his meal while she found every mouthful tasted like ashes.

When she heard him discussing crop yields and estate business she was suddenly overwhelmed by sympathy for both men, knowing as she did that Drew could not remain in England without fear of being arrested. How was it possible, she wondered, to hate Drew for the way he had treated her yet at the same time to want him to be happy?

She loved him. As she pushed the food about her plate she could only hope that the misery she felt now would ease once she and Drew were parted.

'Miss Salforde?'

'I beg your pardon, Sir Edward, what were you saying?'

'I only asked if you would care to try a little of the claret with the venison, it is very good.'

'No…no, thank you, Sir Edward. I prefer to keep a clear head.'

The old man was regarding her with such a sympathetic smile that she felt the colour rising to her cheeks.

'Are you fatigued, my dear? You were miles away.'

Even without looking at Drew she knew he was watching her closely.

'I am a little tired. If you will excuse me I think I will retire now. I want to look my best to meet my betrothed tomorrow.'

It gave her some satisfaction when Drew dropped his fork with a clatter but she affected not to notice as Sir Edward got up to help her from her chair.

'Goodnight, sir, and thank you for your generous hospitality. I shall not forget it.'

He walked over and opened the door for her.

'And I shall not forget *you*, my dear.'

He picked up her hand and kissed it. Her eyes slid to Drew. He, too, had risen, but was busy folding his napkin, his face inscrutable. The lead weight that had been permanently lodged in his stomach all day grew a little heavier. Swallowing a sigh she walked away.

Elyse took an early breakfast in her room and presented herself in the hall as soon as the carriage was at the door, shortly after seven o'clock. Sir Edward appeared with Mrs Parfitt and Jed behind him.

'By heaven, mistress,' cried the housekeeper, bustling up, 'You are keen to get away from us.'

'My chamber overlooks the drive and I came down as soon as I heard the chaise at the door. I do not wish to keep Mr Castlemain waiting.'

Sir Edward's brows shot up.

'Mr Castlemain? You were wont to be much less informal with my son.'

She felt the blush stealing into her cheek.

'It is not seemly that I should call him anything else, unless it is Mr Bastion, which is what I must remember to do in Bath.'

He looked at her closely.

'Have you quarrelled with Drew?'

Her blush deepened.

'We are not…friends.' She added quickly, to change the subject, 'I have left the gowns you loaned me in the linen press.'

'Do you not wish to take them? You will hardly turn up in Bath with nothing.'

'That is precisely what we shall do, sir. Thieves took everything we had with us, Lord Whittlewood must understand that.'

'But I would happily give you the clothes—'

'No, sir, I thank you. I could not take them.'

She could not bear to carry with her anything that would remind her of Hartcombe, save the scars on her heart.

'Ah, good. You are ready.' Drew ran lightly down the stairs, drawing on his gloves. 'We should reach Bath within the hour.' He came to stand beside her. '*Au revoir*, Father.'

Sir Edward nodded.

'Do you go on out, my boy, and tell the postilion where in Bath you wish to go. I will escort Miss Salforde.'

He did not appear to be overly affected by his son's departure and as she placed her fingers lightly on the crook of his arm she urged him not to lose touch with Drew again.

'No, no, I shall not do that,' he responded in a comfortable tone.

They followed the others out on to the drive. Drew was talking to the postilion but as she approached he went to open the door of the travelling chaise.

Sir Edward stopped and turned to Elyse.

'I want you to have this, to mark your coming of age.' He handed her a small square box. 'Do not look at it now, I do not want you standing about in this chill wind. You may open it once you are on your way.' He stood back as Mrs Parfitt came to hug her and she said goodbye to Jed, then he helped her into the carriage, saying as she arranged her skirts, 'And remember, my dear, that if Bath loses its charms, or you need a place of refuge, you will always be welcome at Hartcombe.'

'Thank you, Sir Edward.'

He turned to Drew and held out his hand.

'I pray fortune favours you in Bath, my boy.'

'I shall not stay there a moment longer than necessary.'

Drew gripped his father's hand then jumped into the carriage. The door was closed behind him and the chaise pulled away. Elyse waved to the little group standing on the drive, only settling back in her seat when they had passed through the rusty gates and were bouncing over the neglected lane that led to the main highway. She stared down at the little box in her hand.

'Well, are you going to open it?'

She lifted the lid to reveal a small ring nestled into a velvet pad. A single pearl glistened, surrounded by a ring of tiny sparkling diamonds.

'Oh, it is beautiful,' she breathed.

She drew off her gloves and slipped the ring on to her finger, holding out her hand to show him.

'I remember that ring. It belonged to my mother,' said Drew quietly.

'Oh, then I cannot—' She began to pull the ring from her finger but he stopped her.

'No. My father wanted you to have it. It is a sign of how much he esteems you.'

'I must write and thank him, once I am settled.' She turned to fix her gaze on the passing landscape. It was a beautiful gift but she wished Sir Edward had not bestowed it upon her, because it would make the past few days all the harder to forget.

'And sole control of everything now passes to Miss Salforde.'

The lawyer in his black robes made his pronouncement in a voice laden with foreboding. Elyse watched him sprinkling sand over the newly signed documents to seal the ink, then rose to her feet.

'Thank you. I shall be obliged if you will act for me during my time in Bath.'

'Of course, but since you have taken the trouble to consult me, I am bound to say that in my opinion it would be advisable to leave your affairs in the hands of your guardian until everything can be made over to your husband.'

'Mr Bastion is leaving Bath as soon as we have met with Lord Whittlewood,' she replied crisply, before Drew could speak. 'And I am more than capable of looking after my own affairs.'

The lawyer inclined his head, his doubts of her ability evident in every line of his spare body. Elyse took no notice. She waited in frosty silence for Drew to open the door for her, then she swept out of the office.

Drew followed Elyse down the stairs and handed her into the waiting chaise before directing the postilions to drive to Lord Whitlewood's residence in Queen Square. It was a short journey and undertaken in the same stiff silence that had characterised most of the journey from Hartcombe. Apart from her initial gasp of delight when she had opened the little box and seen the ring his father had given her, Elyse had maintained an attitude of stony indifference towards Drew and he had made no attempt to coax her out of it. She was betrothed to William Reverson, he had no right to come between them. His body burned with desire to sweep her into a fierce embrace, to break down the barriers she had put up between them and awaken the passion he knew she possessed, but that would only be a further betrayal of the trust Harry had laid upon him. And even if he seduced her, would she ever forgive him for his past cruelty towards her?

Perhaps, if she loved him. His father seemed to think she did but how long would that love last? He might persuade her to become his wife, but what then? What would she think of him when the passion was spent and she found herself chained to a man of moderate means, heir to a struggling estate, when she could have been allied to one of the most illustrious families in the land? Then all the old hurt and injustice would be remembered, love would be replaced by bitter regrets that would last a lifetime.

No, better that she should think him a rake than he should ever see that disappointment in her eyes.

His niggling fear that Lord Whittlewood might not be at home was soon banished. The family, they were informed by a wooden-faced lackey, was in the drawing room. They were shown to an impressive chamber on the first floor where upwards of a dozen people were gathered and engaged in noisy conversation.

Good God, thought Drew as he followed Elyse through the door, *this is not merely family, they are entertaining.*

A hush fell over the room as they were announced. All eyes turned towards them and Drew thought how shabby they must appear in their travelling clothes. He sensed rather than saw Elyse hesitate and immediately stepped up beside her, placing his hand under her elbow in a gesture of support. At least there would be witnesses that he had delivered Miss Salforde on time.

An elderly man in a powdered wig came towards them, limping slightly and leaning on an ebony stick. A quantity of snowy lace at his throat and wrists adorned his suit of burgundy cut velvet. The viscount, Drew guessed. He bowed.

'Lord Whittlewood, your servant, sir. I have brought Miss Salforde to you, before the end of Michaelmas Day, as agreed.'

'Indeed.' The viscount returned his bow. 'I had begun to give up hope. My secretary lost track of you after you left Marlborough.'

'You did not think to send out a search party to find us?' asked Drew.

'I did not. We thought it most likely you had taken Miss Salforde back to the north country.'

Drew's anger rose at his indifferent tone but before he could speak again Elyse addressed the viscount.

'I hope Mr Settle is recovered? He was very poorly and we were obliged to go on without him.'

'He is, quite recovered I believe, and will be relieved to know you are safe.'

'He has reached Bath, then?' asked Elyse.

Lord Whittlewood bowed again. 'He reached us a week since.'

'Then he was more fortunate than we were,' said Drew. 'We had the misfortune to be waylaid on the road. The villains made off with the coach and all our baggage and left me with a bullet in my arm.'

There was a general muttering and expressions of outrage from the gathered assembly, one gentleman in a full-bottomed wig exclaiming, 'Good heavens, did you not have outriders, sir?'

'We were travelling as the viscount's guests,' Drew responded, watching the viscount carefully. His surprise and displeasure looked genuine enough.

'That was certainly an error, and one I shall investigate,' said his lordship, frowning. 'May I ask when this attack occurred?'

'On the twenty-first,' said Elyse. 'We took refuge at—at a gentleman's house until Mr Bastion was well enough to travel again.'

The viscount's cool gaze gave nothing away when he turned to Drew again.

'And you have managed to keep our agreement and bring my son's future wife to him, sir.

I congratulate you. I know William will want to thank you himself.'

Lord Whittlewood raised one white hand and beckoned towards the throng gathered behind him. A young man stepped out of the crowd and Drew's stomach lurched with sudden disappointment. No wonder Elyse thought herself in love. The fellow had the classical beauty and bearing of a Greek god.

Elyse had been unable to see William, who now emerged from the far corner of the room. As she watched him approach she could not suppress her smile of delight. He was every bit as handsome as she remembered, the elegantly styled wig, his wide brow and soft brown eyes, the classical nose and sculpted lips—if anything he look more handsome than when they had last met three years ago. He came towards her with the same boyish smile that had charmed her from the start.

'Miss Salforde. Elyse.' He kissed her fingers. 'You are even more beautiful than I remember. How can I have kept away from you for so long?'

She was silent, surprised that she wanted to say tartly, *Yes, why did you do so?*

'When you did not arrive I thought you had

changed your mind about marrying me,' he continued, gazing into her eyes. 'I was *desolé*.'

'Really?' she sighed. It was impossible not to melt beneath his blatant admiration. It provided some balm to her wounded spirits.

Lady Whittlewood glided up, the lappets of her exquisite lace cap flowing out behind her as she gently moved her son aside and addressed Elyse.

'Oh, my dear, what a most shocking tale. To have lost all your baggage, too, you poor child. But what fun we shall have dressing you. La, but you were always a pretty little thing and now you are decidedly a beauty.' She looked past Elyse and directed a smile at Drew. 'We are truly most obliged to you, Mr Bastion, for bringing dear Elyse to Bath. You may leave her safely in our care. I would ask you to stay and dine but…'

She trailed off, her glance leaving Drew in no doubt that his attire was quite unsuitable.

He stood his ground.

'Thank you, my lady, but before I go I would like a few words in private with Lord Whittlewood.'

'Is it really necessary?' The viscount glanced over his shoulder at the murmuring group behind him. 'My lawyer is fully conversant with the settlements. You may talk to him in the morning.'

'I wish to assure myself upon certain points before leaving Miss Salforde.' Drew's reply was smooth but decided.

'Very well.' With the faintest of shrugs Lord Whittlewood limped towards the door.

'I should like to come with you,' said Elyse. She added, as the viscount raised his brows, 'I came of age today, my lord. Mr Bastion is no longer my guardian and if he has anything to say that concerns me I should like to hear it.'

William touched her arm. 'It will be very dull, I am sure. I should much rather you remain here and meet our friends.'

But Elyse would not be moved. Drew recognised the stubborn set to her chin and was not surprised when the viscount capitulated. As they went out the drawing room began to hum with chatter and speculation, even before the door was closed behind them. Drew felt a grim satisfaction that their arrival had certainly not gone unnoticed.

Lord Whittlewood led the way to a small study on the ground floor and Drew began without preamble.

'First, my lord, I wish to look over the marriage settlement, to make sure there is no difference between your copy and the one given to me by Mr Salforde.'

'Would you accuse me of trying to change the agreement?' asked Lord Whittlewood coldly.

'Of course not,' said Drew. 'But you will appreciate that I am concerned for Miss Salforde's interests.'

The viscount unlocked a drawer in the small mahogany desk and took out a sheaf of papers. He handed them to Drew, who read through each sheet steadily, then silently handed them back.

'I trust you are satisfied?' The viscount moved towards the door. 'If that is all—'

'Not quite.'

Lord Whittlewood stared at Drew, who met his eyes coolly. At length the viscount nodded and reluctantly invited his guests to sit down.

'Now, what else may I do for you, Mr Bastion?' he asked, lowering himself into a chair. 'As Miss Salforde said, she is of age now and mistress of her own affairs.'

'That is correct, but I was a close friend of her late father and retain a certain, er, responsibility for the lady.'

'Naturally.'

Drew considered his next words carefully. This would not be easy if he was to avoid insulting his host.

'Miss Salforde's position is a delicate one. She is alone—'

Lord Whittlewood raised his hand.

'Settle informed us that Mrs Matthews was indisposed and obliged to remain in Scarborough.'

'She has broken her arm, my lord,' explained Elyse.

'Then we shall hire a chaperon for you until your aunt can join us,' the viscount told her kindly, before turning his enquiring gaze back to Drew. 'Is there anything else?'

Drew hesitated. With Elyse present he could not be as frank as he would like. 'I am aware that the settlements are drawn up very much in Miss Salforde's favour, including the sum to be paid should your son decide not to marry her. Your letter indicated that you would consider the agreement cancelled if the lady was not with you by today. If I had not been with Miss Salforde when her carriage was attacked...'

Drew let the words hang. Lord Whittlewood

was very still and the air around them swirled with tension.

'I hope you are not implying,' the viscount began in a voice as quiet as steel, 'that I was in any way involved in the attack upon you?'

'Not at all.' Drew's response was equally quiet, equally steely. 'Although you cannot deny that if you *had* changed your mind about the match, a delay in our reaching Bath would be in your interests.'

'True, but I would not stoop to highway robbery to achieve my ends.'

'But you *would* remove to Bath from London.'

Drew saw from the sudden flash in the viscount's eyes that he had hit a nerve, but the shutters came down. Lord Whittlewood waved one hand towards his leg.

'My doctor advised me to take the waters. For my gout.'

'And not one of your family could remain in London to meet Miss Salforde?'

'No.'

Drew kept his eyes fixed upon the viscount, whose next breath escaped in a hiss.

'I confess it occurred to me that Miss Salforde might decide against the match when she reached London and found no one there to receive her, but I was doing no more than taking advantage of an existing situation, not creating one.'

'If I had not changed my mind in three years, my lord, it is unlikely I would do so because of a further delay of three days,' put in Elyse.

Lord Whittlewood inclined his head.

'No, of course not. I beg your pardon, Miss Salforde.'

She pressed on. 'And you knew nothing of the attack upon us?'

Drew would not have asked such a direct question but he waited silently to hear the answer. The viscount met Elyse's gaze steadily.

'I did not, and would not condone such dishonourable conduct.' He drew himself up in his chair and addressed Drew. 'Let us be clear—and I have no reluctance for Miss Salforde to hear this—I might regret making this match. From my son's perspective it is far from ideal, but having put my name to the contract I shall honour it. Miss Salforde may be assured that she will be treated with every courtesy and respect while she remains under my roof. I welcome her now as a daughter.'

Drew studied the viscount intently, listening

to his words, watching every gesture, his senses alert for anything that might give him an excuse to challenge him. He had lived on his wits long enough to know when a man was lying and he wanted more than anything in the world to believe this man a villain, but he could not. The worst he knew of Lord Whittlewood was that he was a gambler and that was a national affliction amongst the English. The fellow had made a half-hearted attempt to make Elyse cry off but Drew believed he was sincere when he said he had not been involved in the assault upon their carriage. He could do no more.

'Then I am satisfied to leave Miss Salforde in your care.'

'Thank you.' The viscount sat back and steepled his fingers. 'My health dictates that I remain in Bath, but to comply with the late Mr Salforde's wishes the wedding must go ahead at the end of October. We shall therefore make the necessary arrangements at St Michael's. The wedding will be a quiet affair, since Miss Salforde is still in mourning for her parent. We shall inform you of the exact date, sir, so that you may attend—'

'Mr Bastion will not be attending,' Elyse put

in quickly. 'He is leaving England almost immediately, is that not so, sir?'

Her eyes challenged him to contradict her. Drew inclined his head, as if in agreement. After all, what did it matter? 'Mr Bastion' would cease to exist very shortly. He rose from his chair. He had done his duty; Elyse clearly no longer required his services.

'Thank you, my lord,' he said. 'You have addressed my concerns and I will now take my leave of you.'

They went out into the hall, where William Reverson was coming down the stairs.

'Ah, Miss Salforde, there you are.' He ran down the last few steps. 'Mama sent me in search of you. Her dresser is even now looking out some gowns you might wear, at least until she can have new ones made up for you.' He crossed to Elyse, smiling down at her in a way that set Drew's hackles rising. 'I am to take you to her and she will find something suitable for you to wear at dinner.' He picked up Elyse's hand and placed it on his sleeve. 'I shall carry you away now, if your business is finished?'

'Yes,' she said quietly. 'I believe it is.'

The viscount and his son were looking at Drew, who fixed his eyes on Elyse.

'If Miss Salforde has no further need of me, I shall take my leave.' No response. He bowed. 'It only remains for me to wish you joy in your forthcoming marriage, ma'am.'

She curtsied to him, her shuttered face and cold demeanour telling Drew he was not forgiven, nor ever would be. And that was for the best, since she was to marry another man.

Elyse stood in silence, flanked by William and Lord Whittlewood as Drew turned on his heel and walked away from her.

He is going. The words rattled around in her head *He is going and I shall never see him again.*

She watched him cross the tiled floor, willed him to look back but he kept on, his step swift and steady. A flunkey ran to open the door and he disappeared into the street, leaving her feeling more desolate and bereft than ever before.

Chapter Ten

'Well, now, here's a to-do.'

Lord Whittlewood's utterance brought forth little response. The family were at breakfast, where it was the habit for the viscount to peruse the London papers while his son, wife and any guests applied themselves to their food. Elyse had been at Queen Square for over a week now and was well aware of the ritual. Lady Whittlewood might put a question to her husband but it was not necessary for anyone else to react unless the news was of particular interest.

As she expected, the viscountess paused in the act of drinking her coffee to say, 'What has caught your attention, my lord?'

'A gentleman has been pardoned for his part in the 'forty-five.'

'Is that all?' Lady Whittlewood signalled to

a servant to refill her cup. 'I would not have thought that anything remarkable.'

'Not in itself, perhaps, my dear.' The viscount folded the newspaper and passed to her. 'Except that the fellow has been masquerading under the name of Bastion.'

'Good gracious!' William exclaimed.

Elyse dropped her knife onto her plate. Lady Whittlewood took the paper and began to read. Elyse wanted to snatch it from her hands but she was obliged to curb her impatience.

'How does that reflect upon Miss Salforde, Papa?'

Dear William, to be concerned for her!

'Not at all,' replied the viscount, giving Elyse a reassuring smile. 'It seems the fellow was granted a full pardon several years ago, but the family made no formal announcement and the gentleman was unaware of the change in his circumstances. Now, however, it appears he has returned to his home. He is heir to Hartcombe, in the county of Gloucestershire, and will succeed to the baronetcy when his father, Sir Edward Castlemain, dies.'

Lady Whittlewood's kindly smile flickered over Elyse.

'That does explain why he was living abroad

when he met your papa, my dear. However, I am pleased the young man is now back with his family. That is how it should be.'

Yes, thought Elyse, it is as it should be, but her mind was aflame with conjecture. How had this pardon come about, had Sir Edward known of it? It seemed impossible that he should not, but why had he not said anything? And why had Drew not told her?

He could not have known, she thought. Certainly not before he had left her in Lord Whittlewood's care. Sir Edward must have kept it from him. Her hand went to the thin ribbon around her neck from which the pearl-and-diamond ring was suspended and nestled, concealed, between her breasts. That Sir Edward should give her such a valuable gift argued that he thought highly of her, yet he had not told her of his son's pardon. It made no sense.

'I will send him and his father an invitation to our party on the twenty-eighth,' declared the viscountess.

'Party?' Elyse looked up, jerked out of her reverie. 'But my lady, I am in mourning.'

'I am aware,' nodded Lady Whittlewood. 'But it was your papa's express wish that the marriage go ahead on the date agreed. He wrote to tell you so from his deathbed, did he not?'

'Well, yes, but—'

'Then we are carrying out his last wishes, and that is very important. For the wedding itself you will wear all white with no colour whatsoever—perfectly proper for a bride in mourning, but for the evening party I think you might wear your new grey sacque with black trim. The family will wear black ribbons and shoe buckles, of course, as a sign of respect.' When she saw Elyse's troubled frown she threw up her hands. 'Heavens, my dear, it is only a small gathering, no more than a hundred guests—'

'A hundred!'

'When the younger son of a viscount marries there is naturally great interest in the matter,' the Lord Whittlewood explained.

'Indeed,' agreed my lady. 'Why, how else is everyone to meet you?'

'I take it Henry will be coming?' enquired William.

'Yes, he and his wife will join us here next week.' Lady Whittlewood turned to Elyse to explain. 'Henry is my eldest son, and Whittlewood's heir. He and his wife live in Kent but wrote to say they would post here immediately when I told them the news. And William's sister, Daphne, will be here, too, with Berwick, her husband. They are all eager to meet you.'

'But a party…' Elyse trailed off uncertainly.

'You must be guided by me on this, Miss Salforde.' The viscount gave her a kindly smile. 'It will give William the opportunity to show off his future bride. Is that not so, my boy?'

'Just so, my lord.'

Elyse regarded William thoughtfully. The words were perfectly civil, but she thought the tone lacked enthusiasm. She wondered if it was her imagination, but William's smile did not seem quite as warm this morning. She could not fault his behaviour towards her since she had arrived in Bath. He escorted her everywhere and his attentions were perfectly correct but there was not the same, happy feeling of romance about their meetings that she remembered. That was hardly surprising, she thought, for they were both older. That first, hectic flush of infatuation could not be expected to last. However, she could not help wondering if William was disappointed in her.

She thought of the previous evening when he had come upon her alone in the morning room and had taken the opportunity to steal a kiss.

She had gone willingly into his arms, turning her face up to his, but when their lips met the experience had not moved her at all. Oh, it had not repulsed her, like Mr Scorton's clumsy embrace, but there had been no explosion of the senses, no excitement. William had not seemed dissatisfied. He had hugged her to him, saying with a soft laugh, 'You little innocent. There is such a lot I have to teach you.'

But Elyse feared that in this case she was far from innocent. She had tasted Drew's scorching kisses. He had roused such passion in her that she had not been able to control herself, and she very much feared that she would never experience such heady excitement with William.

Elyse dragged her mind back to the breakfast table, where her hostess was rising from her chair.

'Then it is settled,' declared Lady Whittlewood. 'I shall add Mr Bastion—Mr Castlemain I *should* say—to my list.'

'Perhaps he will not come.'

Only when the words came out did Elyse realise she had spoken aloud.

'Not come? My dear, how can he not?' The viscount's thin brows rose. 'The highest families in the land will be represented here that night and our recognising him will put the seal of approval upon his return to society. What could be better for him?'

What indeed, thought Elyse miserably. So she was to suffer his presence yet again. Was she never to be free of him?

Drew swung the axe and brought it back with a satisfying crack against the trunk of the tree. He had been working in the woods since daybreak, thinning out the trees and clearing paths. It was not strictly necessary, now they had taken on extra staff, but he wanted to prove to himself that his arm had healed. Even in such a short time Hartcombe was looking much better. He had transferred all his funds to the family bankers and he and his father had talked to their attorney to begin the process of buying back some of the lands that had been sold. Drew's small fortune would not buy it all, but the three tenant farms and the Home Wood were a beginning and with good management and hard work he hoped the estate would begin to show a profit in a year or so. And he intended to work hard, although hopefully not at the gruelling pace he had set himself today, as he tried to shut out all thoughts of Elyse Salforde.

It had been two weeks since he had left her in Queen Square but her image was as fresh as ever in his mind. He had returned to Bath several times since then, on business and to replenish his wardrobe, but on each occasion he had taken care to avoid the fashionable places where he might see her, but it was impossible to avoid hearing the local gossip. It appeared that all Bath was alive with the tale of the beautiful stranger who had stolen the heart of Lord Whittlewood's son. Accounts varied wildly. In the hatters he heard two gentlemen speculating upon the fortune of this new heiress from the North Country, while on the street a group of women at a market stall gossiped about the poor orphan who had been snatched from poverty by the Honourable Mr Reverson. Even when he left his horse at the White Hart the ostlers were talking of it, convinced she had arrived in Bath in a gilded coach pulled by six high-stepping greys.

Whatever the tale one fact held true, the young lady was a beauty to outshine all others in the city. And so far she had not been seen dressed in anything but mourning clothes, only wait until she appeared in the latest colourful fashions.

A final, swinging cut from his axe and Drew stepped back as the tree began to topple.

'Well done, Harry,' he muttered, watching the trunk fall gracefully to the ground with no more than a crackle of snapping branches. 'You've achieved a great match for your daughter.'

''Scuse me, sir.' He turned to find the new stable boy running towards him. 'This's just arrived for you.'

He took the proffered note. The elegant handwriting was unfamiliar. What was so urgent that the lad must needs be sent chasing after him? Then he saw the Whittlewood crest stamped into the seal. Quickly he ripped it open to find a gilt-edged card inside.

'"Lady Whittlewood requests the pleasure..."'

His lip curled. So they had discovered his identity! Not so very difficult, when his pardon and history had been broadcast far and wide. He would have eschewed all public announcements if it had been possible, but his father had argued that it was necessary for everyone to know who he was and that no stain now besmirched the ancient name of Castlemain. And it had worked, since he was now invited to enter the viscount's hallowed portals as a guest.

It made no real difference to him. Elyse had not cared that he had been branded a traitor. It was he who had held back, persuaded her he was only toying with her affections. He did not regret it. She was better off marrying her Adonis. If only a half the tales he had heard were true then the couple were devoted to each other. He hoped she would never discover how her father had engineered such a brilliant alliance.

'Sir? Am I to run back with an answer? Sir?'

He glanced at the card again.

'No, Sam. There is no urgency to reply.'

He picked up his frock-coat and slipped the card into the pocket before picking up his axe again. Perhaps he would go and see for himself that Elyse was happy.

And then perhaps he would be able to forget her.

It was raining. Little rivulets ran down the windows, obscuring the view of Queen Square. Elyse knew it would be easy to blame the inclement weather for her low spirits but she was no self-deceiver and she was aware that it would not be the truth. She had tried, truly she had. She'd thrown herself into life at Queen Square, allowed herself to be pampered and spoiled by Lady Whittlewood and dressed as befitted a lady living in the viscount's household, albeit one who must abstain from wearing colours whilst in mourning. Everyone was so kind to her, and they did not yet know that she now brought a small fortune with her. She had decided not to tell them about her inheritance until the wedding day, deeming it a fitting wedding present for William.

Aunt Matthews had written, distraught because she had contracted a fever and Dr Carstairs had forbidden her to travel for several more weeks. Elyse had suggested that because of this they should delay the wedding. Lord Whittlewood had patiently explained to her that the contract drawn up between himself and her father was quite clear; the wedding must take place before the end of the month.

So here she was, one week away from marrying William and feeling none of the excited anticipation one might expect in a young lady on the verge of matrimony. All she could think of, when she was not strenuously keeping herself occupied, was Drew Castlemain and the way it had felt to be in his arms, exchanging kisses.

Just the thought of it sent the searing, heart-stopping excitement running through her again, hot desire tearing at her insides and such an ache of longing in her heart she almost groaned aloud. She could not believe it had meant so little to him, that he had not felt the connection between them. How might it have been if he had known of his pardon earlier? Would he have treated her differently, perhaps even considered making her an offer?

She turned away from the window, wrapping her arms about her as if to ward off a sudden chill. Now she was deceiving herself. He did not care for her, did not desire her, save fleetingly, as an object of lust. She must be thankful he had not seduced her thoroughly. He had told her as much. But he had just as thoroughly ruined her, since she could not forget him.

There was a knock on the door and the maid appointed to wait upon her entered the room.

'Oh, I beg yer pardon, mistress, I thought the family had all gone out and I come up to tidy the room…'

'Come in, Hetty, I am leaving now.'

She glanced in the long mirror for a final check upon her appearance. Lady Whittlewood had taken great pains to provide Elyse with dozens of new clothes, all suitable for a young lady in mourning and the one she had chosen today was no exception, a pewter-grey silk morning gown with black lace trim. Elyse had decided not to add the fashionable black apron but she had placed a straw bonnet with new black ribbons over her lace cap. Her only ornament was the diamond ring William had given her to mark their betrothal. All very sober, nothing to give the Bath quizzes cause to gossip.

William was waiting for her when she came downstairs.

'So there you are. My mother is gone with Papa to the Pump Room and I waited behind to escort you. Shall we go?'

Elyse smiled and took his proffered arm. Apart from that one kiss soon after her arrival he was treating her like a guest rather than a fiancée. She tried to be charitable. It was only to be expected since they had not seen each other for three years. Despite their letters they were a little shy of one another.

The rain had stopped but the air was cold and damp. The overcast sky would lower anyone's spirits, Elyse decided. After all, what had she to be gloomy about? Her future was secure, as Mrs William Reverson she would be a woman of substance and standing, married to the man she had dreamed of since she was seventeen.

Elyse stole a peep up at William as they strolled along Bath's busy pavements to the Pump Room. She had thought him the most handsome man of her acquaintance when they had met and now, at one-and-twenty, his classical looks were even more striking. His fair colouring was evident despite his powdered wig, the pale brows and lashes only accentuating his liquid-brown eyes. So why, when he turned his head to smile at her, did she think him less attractive? Was it that she had recently conceived a penchant for darker hair and blue, blue eyes?

No! She must not even think of that.

'You are very pensive,' said William. 'Is anything the matter?'

'No, no, of course not.' Her doubts resurfaced. 'Only, are you *sure* you want to marry me, William?'

'Nothing I would like more,' he replied promptly. 'It is all agreed, is it not? My father says he will let us have one of his properties, a snug little house in Berkshire where we may set up our nursery.' He squeezed her hand, where it rested on his sleeve. 'A few more days and we will be man and wife. I cannot wait to have you to myself.'

Elyse remembered the delicious thrill of excitement she had felt when he had whispered such things to her in Scarborough. He had even stolen a kiss, which she had thought the most wonderful, daring and exciting thing in the world, but the kiss he had recently bestowed upon her in the morning room had left her strangely unmoved and now the thought of William taking her in his arms, of kissing her passionately, touching her the way Drew had done, made her shudder. Mistaking her reaction William laughed.

'You are eager for it, too, I know, but we must be patient. It would not do to behave with any hint of impropriety while we are living under my father's roof.'

'No, of course not.'

But once they were married, what then? she wondered. She could only pray that she would learn to love him again.

The week passed slowly but inexorably and Elyse tried to feel something other than growing apprehension for the approaching nuptials. She kept her anxiety hidden from her hosts and presented a cheerful smiling countenance whenever she was in company. Nothing could have exceeded Lord and Lady Whittlewood's kindness to her. She might not be the bride they would have chosen for their son but they had accepted the inevitable with a good grace and Elyse was grateful. For her it was a splendid match, arranged by Papa to secure her future comfort and it was churlish of her to want anything different. Churlish and futile, she scolded herself. Drew might be a free man now but he was lost to her. He did not love her and he was a rake: even if by some miracle she could marry him it would not work, his amours and intrigues could only result in repeated heartbreak for her.

Elyse was thankful her days were so busy. Her arrival in Queen Square without any luggage had scandalised Lady Whittlewood, who had hurriedly procured a few new gowns for her and taken her on numerous shopping trips to provide her with everything she would need for her new life as the Honourable Mrs William Reverson. Parcels arrived every day containing dresses, shoes, hats and myriad other items the viscountess considered essential for a lady's wardrobe. In addition to this Elyse threw herself energetically into all the arrangements for the marriage, as well as the party that had been arranged for the evening before the wedding.

Because Elyse was still in mourning for her father the marriage must be a very private affair. Only close family were to be present, and in Elyse's case even that was impossible since her only relative, Aunt Matthews, was still laid up with her broken arm. Aware that she would have no one to support her, the kindly viscountess had suggested that Mr Andrew Castlemain should be invited to the ceremony, but Lord Whittlewood had firmly but gently counselled against it.

'He may be a very fine young man and of course he is pardoned now,' he said. 'But the fact is he has been masquerading under a false name. Also his connections with the Jacobite cause are not something we should be seen to condone too much.'

'That may be so,' replied Lady Whittlewood with unaccustomed firmness, 'but he was Elyse's guardian and the poor young man's role in bringing her to us must be recognised.'

'Then you must content yourself with the fact that you have invited him to your party, my dear.

Such a distinction will do much to reinstate him in the polite world.'

Elyse found herself remembering those words as she took a leisurely breakfast on the morning of the party. She had hoped Drew would not come, but when she had been helping Lady Whittlewood with her correspondence she had seen the letter from Hartcombe. 'My esteemed father is unable to attend,' it read, but any hopes that Drew might also stay away were dashed by the following line, a brief acceptance written in a bold, firm hand. Just the sight of Drew's name, written with a flourish at the bottom of the page, had caused her heart to thud erratically. Dear heaven how was she to face him again, knowing how much she still cared for him?

It would be best, she decided, if William could remain at her side this evening. Surely he would think it very natural that she should want his support. She would tell him she was nervous at the thought of being introduced to so many new people. It was not true, of course. She was naturally gregarious and relished such events, but she knew it would not be wise to confess to William that there was only one gentleman invited that evening whom she did not wish to meet.

With that problem resolved Elyse dressed quickly and made her way downstairs. She had left her reading book in the morning room last night and thought she should retrieve it before some eager servant tidied it away. She entered the room with her usual briskness to find William standing in the middle of the room with his arms around the second housemaid.

They jumped apart when Elyse came in but not before she had seen them kissing. The doubts and indecision, the sympathy Elyse had felt for William when she thought that she might be deceiving him, all were washed away by the huge wave of anger that surged through her. She stepped to one side to allow the maid to scurry away, her cheeks scarlet with mortification. Then with silent deliberation Elyse closed the door.

'Is this a foretaste of what I am to expect as your wife?'

William shot her a resentful glance from beneath lowered brows. He looked very much like an errant schoolboy.

'It was merely a little dalliance. There is not so very much wrong with that.'

'Dalliance,' she repeated with a scornful curl of her lip. 'On the eve of our wedding?'

'Come along, Elyse, you must see that it was nothing more than a harmless little kiss.'

Elyse was outraged. 'Your actions could result in that servant being turned off without a character.'

'Not unless you tell Mama what has occurred here.' He drew himself up. 'I am a man, Elyse, and I have needs. Since I cannot have you I must find solace elsewhere.'

'You could not wait one more day?' She took a long deep breath, trying to control her temper. 'When we were apart, then mayhap there was some excuse, but not here, now—'

He scowled at her.

'You can have no reason to complain of my treatment of you. I have put myself out to dance attendance upon you ever since you arrived in Bath.'

'I thought you wished to do so.'

'Naturally I do not want to be thought backward in my attentions to my future wife.'

'You make it sound like an onerous duty.'

'Well, so it is.'

Her chin went up and she said frostily, 'No one is forcing you to marry me.'

'Of course they are!' he flashed back at her. 'Do you think I would be marrying you if it wasn't for that damned wager...'

His words trailed off and in the deep silence that followed he gazed uncertainly at Elyse. She suddenly felt a little dizzy and sank down on the nearest sofa.

'Wager? What do you mean?'

He flung himself down into a chair opposite and dropped his head in his hands. She said with quiet firmness, 'The truth, William, if you please.'

'It was when we met, three years ago in Scarborough.'

'I remember. You asked me to marry you.'

He shrugged.

'While we were dancing at the assemblies our fathers were engaged in games of chance. My father had lost a great deal of money to yours. Twenty thousand pounds.'

'Twenty thousand!'

'Such sums are regularly won and lost.'

Elyse paled. 'Oh, heavens. I had heard that gambling was rife in London and Bath, but I never dreamed that such a thing could happen in Scarborough.'

'Why not? It is a spa town and wherever the rich gather they need their amusements. Papa told me Salforde was willing to offset the debt in a marriage settlement. I was young, and you were very engaging,' William shrugged. 'It seemed an excellent solution.'

'Papa told me nothing of this.'

'Why should he? You were only seventeen.'

'As were you!'

'But you are a female, and could not be expected to understand such matters.'

'Instead I was allowed to think you were in love with me.'

'And I was, at first. You know it was agreed we should not marry until I had come of age. There seemed plenty of time to enjoy myself before I had to settle down. Then, this spring, your father wrote to Papa to set a date and I realised it was not what I wanted at all, only by then it was too late. If I cried off the debt would have to be paid. Immediately and in full.' He frowned. 'Our estates are not in good heart. Most of them are mortgaged to the hilt and any excess revenue is eaten up in living as we do.' He gave her a petulant look, as if anticipating her next remark. 'Such expenditure is necessary for someone as prominent as my father. Then there was all the expense of Daphne's wedding to Berwick last year. Father could not possibly pay you the twenty thousand pounds to prevent our marriage. He called in his lawyer to go over the agreement again but there was no way out, save one, faint possibility. Papa wrote to insist that you join the family by Michaelmas or forfeit the contract. Then he removed us all to Bath, hoping you might not follow.'

'And the attack upon our carriage?'

'I swear my father had no hand in that.'

Elyse clasped her hands together in her lap. She had been waiting to announce to William and his family that she had a small fortune of her own now. Tomorrow when she became Mrs William Reverson it would become her husband's property. She had thought it would be a delightful surprise for him. Now it paled into insignificance against the debt her marriage would write off. She said slowly, 'So we are to marry, to save your family from ruin and disgrace.'

'Yes.' William rose from his chair. 'We shall just have to make the best of it.'

She made no attempt to stop him as he left the room and when the door clicked shut she remained in her chair while the silence settled around her like a heavy cloak.

So William did not love her. The revelation following so closely upon Drew's rejection made her wonder if she was too romantic in her notions. Perhaps the love she had read of in books did not exist. Or perhaps it was exceedingly rare.

Elyse sighed and pushed away such dismal thoughts. She had so much to be thankful for. She and William might not be in love but many marriages began with no more than liking and were perfectly happy. There was no reason why theirs should not be so.

She heard the sounds of an arrival and peeped out to hear the butler's sonorous voice welcoming The Honourable Mr and Mrs Reverson to the house. So William's brother had arrived. She remembered that his sister and her husband were also expected, but she was in no mood to meet anyone just yet and slipped away to her own room, where she remained until dinnertime.

When Elyse entered the drawing room she found all the family gathered there. Introductions were performed and everyone greeted her civilly, but from the lack of interest they showed in her circumstances she inferred that they all knew about the terms of the marriage, and she was consequently very subdued as they went into dinner.

Chapter Eleven

'Well, my dear, are you ready to meet the cream of Bath society?'

'I am, my lady.'

Elyse was standing between the viscountess and William at the top of the staircase. She was very conscious of her grey silk, its neckline decorously filled with a white fichu, a stark contrast to the sea of coloured gowns milling below them as the first of the guests prepared to mount the stairs to the reception rooms. She smiled politely as she was presented to Lord This and Lady That, made her bow to an earl and his countess. Some of the guests she had met before when she had been out with William, but most were strangers and she tried to ignore the speculation their eyes, the whispered questions about her birth, her fortune and how had she managed to make such a splendid alliance.

In the noise and confusion of the arrivals she heard Lady Whittlewood's laughing response to one matron's assertion that Miss Salforde was a very pretty young lady but quite unknown.

'Oh, she is from the north, dear ma'am, but *perfectly* respectable. William was quite smitten from the first, and since Henry already has two sturdy boys to follow him the succession is secure. So who are we to stand in the way of love?'

And so it went on, lords, baronets and gentlemen, dowagers and ladies. It seemed to Elyse that the whole of Bath was present in the viscount's rooms but there was one exception, the one person she longed to see, the one she most dreaded meeting. Then he was there in the hall below her, handing his hat and cloak to the footman. Her heart lurched. He looked so tall and elegant in his new coat of blue Genoa velvet with the silver buttons. He was shaking out his ruffles, climbing the steps towards her, looking straight ahead, never glancing up.

'Mr Castlemain. I am delighted you could come, sir.'

Lady Whittlewood held out her hand and Elyse watched as he bowed over it with exquisite grace. He was one of the few men to wear his own hair, long and confined at the nape of his neck by a black ribbon, but the thick, unpowdered mane glowed like dark honey in the candlelight, proclaiming the health and vigour of the man. Elyse clenched her hands around the stem of her fan. She remembered driving her fingers through those same silky locks, clinging on as Drew's mouth worked unspeakable delights on her body. She had been right to dread seeing him again.

'Miss Salforde.'

His voice, deep and smooth as velvet, recalled her attention. He was standing before her, tall, broad-shouldered, achingly desirable but he could not be hers. Never hers. He was a rake, he stole hearts for a pastime. Angrily she drew herself up, gave him a haughty look and kept her hands firmly wrapped around the fan. She would not extend her fingers for him to kiss. Their eyes locked and she hoped her gaze conveyed the haughty disdain she wanted him to see and not the searing pain of her breaking heart. His showed nothing more than light amusement.

After a moment he gave a little bow and moved on. The viscountess touched her arm.

'My dear, your greeting for Mr Castlemain

was less than cordial. I know the revelations about his past came as a shock to us all, but he has been granted a full pardon and he *was* your guardian, Elyse. It would not do for you to be thought ungrateful for his care of you.'

Lady Whittlewood's gentle rebuke brought the colour stealing into Elyse's cheek but there was no time to respond, for more people were demanding their attention.

At last the line of guests dwindled away to nothing and Lady Whittlewood allowed William to take Elyse into the drawing room where there was such a crush as must gladden any hostess's heart. The double doors between this apartment and the one behind had been thrown wide to make a spacious reception chamber, glittering with light from the chandeliers and candles in their wall sconces that made the room as bright as day. As if some malicious spirit wished to persecute her, Elyse saw Drew immediately. His tall, dark figure was easily recognisable and a sudden shifting of the crowds created a space so she could see that he was part of a lively group. The gentlemen were laughing, the ladies fluttering their fans. As William led her past them Elyse noticed that each of the ladies had her eyes fixed upon Drew. She recognised the tell-tale gestures as they vied for his attention, the playful tap upon his sleeve, the fluttering of lashes. She dragged her eyes away, resolving to think of him no more.

William led her through the crowd, stopping for a word here and there. He was smiling and attentive, his manner a nice mixture of pride and pleasure as he showed off his future bride. Elyse began to relax. She was used to social gatherings such as this, could parry words with the wits amongst them and laughingly turn off the more impertinent enquiries about her background. William seemed pleased, too, for he patted her hand, saying,

'We are a good pair, I think. We shall deal very well together.'

She smiled. 'I hope so.'

She felt his hand on her waist, drawing her closer and he lowered his head to murmur in her ear. 'You are looking dashed irresistible, too. Send your maid away as soon as you can tonight and I will come to your room.'

The scene she had witnessed in the morning room flashed into Elyse's mind and she stiffened, yet what could she say? Tonight or tomorrow, after the ceremony, what difference would it make?

A sudden flurry of activity near the door caught their attention. Latecomers had arrived, a group of young bucks, flamboyant in their powdered wigs and lavishly embroidered coats. They erupted noisily into the room, making loud, laughing apologies to Lady Whittlewood for their tardiness.

'Who can these young men be?' wondered Elyse, standing on tiptoe to see what was happening. She chuckled. 'I vow I have not seen them in the Pump Room taking the waters.'

'No, indeed, they are friends of mine,' said William. 'I had best explain to Mama that I invited them.' He hesitated. 'Would you mind if I did not present them to you immediately? I should like to talk to them first, alone.'

'I do not object to their high spirits, William.'

'But I do. I would not have them put you to the blush.' He released her. 'Give me a few moments, my dear, no more, I vow.'

He kissed her cheek and left her, pushing his way through the press of people until he was swallowed up in the crowd.

'Very affecting.'

She swung around to find Drew standing beside her.

'Do not sneer at William, he is very considerate to me.'

She hunched a shoulder and turned away from him.

'I do not sneer. It was an observation.' He stood beside her. 'Was it your idea to invite me?'

'No. Lady Whittlewood suggested it. She thought it would help your standing, if you are going to remain at Hartcombe.'

'Then I am in her debt.'

'Is that why you came?' She could not resist the question, any more than she could prevent the wistful note creeping into her voice. She wanted him to say he had come to see her, to assure himself that she was happy.

'Of course. If I am to restore Hartcombe such connections as I am making this evening will be invaluable.'

The tiny spark of hope died.

'I am glad. How is your arm?'

'It barely troubles me now.'

It had not troubled him at all when he had embraced her in the pavilion. She must not think of that. It was over.

With the faintest inclination of her head she moved away. She could be happy without Drew Castlemain, she would do her duty to William and *learn* to be happy. The room had become even more crowded, if that was possible, and noisy with chatter and brash laughter. The crush of bodies added to the heat from the candles and the fires blazing in the hearths. Elyse found it rather oppressive and her head was beginning to ache.

'Tomorrow you become Mrs William Reverson.'

Drew's voice in her ear made her jump. He had followed her.

'Yes.'

'And you are happy at the prospect?'

Anger surged within Elyse. How dare he come here to taunt her?

'Of course.' He chin went up and she forced herself to turn her head and meet his eye. 'William and I are very well suited.'

Wish her joy and leave, now.

Drew recognised the wisdom of the thought but could not act upon it. He had glimpsed the sadness behind the fire in Elyse's brown eyes, the same sadness he had seen there that day in the pavilion. It had haunted his dreams ever since and made him question if he had been right to push her away so ruthlessly. He determined that if she had any doubts at all she should not marry Reverson.

'Elyse.' He took her arm. 'Pray, if you will, spare me a few moments alone with you.' He saw her look of alarm and added quickly, 'I wish to talk to you, nothing more, you have my word.'

She regarded him for a moment, then seemed to come to a decision. With a slight, decisive nod she set off through the crowd. Drew remained a discreet distance behind her. A screen had been set up to shield the service door through which the servants made their way to and from the room. Elyse slipped behind it and Drew found himself on a narrow landing at the top of the backstairs. It was mercifully empty and he followed her to another door just beyond the staircase.

It led to a small sitting room. A few candles burned but the room's plain furnishings indicated that it was not used for entertaining. Elyse turned to face him, hands clenched nervously before her. Drew noted that the stomacher of her pewter gown was decorated with tiny jet beads that caught the light and he found himself thinking of the first time he had seen her. She had been wearing dull black bombazine but it had only served to emphasis the beauty of her dark eyes and lustrous dark hair. He had thought her beautiful even then.

'Well, sir, what is it you want to say to me?' Her cold tone brought his wandering thoughts back to the present. 'Be quick about it, if you please. I shall be missed.'

'I owe you an apology,' he began. 'I have behaved abominably to you.'

The angry look did not fade from her face.

'You have indeed, but it taught me a valuable lesson.' Her tone was light and brittle as glass. 'It showed me how close I had come to ruin. It made me appreciate everything William has to offer.'

'Does he love you?'

Elyse blinked. She had not been expecting such a direct question.

'Of course.' Her eyes slid away from his searching look as she pushed aside the vision of William and the housemaid. 'Why else would he have offered for me?' She added defiantly, 'I know the truth now. I know of the wager, and why the viscount allowed the match. William told me of it, to assure me it made no difference to him.' She recalled Lady Whittlewood's words. 'He was smitten from the first, you see.'

'And do you love him?'

She felt the prickle of tears behind her eyes. This was intolerable. He had no right to question her like this.

'I do. Now pray let me return to the party.'

He caught her arm as she tried to walk past him.

'I do not believe you. The way you responded to my kiss—'

Her head went up.

'That was merely a—a foolish, lustful interlude. It had nothing to do with love.'

'And what do you know of that?' he demanded angrily. 'You think yourself in love with a boy you met when you were seventeen and whom you did not see again until a few weeks ago.'

'I know more of love than you,' she flashed. 'You know only lust and seduction and deceit.' She pulled herself free from his grasp. 'Tell me, was I still at Hartcombe when you learned that you were a free man?'

'What?' He looked at her as if her question had caught him off-guard. 'Yes, my father told me, the day before we left.'

The day he had made love to her in the pavilion.

'But you kept the truth from me.'

He rubbed a hand over his eyes. 'What good would it have done to tell you?'

'And you persuaded Sir Edward not to say anything?'

'I did. I did not wish him to—' He spread his hands. 'It was not important. You were coming to Bath to marry Reverson.'

A chill ran through Elyse, as if there was ice in her blood.

'You are right,' she said stiffly. 'I *am* going to marry William. Did you think your scorn that morning was not rejection enough? Perhaps you were afraid I would cling to you even more if I had known you were no longer an outlaw.'

'No! I did not know *then*—'

She broke across his protest, unheeding. 'You are despicable. I am only thankful that after tonight I need never see you again.' She dashed a hand across her eyes. 'Now, let me go back to my fiancé.'

'And if I said I loved you?'

His words hit her battered heart like heavy stones. What was he trying to do? Was he merely taunting her, or did he want to establish her as his flirt, his lover even before she was married? He was testing her, playing his rakish games, but she would not rise to the bait. Misery and anger was a potent mix, but it kept her tears at bay and allowed her to speak with unwavering and icy deliberation.

'You have my sympathy, but you can hardly expect me to rejoice at such a declaration. It is as unwelcome as it is unlooked for.'

His eyes were blazing and she stepped back, out of reach. If he dragged her into his arms and kissed her now he would know she was lying. She loved him with an intensity that terrified her. She summoned up the last shreds of control.

'Please leave now, Mr Castlemain. It is best if we do not meet again.'

Drew saw her step away from him; saw the fear in her eyes and silently cursed himself for seven kinds of fool. For a man famed for his address he had handled this very badly. He had intended to suggest to her in a reasoned way that she need not marry Reverson, that she need not marry anyone, if she didn't wish to do so. Then he had planned to declare himself, to tell her that his hand and his heart were hers for the taking. Instead he had blurted out his feelings like any mooncalf and she had recoiled in disgust. He reached out for her.

'Elyse, I—'

She turned away from him.

'Just go. For pity's sake leave me!'

Her anguished whisper cut him to the quick. His hand dropped back to his side.

'I will inflict my presence upon you no longer,' he said quietly. 'I wish you every happiness, Miss Salforde, and ask you to believe that I am, now and always, your obedient servant.'

Elyse heard the door close and knew she was alone.

I will not cry.

It was tempting to throw herself down in a chair and give way to her misery but Elyse knew that if she wept now she might not be able to stop. Without giving herself time to consider what had just occurred she went swiftly back to the reception. Pride would not allow her to show an unhappy face in such a gathering and she stretched her mouth into a smile that soon made her cheeks ache. The room was as noisy and crowded as when she had left it. She spotted Drew's dark head immediately, her glance drawn in his direction as if by some force of magnetism. He was making his way towards the door but his progress was slow, impeded by well-wishers, smiling and bowing, anxious to welcome him back into society.

She dragged her eyes away from him. His future was assured, as was hers. She would think of him no more.

But when did Sir Edward tell him about the pardon? It could not have been before he found me in the pavilion.

'I did not know then...'

She pressed her fingers to her temples. She would *not* think of him. A brief break in the crowd gave her a glimpse of William standing with his friends on the far side of the room and she made her way across to him. The group stood by themselves, the other guests having moved away and Elyse soon realised why. The immoderate laughter and reddened faces of the young bucks suggested they had been imbibing freely. Even William was looking a little heated and when he saw her his words of greeting were suspiciously slurred.

'Ah, and here is my blushing bride. Come along and meet my friends my dear. Almondsbury, Pendle, Griffin, make your bows to Miss Salforde.'

The young men attempted flourishing bows with varying degrees of success. Mr Almondsbury straightened and raised his quizzing glass, subjecting her to a prolonged scrutiny. Mr Griffin came forwards to take her hand.

'Ah, fair lady! 'T-T-Tis an honour to meet you at last.'

She regarded him as he bowed over her fingers, a slight frown creasing her brow.

'Have we met before, sir? In Scarborough, perhaps?'

He unbent and there was no mistaking the alarm in his rather protuberant eyes. It put her on her guard.

'S-S-Scarborough, oh, d-dear me, no, Miss—'

She snatched her hand away.

'It was you,' she exclaimed. 'You were one of the attackers.'

Her horrified glance swung from Mr Griffin to William, who began to bluster loudly, but the reaction of the other gentlemen gave the lie to his denials. Elyse looked about her. Everyone was still resolutely ignoring them. Such was the noise in the room she doubted if anyone could overhear their conversation.

'Did you think it a good joke?' she demanded in a furious undertone.

'I said we shouldn't take loaded pistols,' muttered Mr Pendle.

'Be quiet,' snapped William. 'Elyse, this is not the time to discuss this.'

'Oh, and when would you suggest we discussed it?' she retorted. 'I want to know which of you wounded Mr Castlemain.'

She glared at the little group, who shuffled uncomfortably beneath her stern gaze.

'I regret to say that was me,' admitted Mr Pendle. 'But only after he had fired at Almondsbury.'

'He pinked me,' complained that gentleman, holding up his right hand to show a healing gash on the side of his palm.

Elyse was not impressed. 'You could have killed him. How dare you! It is a good thing Mr Nash has decreed you do not wear your swords in Bath or I would use yours to run you through.'

Mr Pendle blanched and retreated in the face of such blazing anger. She turned towards William. 'And the coachman, was he a part of your plans? He said Lord Whittlewood had paid him to drive us to Bath.'

'My father had nothing to do with it,' said William quickly. 'It was entirely my notion. I knew from the start that my father's plan would not work. If you had come all the way from the north then you would not be put off by a few extra miles to travel to Bath. We decided we must try to stop you.'

'We? Your friends were a party to this?' her scorching glare encompassed all four of them.

'Yes. I told Settle how it would be if you followed us.'

'Settle *knew* you were going to attack the coach?' she asked, incredulous. It certainly explained why he had been avoiding her since her arrival in Queen Square. 'And he did nothing to stop you?'

William's scowl deepened. 'He had no choice, short of telling my father, and he has always been too loyal to me for that. Settle thought he could delay you if he said he was ill, but that dashed guardian of yours was determined to fulfil the contract.'

'And he was seriously injured for his troubles,' said Elyse, her anger against Drew fast disappearing. 'What a despicable thing to do, William!'

'What does it matter?' demanded Griffin peevishly. 'The fellow's a dashed traitor.'

'He has been granted a full pardon.' Elyse flashed back. 'He a free man, and a far more honourable one than any of you.'

He was closeted with his father while I was in the kitchen. Perhaps that was when he learned of it.

'It was an accident, we never meant you any harm,' said William in a sulky tone. 'I will arrange for the baggage to be returned, anonymously, of course. And Castlemain's purse, too.'

'That is the very least you can do,' she told him angrily. 'Whatever were you thinking of, to try such a trick?'

William's scowl deepened. 'We merely planned to hold you at Griffin's house for a week or so, until Michaelmas passed and the contract was breached.'

She stared at him in dismay.

'Oh, William. Are you so averse to marrying me?'

'I had not seen you for three years,' he protested. 'You are a stranger to me.'

'But your letters!'

He shrugged. 'While our marriage was but some vague future event it was easy to write, but as the time grew closer I began to regret my rash promise. Father would not let me cry off, or give you any hint that I was reluctant to wed you.'

'Dear Miss Salforde, Reverson is but a few

months older than yourself,' cried Mr Almondsbury, jumping to the defence of his friend. 'He is too young to be setting up his own nursery.'

'He is right,' declared William. 'There is much I wish to do.'

'Oh?' she countered with deceptive sweetness, 'like kissing housemaids, perhaps?'

'You know that is not what I mean. I had intended to go on the Grand Tour, for example.'

'I see no reason why you should not still do that.' She added, determined to be cheerful, 'We might go together.'

'Impossible.'

'Why?' Elyse bridled at William's swift dismissal. 'I should like to travel just as much as you.'

'I am not free to settle down. I must travel constantly.'

Drew's words came back to her. She was certain now that he could not have known about the pardon when he uttered them.

'Once we are married you will remain in Berkshire with the children,' declared William. 'I have no doubt you will like to have a large family, but of course that will preclude your going abroad.' He looked up. 'Enough of this, we have been talking here too long and my father is beckoning to us.' William held out his arm to her. 'Come along, Elyse. I am very sorry for what occurred. We all are, but the terms of the contract have been met, so tomorrow you and I are to be married and we must resign ourselves to the fact.'

Elyse was too angry and distracted to resign herself to anything. Sir Edward must have told Drew about the pardon while she was in the kitchen with Mrs Parfitt. Why did Drew not come to tell her afterwards? If he loved her, surely he would have told her. Unless…

Her thoughts racing, she accompanied William through the crowd to where Lord and Lady Whittlewood were standing. She looked around the room but there was no sign of Drew. Lady Whittlewood put out her hand to draw her son closer and Elyse turned to the viscount.

'My lord, you are fully conversant with the terms of the settlements, are you not?'

'Naturally, but I do not think this is the place to discuss—'

She interrupted him ruthlessly.

'And it is impossible for William to withdraw from the marriage?'

'Quite impossible. If the marriage does not go

ahead then the full sum agreed in the settlement would go to you.' The viscount looked grim and shook his head at her. 'Your father drove a hard bargain, Miss Salforde.'

She fixed her eyes upon him. 'But what if *I* were to cry off?'

His thin brows went up. 'You? But why should you do that? This is an excellent match for you.'

'Nevertheless, what penalties are in place should I withdraw?'

'Why, none. Your father and I never contemplated such an eventuality. His lack of fortune made it irrelevant.'

She met his eyes with a steady gaze.

'As I understand it, the sum at stake is considerable. Twenty thousand pounds, to be exact.'

His brows snapped together.

'Who told you that?'

'William let it slip. Our marriage is payment of a gambling debt, is it not?'

'I think we would prefer not to mention that, my dear.'

'You are right.' She smiled. 'I do not intend to think of it again.'

She stepped away a little and took a deep breath. A sudden lull in the noise around them seemed providential. She raised her head and proclaimed in a ringing voice.

'My Lord and Lady Whittlewood, I am very conscious of the honour you do me, but I regret that I cannot marry your son.' The lull became a stunned silence. She turned to William. 'I am very sorry, Mr Reverson, if this gives you pain.' She tugged the diamond ring from her finger and held it out to him. Automatically he put out his hand to receive it. She smiled at him. 'I hope one day we may be friends.'

Elyse turned and hurried towards the door, the crowd parting silently to let her pass. William had been staring, perplexed, at the ring lying in his hand but now he looked up.

'Elyse! Where are you going?'

She glanced back.

'To find happiness, if it is not too late.'

When Drew left Elyse the clatter of dishes and cacophony of voices suggested that the backstairs would be swarming with servants. He had no choice but to return to the reception and make his way through the crowds to the door. His progress was impeded by the number of his father's acquaintances waiting to pounce on him. They wanted to wish him well and enquire after his family. He thought bitterly that Lord Whittlewood's intention to help re-establish the good name of Castlemain had been only too successful. Duty dictated that he bury his hurt and impatience and respond civilly to each and every one of them.

At last he escaped and ran down the stairs, curtly ordering his carriage. A servant was despatched immediately, but with such a crush of guests he suspected that his coachman would have had to go some way to find a spot where he could wait without blocking the road. He paced the hall, impatient to be away before anyone came downstairs in search of supper. He should not have come. His father was wrong about Elyse. She might have loved him, if he had courted her properly and treated her with respect. Perhaps then she might have considered him as a serious rival to Reverson.

He thought of the way she had responded to him in the pavilion, the melting look in her eyes. He could have offered for her then. She would have accepted him and thought the world well lost. Instead he had done everything in his power to disgust her.

'Fool,' he muttered furiously. 'Imbecile.'

A lackey bringing Drew's hat and cloak stopped and began to back away.

'Not you,' said Drew irritably.

There was a sudden burst of noise from above as the drawing-room door opened and it was with relief that he heard the footman announce that his carriage had arrived. He grabbed his hat and cloak and headed for the door. He wanted to be gone from this damned place without speaking to another soul.

The flaring torches outside the viscount's residence lighted his way to the coach and Drew climbed in, feeling very weary. He would be able to tell his father that his reception in Bath had been more than cordial, but he himself would not count the evening a success, because he had come away without Elyse.

He threw himself back in a corner and closed his eyes, anxious to be home. Suddenly the commotion outside became louder. He heard the squeak of the handle as the door opened, felt the carriage rock and heard the whoosh of a whirlwind. He opened his eyes to discover it was not a whirlwind but a rustling cloud of grey silk.

'Elyse!' He sat up with a jolt. 'What the devil—?'

She fell on to the empty seat opposite him as the carriage set off, saying breathlessly, 'I am *so* glad I did not miss you.'

Before he could form a reply she leaned forwards and slapped him, hard, across the face.

Chapter Twelve

'You are the greatest knave that has ever drawn breath, Drew Castlemain!'

Drew peered into the darkness, trying to see the termagant sitting opposite him. They had driven out of Queen Square and now there was only the sliver of moon riding high above them to light the way. The shadows inside the carriage were inky black.

'I think I must be,' he murmured, rubbing his cheek. 'I don't *think* you have broken my jaw.'

'It would serve you right if I had,' she told him furiously. 'Why did you keep your pardon a secret from me?'

Drew leaned back. He was bemused, but somewhere deep inside his heart was singing like a lark. Elyse was here, in his carriage and they were on their way to Hartcombe.

Home.

'You were going to Bath to marry Reverson,' he said. 'To…er…"make him the best, most loving wife there ever was". Those were your exact words.'

'That was your intention, was it not, when you rejected me so thoroughly, to drive me into William's arms?'

'At that time I did not know I was a free man. I thought I was still an outcast, forced to wander abroad, never settling in one place. I could not inflict that life upon you.'

'And you gave no thought to what I might want. But that is irrelevant now. When you did learn that you were pardoned, why did you keep silent?'

'I had given you enough cause to hate me. Even with the pardon, what could I offer you, compared to the life you would have with Reverson?'

'How idiotically noble of you.' Her scornful voice cut through the darkness.

'And what would you have had me do?' he demanded, rattled.

'Allowed me to make the decision for myself.'

He exhaled.

'You are right,' he said at last. 'I realised it

soon after you had gone, and I intended to do so this evening, only I made a mull of it.'

'Very true,' she said bitterly.

Elyse leaned back against the squabs and waited. The anger and excitement that had carried her out of Lord Whittlewood's house and into Drew's carriage had abated. She was beset by doubts when he did not reply. Perhaps he had thought better of his rash declaration. Perhaps he had no wish to marry someone who scolded him so roundly. The enveloping darkness did not help. She could not see Drew's face. She had no idea what he was thinking.

'I am not going to marry William,' she told him, when she could no longer bear the silence. 'I have broken it off irrevocably and there can be no question that I jilted him. The viscount's debt to my father is cancelled.'

The unnerving quiet continued.

'Pray do not think that I expect you to marry me,' she said, trying to keep the note of uncertainty out of her voice. 'Sir Edward offered me sanctuary at Hartcombe and I will accept that until I can return to Scarborough. Th-that is why I wanted to share your carriage, sir, not for any other reason.' Her voice faltered. 'And I d-did not have time to collect my wrap...'

'Damn this darkness.' Drew muttered as he moved across to sit beside her. He put his arm around her shoulders. 'Is that better, or would you like my cloak? It is here somewhere.'

'No, I am warm enough now.' Reassured by the feel of his arm about her, she leaned against him and slipped one arm around his waist. 'I discovered that it was William and his friends who held up our coach.'

'I guessed it was some such thing.'

'They did not mean to shoot you. They intended merely to prevent my reaching Bath before Michaelmas.'

'The devil they did. Would you like me to call them to book?'

'No, no.' She held him close. 'I want merely to forget it all. Although you might wish to be revenged upon Mr Pendle for putting a bullet in you.'

'No, no, 'tis almost healed now. Besides,' he added, a laugh in his voice, 'Why should I wish to do that, when he has done me such a service?'

'That is true, I suppose. If you had not been wounded we would never have gone to Hartcombe, and you would not have made it up with your father and learned that you had been pardoned.'

His arm around her shoulders tightened.

'And I should not have had time to discover just how much I love you.'

'Oh.' Hot tears prickled behind her eyes. 'Oh, if only that were true.'

'It is.' He put his fingers beneath her chin and she responded to their gentle pressure to look up. His face was a pale blur in the darkness yet she could feel the heat of his gaze. 'I have not led a blameless life, my love. I have made mistakes but I have paid for them.'

'I do not care about your past,' was her swift reply.

'But you must care about the future,' he told her. 'You must understand what it is that I can offer you. It will take years to make Hartcombe truly profitable again. And of course in time I will inherit the baronetcy, although I hope that event is many years distant.'

'So, too, do I. But is that all you can offer me?'

His arm tightened around her.

'That and my heart, now and always.'

She gave a little sob and threw her arms around his neck.

'Oh, Drew, that is all I ever wanted from you. I love you so much!'

* * *

When Elyse gave herself up to Drew's kiss, she was not prepared for the assault upon her senses. They had been battered and bruised by the events of the evening and when their lips met there was no soft easing of the rigid control she had placed upon herself. There was no melting tenderness, only raging fire. She was consumed by desire, a shockingly powerful need to have him love her. She returned his kisses forcefully, eagerly tangling her tongue with his, revelling in the hot, erotic sensations it was creating throughout her body. When Drew would have pulled back she clung to him, urging him to go on.

'Oh, my love,' his words were a thread, whispered against her skin as he dipped his head to run a line of kisses over her neck. 'Bid me stop now, or there is only one way this will end.'

'Never.' Her head was thrown back, her skin burning where his mouth had touched it. 'I want this as much as you.'

She had no doubts. She needed him to finish what they had begun in the pavilion. The carriage rattled on, its gentle swaying joined with the pale moonlight to create a darkly magical world for their lovemaking. Drew's hand was on her waist, sliding up over the stiffened bodice towards the rise of her breasts. Her skin tightened in anticipation, nipples hardened, aching for his touch. She clutched him, one hand pushing past the lace at his neck, tearing open his shirt, desperate to feel the skin beneath.

Drew pulled away, but only to remove his jacket and while he did so she dragged the fichu from her neck and it fluttered pale and ghostly to the carriage floor. When he reached for her again she went into his arms, the cool softness of his lawn sleeves wrapping around her while she was devoured by his kiss. She felt lightheaded, almost swooning with the pleasure he was inflicting on her. She did not resist when he eased her down on the seat, his hands pushing aside her heavy skirts. She returned his kisses, driving her hands through his hair, revelling in its silkiness between her fingers. A little shudder of delight ran through her when she felt his hand smoothing over the skin of her thigh. Her very core was melting, opening, and she shifted a little, lifting her hips to offer herself up to the delights of those questing fingers. Suddenly his hand was cupping the hot, aching mound between her thighs. She moaned, her body shifting restlessly as he teased and explored. Little tremors were pulsing through her, threatening to overwhelm her senses. She slid her hands to his waist, to the fall of his breeches, fumbling with the buttons. She could feel his iron-hard erection through the thin material and it took her breath away. She had no knowledge of this, yet heat flared through her, combined with an overwhelming need for satisfaction.

'I want you, Drew,' she whispered. 'I want you now.'

He brushed aside her fingers and she sank back on to the padded seat, reaching for him, pulling his head down until she could kiss him, which she did with a kind of desperation. Her petticoats were bunched between them but she barely noticed, nor the cool air on her naked limbs. Her body was arching and trembling with need. His hands slid around her buttocks, lifting her towards him and she gave a soft gasp as she felt him at the hinge of her thighs. He was teasingly close to entering her and she tilted her hips a little more, inviting him into her very core. She pushed herself towards him, catching her breath as he slid inside her. It was a small pain, soon forgotten. Her hips came up to meet him as he drove deeper, harder, again and again. When she would have cried out he covered her mouth for another searing kiss that made her whole body shudder with desire.

Her senses took flight, her body trembled out

of control. She was ready to tip over into ecstasy. She clutched at him, dug her fingers into his back as tremors of pure pleasure began to ripple through her, building in intensity. They were moving as one. Elyse tore her mouth free and gasped out his name even as he plunged even deeper into her core, taking her over the edge and into the abyss. It was as if she had stepped off a high cliff and was held, suspended for one brief, exhilarating moment. She felt his release, heard his shout of triumph before her mind shattered and she lost all comprehension of time and space.

Drew's body was heavy above her, gently rocking with the continued swaying of the carriage as it rattled on. At last she felt at peace. Complete. She did not move, savouring the moment, the joy of it. It was as much as she could do not to sigh out loud when Drew eased away from her, a deep black shape against the faint moonlight shining through the windows.

'The die is cast, my dear. We must be married now, and with all speed.'

The night air chilled her bare skin and she sat up, carefully pulling her skirts back into place.

'Is that what you truly want, sir?'

She could not quite accept it, even now. That

he loved her in his own fashion she did not doubt, but he loved honour more. He had done his best to prevent her falling in love with him, determined not to raise hopes he could not fulfil. She would take full responsibility for what had just occurred. After all, she had thrown herself into his arms, begged him to love her and he had done so. She would demand nothing more of him. She had money. She could return to her aunt in the north and live out a single life, but she would carry the memory of this moment with her to the grave.

'You are no longer a maid,' said Drew. 'I have taken that which I told you was a husband's right. Therefore I must now become that husband.'

'I shall not demand that you make an honest woman of me.'

Elyse bent to scoop up her fichu and as she did so the ring around her neck fell forward. Drew reached out and caught it. In one swift, decisive move he tore the ring from the thin length of ribbon.

'But *I* shall demand it, if you will have me.' He slid to his knees on the carriage floor. 'Will you marry me, dearest Elyse? Will you take this flawed, foolish man and trust him to make you happy?' He took her left hand and held the ring over the tip of her third finger. 'My father knew your worth. This is my mother's ring, the one he gave her when she agreed to marry him. Will you wear it now as a token of our betrothal until I can buy you one of your own?'

Hot tears burned her eyes and she said unsteadily, 'Oh, Drew, I do not need any other token, if you really, truly wish to marry me.'

'Can you doubt it?'

He pushed the ring on to her finger and leaned forwards to kiss her. When at last he let her go he sat down on the bench beside her, pulling her against him and settling her comfortably in his arms. He sighed.

'I warned your father how it would be if he made me your guardian.'

'He entrusted me to your care,' she murmured. 'Upon your honour, which was certainly very tiresome, since it prevented you from declaring yourself.'

'A rebel's honour,' he retorted bitterly.

Elyse pushed herself away and put one hand up to his cheek, saying softly,

'It is what makes you the man you are, Drew Castlemain. It is the honour of my one and only true love.'

* * * * *